UXBRIDGE College Learning Centre
Coldharbour Lane, Hayes, Middlesex UB3 3BB
Telephone: 01895 853740

Please return this item to the Learning Centre
on or before the last date stamped below:

WITHDRAWN

LEARNING RESOURCES AT UXBRIDGE COLLEGE

Uxbridge College Hayes Campus

'*Endangered Species* displays an astonishing virtuosity in bringing together the multiple narratives that define the Atlantic adventure. From Bermuda to Gambia/Senegal and South London is a new and audacious rendering of colonial encounters.'

George Lamming

ENDANGERED SPECIES
AND OTHER STORIES

ANGELA BARRY

PEEPAL TREE

First published in Great Britain in 2003
Peepal Tree Press
17 King's Avenue
Leeds LS6 1QS
England

ISBN 1 900715 71 6

CONTENTS

For my sons Ibou and Douds
and in memory of my mother and father

VOICES OF A SUMMER NIGHT

VOICES OF A SUMMER NIGHT

Voice One:

"Philip! Don't you slam the door on me! You know what you can do...you can go straight to hell, you and that woman of yours..."

Oh God! My head's bursting. Everything in the bedroom's spinning. Look out over the water... Look out there. The white tablecloths and the flowers and the china and the sun setting over the ocean – they looked so beautiful only a few moments ago... Now... Everything shot to hell, ruined. "You're just going to have to put up with it, aren't you, Eve?" he says calmly. So what does he think I've been doing these past five years, since that green-eyed bitch clawed her way into my life? I've put up with it and put up with it and now she's going to set foot in *my* house, on *my* lawn, turn up at *my* dinner party as though it's her God-given right. And he tells me to put up with it! Dear Lord, tell me which one of them I should hate more. Mr. or Ms. Civilised! If I run into her at the office, or should I say, at *their* office, she's so polite it makes me want to puke. I should have slapped that high-yellow face of hers long ago. It's her voice I can't take. Well-bred Barbadian mixed with the University of Toronto rounded off with the English Inns of Court. Little Miss Cultured. But underneath it all, nothing but a cheap husband-snatching slut. Yes, that's what you are, Georgia Shillingford. Whatever the world says, that's what you truly are.

9

And the evening starts so well. I'm feeling good. My diet's paying off. I've lost five pounds and it shows, especially around the middle where all my excess goes. And this black dress really suits me, flatters my tummy – which has never been right since the children were born – and shows off my legs with that outrageous slit. We're getting ready. He zips up my dress; I fix his tie. No tension. That invisible Berlin Wall running through the room, slicing through the centre of the bed, crumbles away. It almost feels like it once was.

He reminisces about when he first started to work for Clyde James, what a tyrant he seemed then and now, twenty-five years later, it's "Old Man James", retiring and leaving Philip as the firm's senior partner. I feel a warm glow because I know that all that time, I'm right there by his side. I tell him what's planned for dinner, how it's going to be the social event of the summer. He nods his appreciation – this is going to make him look good. After a run-down of the menu and the wines, I tell him I've ordered fifteen white orchids for each of the women from the firm – a classy detail, if I say so myself.

"Fifteen? You ordered fifteen?" he says.

"No actually, sixteen, including the one for myself."

"There are sixteen women at the office." His voice goes tight. "You know that."

And there's that Berlin Wall back up again.

"You don't mean that... that..." I leap to my feet and without needing to see myself in the mirror, I know my face is ugly. "Philip, you can't be serious!"

"Of course Georgia is coming! What did you expect?"

"That whore's coming here?" I glance about me, looking for something to smash. I remind him how, four years ago, when I confronted him with their disgusting affair – then already a year old – he'd promised that she'd never set foot in this house again.

"This is different. And you know it." He tugs at his tie. He speaks as if I'm some slow-witted child. "You know very well that tonight is business. Old Man James's retirement. And Georgia happens to be a partner. Or had you forgotten?"

"How could I forget? How brilliant she is, how beautiful, how talented. Of course we all know one place where she's got plenty of talent..."

He heads for the door, sucking his teeth. Stands for a moment, saying nothing. I put my hand to my mouth, trying to hold back the torrent of words about to burst out.

"I hate the life you've given me," I blurt out at last.

Which is when he delivers his parting shot about me having to put up with it. Well they weren't exactly his last words. The last thing he said was, "And she isn't a whore, no matter how badly you want her to be."

I look outside again. The day is staggering along like a drunk. Soon, very soon, it will collapse into the sea and be gone.

Voice Two:

How many times does a door have to slam before it undermines the foundations of a house? Good thing I was there to see them cutting into the hill, see that seam of hard white rock and the steel foundations and the concrete block rising from it. A strong house, that's what I thought. But now? Is there any material made by God or man that can withstand the way she makes me feel? She knows that of all the things that I hate in this life, it's noise. And for the past four years there's been nothing but noise. Ever since she found out about Georgia. Since then nothing but slamming doors and my property at risk.

I try to see her point of view. She *is* my wife and the mother of my children. It can't be easy to see me in love with

11

another woman. But that's all she can see – the fact that I have the almighty gall to find someone who really understands me, who I can really be myself with. She should be grateful I don't screw around and bring something nasty back home. I'm still here, aren't I? She see me leaving? I've stuck with this marriage and my family wants for nothing. Does she give me any credit? All she can do is rant and rave and humiliate us all. And the house she lives in, the clothes she wears, the trips she goes on – where does the money come from? Does she ever think about that? If she's so unhappy, why doesn't she pack her bags and go and do some work for the first time in twenty years. A nice little job teaching Art at Warwick Secondary. Huh! My girl may be crazy but she's not stupid! So she stays, her life's work to make my life hell. My God! She was such a lovely girl when she was young. I could do no wrong in her eyes nor she in mine. Who would have thought she had this vicious, jealous streak? I guess I should count myself lucky that she didn't pick up the bedside lamp and throw it at me.

Take up Yoga. That's what I have to do. My body's in good shape from the morning runs and workouts at the gym, but my insides feel wound up like a coil. Pressure at work. Pressure at home. No hiding place. I need to talk to Georgia about it. Oh Georgia, my love, you are perfection ...

Get a grip, man. Forget it, delete it from the screen. I won't let Eve spoil this occasion. I've worked my guts out for this and I don't think even she's so unhinged she'd cause a scandal in the middle of the farewell speeches – though look what she did to Georgia in the Board Room! I'd better make sure she doesn't drink too much. There's nothing more loathsome than a loud and drunken woman and that's what my wife is becoming. But tonight, she will behave like a lady. Or else.

Control my breath. I must learn to breathe and block out

this anger. It wastes my time and my energy... This evening is special. I can't wait to see the old man's face when we announce the scholarship fund to be set up in his name. And Georgia doesn't know how much she touched me with the idea of setting up another fund in memory of Mother – The Daisy Blyden Award for Legal Education. She can't know how moved I was. Maybe she does know. She knows everything there is to know about me.

Voice One:

It's just before nine when the sound of the doorbell rises slightly above the buzz of voices in the living room. I'm standing here by the open French doors, doing nothing in particular, waiting and watching. Cute young waiters dart about, moving a fork by a millimetre, whisking away a fallen rose petal, relighting a citronella candle. I allow myself a smile. This is my handiwork. Look at the living room. Rugs from Morocco, paintings by Haiti's finest naïf artists, mahogany masks from Burundi, bronze figures from Benin. Nowhere in Bermuda – many people have told me this – is there such a collection of treasures from the Caribbean and Africa, bought in the days when we would go on cultural head-hunting expeditions armed with Philip's wad of dollars and my artist's eye. Just look at it all. Wouldn't Philip's mother have been proud. Poor woman, didn't even last out to see the twins' birth. Such a shame she didn't live to see how well Philip did. She would have given *him* all the credit, of course, for being the poor boy who made the big time. But I think, though she died over twenty years ago, she knew where Philip was headed, knew he would end up in a house on the hill overlooking the water. But I did my part, Daisy. Pity you aren't around to remind your son of that!

A few quick cocktails inside me and I'm feeling a whole lot

calmer. No going off the rails tonight. That's a promise. After this one, no more martinis. He's not going to have the satisfaction of being able to give me that "You're drunk" look.

So I take my ease by the patio doors, sneak a look at the guests. Talk about chic! "Smart casual" in Bermuda means extremely formal – or at least extremely expensive – in the rest of the world. Two unfortunate ladies have arrived wearing the same outfit from the it's-a-steal-at-$400 rack at Cecile's. They keep to opposite ends of the room. Although the competition is fierce, the winner, by two outstanding breasts, is Cherie Clarke, the newest lawyer in town, who's poured herself into a tiny tube of white stretchy material. Not even room for the orchid. The men buzz around her like horse-flies on a dung heap. In my black dress I feel like a sparrow among peacocks.

The bell rings again. This time Philip hears it and bounds over to open the door. In steps Old Man James, last of a generation of lawyers whose clients sometimes paid them in crocus bags full of new potatoes. Here he comes, a bit unsteady on his feet, walking into the house of his heir apparent, with Georgia on his arm. I tell you, my stomach heaves as the martinis rush to my brain. But I'm not so gone that I can't see the beauty of the scheme to get her into my house with maximum legitimacy. My hand starts to shake and I only just put my glass down in time. Keep your promise, girl, keep your promise. I raise my head as high as it will go and make the long journey towards the door. Eyes bore into my back. Have these people dressed up like this to see a repeat of the time when I cursed Georgia in the Board Room? In my own home, surrounded by enemies.

As I make that exposed journey, my eyes light on three small pastels of local flowers that I did a while ago. They're more than good, I tell myself. They're exquisite. But who the hell cares that I can paint pretty pictures and know the difference between good art and bad art? If I'd filled this house with cheap junk, most of these people would be none the wiser. Philip included. For him, they're investments, pure and simple. How could he know any different? All he had was Daisy who scrubbed white people's floors all day then went back to a room on Till's Hill where she raised him. How could he know different? My family had money and education for three generations. So was it revenge when he made fun of me – nothing overt, but mockery nonetheless – when I started painting again? Shit! You killed that thing in me, Philip, and I hate you for it!

I arrive in front of Philip, Georgia and Old Man James, inwardly fuming.

"Sir Clyde, darling," I say, putting my arm around the old man. "Welcome to our humble abode." I stamp a fuschia-coloured mouth on his papery cheek. A slight but constant tremor comes from his body. This retirement's coming not a moment too soon.

"Eve! Eve!" Despite the nodding of the grizzled head, his voice has lost none of its vigour. His hand is still around my waist, for support perhaps, but also because he has always fancied me. "You know I would never pass up the chance to come to your house, give you a little squeeze," – which he does, the dirty old man! – "and make your husband jealous."

"Oh, Sir Clyde!" I raise my voice a notch. "Don't be so old-fashioned. Jealous husbands and jealous wives are a thing of the past. Nowadays, everybody just does their own thing. Don't you agree, Philip?" I don't pause. "Good evening, Georgia."

For a split second, I feel them squirm, my husband and his lover, as we stand almost shoulder to shoulder next to Old Man James. Georgia recovers before Philip does.

"Hello, Eve," she says in that maddening voice. I think she smiles but can't be sure because I'm gazing at a small space between Old Man James's head and her own. Out of the corner of my eye, I can see Philip's bottom teeth glinting, a sure sign that his lips are pulled back in a hard angry line. Around us, the assembled staff of James and Blyden, Attorneys-at-Law, take it all in. For them, the banquet has already begun.

Philip seems to come out of a daze and takes the old man's arm, a broad smile making him look suddenly boyish. I have to admit it. He's still very attractive, looks better than he did when he was young. All of that "my-body-is-my-temple" stuff has paid off. See the unfairness of life! Older men are called distinguished; older women are just past it. My eye catches Cherie Clarke's. Your turn's coming, my girl. You just don't know it yet.

"Come on, Sir Clyde," says Philip. "Everyone's waiting for you."

Off they go, the old king, his prince regent and she who would be queen. This trio is enfolded by the others with the affection of a family. I'm left at the doorway needing only a frilly apron to feel like a maid. I find my drink and gulp it down. Only then do I allow myself to look at her. As usual, I'm struck by the fact that there is not one thing about her that you would call beautiful. The forehead is a bit too high, the lips a shade too thin. Her body doesn't scream sex nor is she in the full bloom of youth any more. But there she is, the focus of attention, like she always is, making the other women look like they thought this was a masquerade ball while she alone is perfect in a simple burgundy dress.

I want to tip over the floral arrangements and pour wine down her. But I can't. On a good day, I might have done something really spectacular. That's one thing about me that scares Philip. What I call my sense of theatre, what he calls my "full craziness". Whatever it is, I don't have it just now. All I want is to become invisible.

Voice Two:

Breathe slowly, man, breathe slowly. That was rough. With everyone watching, it was even worse than I thought it would be. But please God, the evening can only get better, though who knows what Eve's going to do next. There's nothing she loves better than an audience. "Jealous husbands and jealous wives are a thing of the past!" she shrieks to the multitude, really enjoying herself. Didn't care that the old man might have been embarrassed. In the old days, he would have been too sharp to let her use him like that. But now ... Before I get senile, somebody give me a pill. I never want to be anything less than I am today.

Isn't Georgia a dream? Isn't she always? That straight back, so very very regal. Drew me to her right from the beginning. Even now, after five years, I find myself gasping for breath when she comes into a room. She looks so beautiful tonight, with her hair on her shoulders. Calm, composed. Eve has no weapons against her. Why did I have to live in the world for fifty years before I knew what love was? And there she is walking out onto my patio, tied to me by an invisible thread that no one, not even Eve, can sever.

Let this night go smoothly. Let Eve do nothing that will bring shame to me, my children, my business and my mother whose memory we honour tonight. Let these tight coils in my stomach loosen. And when tomorrow comes, let my dream woman come to me and let us breathe together.

Voice Three:

I'm back! After four years' banishment, I'm back in Philip's house. Under normal circumstances, I'm not a gloater, but I think that this calls for a little celebration. Maybe tomorrow afternoon. At my place.

The Lady Wife would have done well with the Viet Cong. The consummate guerilla fighter with her surprise attacks, "the night raids, the shamming dead..." What poem does that come from? This love business is making my mind go soft. Five years ago, I would have known the poem and the poet. Now all I know is what it feels like to step on a land mine.

God, that moment seemed endless. My knees were shaking and my skin prickling with sweat. Georgia, you're safe. She can't touch you. You're a lawyer, you see people and situations objectively – you see her for what she is – neither hate nor despise her. I've had clients like her. If you appear to remain calm and unimpressed when they're having a wobbly moment, they stop.

I have to admit that she puts in a flawless performance as the wronged wife – though it's a much easier part to play than mine. I'm not as gifted an actress as she, but still the mistress is an impossible role to play. She's a whore, a money-grabber, a marriage wrecker – or some puny-brained self-loather who's never more happy than when she's in a relationship that will destroy her. There's no moral high ground for the mistress! My academic achievements, my courtroom victories, my work in the community, my all-round delightful nature – all of these vanish in a puff of smoke when the Lady Wife steps into Chambers flashing her wedding band, her children's photos and her bleeding heart. It makes my blood boil. I have to admit that some-times it's been that anger that's kept me determined to make "Philip and me" into a reality. But tonight, with the night falling and waiters hovering, feeling his eyes on me, having his hand brush against mine every few minutes, at such times all I can do is pity her. She never had this with him, even when they were young.

Speaking of the Lady Wife, where's she vanished to? No-where around. Good! I can relax. I love the gardens of this house and the sudden drop of the cliff down to the beach.

The house itself is well designed, but oh, the way she's done it up! What's the saying? A little knowledge is a dangerous thing? She claims to know about art. She waves around a degree from some multiple-choice American university. You can't move inside there for stumbling over great lumps of wood and bronze. Works of art, she calls them. Frankly, I find most of them either childlike or grotesque. Whatever, each one deserves to be in a room of its own. If I lived here, I'd clear out ninety-nine percent of that stuff and leave some uncluttered space. Philip would see that those with real money and class are the ones least likely to put it on parade in public.

The breeze from the sea is sweet. Yes, I'd love some wine. Hmm. A fruity little number. I wonder where she is? When's the next attack coming?

Voice One:

Main course over, just desserts to come. Will anyone out there miss me or will I have vanished like a stone into quicksand? Did any of those buggers notice the moment when I'd simply had enough and quietly and, I thought, graciously excused myself after a few spoonfuls of the cold watercress soup? Will any of those bastards have thought, "Poor Eve, what a martyr to migraine!"? Will they hell! Who cares? Me and my martini are now the tightest of friends. There's a lot of noise coming in here from the kitchen. Hey, you, plates! Do you have to clatter so loud? Well, sister, you've sunk pretty low. Here you are getting hot talking to plates. What a come-down!

My Sun Room. God, how dismal it looks. It's gone to rack and ruin since I was last here. A graveyard for everybody's castoffs – broken chairs, discarded gadgets. How I used to love this place! How long has it been since I was last here? I don't remember. I don't remember. Ages ago. This drink's disappearing too fast. I'll need another soon. I do remember. It's my curse.

I called it the Sun Room because, during the day, it lets in the purest light from off the sea. I did those flower pastels here and quite a few others. It was here that I tried to do something new. The kids were growing up, Philip was immersed in his work and I... I was sinking into purposelessness. I decided I would try to paint a human figure and in a medium I'd never used before: oil. God! Before the void of the canvas my mind went blank, my fingers as if paralysed. Then it happened. My subject padded in and hid behind the blank canvas. I remember shivering, knowing that only I could make her visible.

I had problems with the oils. They would drip and make a mess, want to be bright and separate and refuse to combine into the dark, murky colours I wanted. It was as if they didn't want to let me break into something new. I knew what I wanted, but the medium kept slipping through my fingers. I cursed and raged, abusing the figure on the canvas who would not live. I once threw a jar at her and watched as the efforts of a week dripped onto the floor. Yet my subject seemed to urge me on. That was what brought me back to the Sun Room every day.

Time's so very strange. Here in this room, the events of the past press down on me so hard that I can taste their nearness. I'm back to that day four years ago when Marge, long time friend and full time busybody, came with her gift, the news that my husband was having an affair with the Chambers' newest junior. "And she's not some cheap floozie who'll be satisfied being an outside woman. She's trouble, Eve. You mark my words."

Memory fills my head like a thick dark tide. My limbs are dull and heavy. Only my hand is alive and it's looking for something, moving a broken table, tossing aside a rusty golf club. My hand seems my only living part, drags the rest of me into action. I find myself following my hand's lead, searching, searching. I'm in the corner of the Sun Room, the one furthest from the light, furthest from the laughter of Philip's dinner guests. I rifle through the debris of building projects long dead, of gardening enterprises long rotted away and sucked into the earth.

I find what I'm looking for.

Tears well up as I look at the painting for the first time in four years. She is still there, incomplete, the woman sitting in a dark smoky bar. I see her haggard eyes, the hard line of her neck and shoulders, the droop of her greying, processed hair, the fading glamour of her clothes, the rough hands clasping the glass. Then there is the mouth, wistful, broken, as though she is uttering a prayer. I close my eyes. The painting is still before me, unfinished, tentative, as cruel and as true as it was on the day I abandoned it.

The patter of applause pulls me back. I hear a low, resonating voice that I recognise as Philip's. Ah! The speeches. I'm sure Philip's will be witty and wise and all those other good things he's known for. How wonderful it's been all these years being married to the world's most perfect man. Shame I didn't quite measure up. Before this night is out, I'll show him that if I'm imperfect, so is he and so is she. How, I don't know... My brain's clouding over again. It comes and goes, lucidity, I mean...

Woman imprisoned on the canvas, woman in the bar, exhausted woman, broken woman, woman of spent joy, woman of lost hope, woman of hard labour, incomplete woman, unwhole woman, tell me what I should do...

Voice Two:

Oh, Mother! You're here in spirit tonight! When I announced the scholarship fund in your name, I read from that composition I wrote about you when I was nine. Could only read a sentence or two. "My momma makes sure I'm clean and tidy and that I always do my homework. She gives me lots of hugs and tells me I can be a big man one day." That's all I could trust myself to read in public, but there was so much more and I remember forming the letters with my fountain pen on the rough exercise book paper. "She has to work hard at Mrs. Cooper's house and Mrs. Spurling's house. Sometimes I have to wait until dark for her to come home but when she does, she cooks me a nice dinner. Every September, I get a new pair of school shoes. I have to put cotton wool in them and make them last until summer. On Christmas Eve, we go over my Granny's house and I get toys and candies and see my aunties and cousins. But mainly it's Momma and me because nobody loves me like Momma." I carry that composition in my breast pocket next to my heart, Mother. You've been gone for almost twenty-three years but I miss you as though I buried you only yesterday. If only I could find a way to truly honour you. The scholarship fund is so little...

Old Man James is finishing. His voice is dropping to a whisper, a technique he perfected in court. Makes the jury listen by having to strain to catch every word. In an hour or so, this'll be over and Georgia and I'll have a few moments together before she goes home. Where is she? There she is, getting some water for C.J. Typical. Brilliant and kind. A rare combination and she has them both. I'm sorry Daisy never knew her. She would have known from the first that this was the woman who was destined for me, my glory and my reward. How I wish our time together didn't have to be measured out in chunks, in fits and starts. Unfair! Unfair!

The old man's finished. Time to wind up the proceedings. Things have gone well. My wife's disappearing act doesn't seem to have caused even the slightest comment. Wherever she is, for whatever unfathomable Eve-ish reason, let her please stay there until all the people have gone. She used to have a way about her, I have to admit. She had style, she had a way with words and then there was the famous artistic streak. But all that's a memory. Today's Eve is better kept out of sight.

Voice One:

On my way back to my station at the patio doors, I stopped in the kitchen and drank bitter black coffee to push back the fog curling around my brain. The guests are all inside, wearing the glazed look of the overfed. Old Man James is supposedly talking to two young men with keen, fox-like faces, crouching in veneration before him. His expression tells me that he's not listening to their urgent queries about how to make it in the world. All he wants is to be taken back home to his bed. I guess almost everyone's feeling that way. Yet at this moment when everything seems to have been done, there is something I still must do, just as the woman on the canvas told me.

Georgia and Philip come in from outside. They freeze when they see me. Georgia is right in front of me, close enough to smell. It's a light flowery fragrance which hangs on top of a strong scent of musk. I know it well. How many times did it invade my bedroom at three in the morning smeared all over my husband's body? Old Man James calls Philip who hurries over to rescue him from the fox-faced boys with the bristling moustaches. I turn to Georgia and look her full in the face for the first time in a long while. There are some fine lines cut into that patrician brow and a scattering of grey in the midst of the curly brown hair. Life has *some* nice touches.

"I want to talk to you. I have something to say."

"Excuse me?" Georgia's mask of composure remains solid.

"You heard me. I want you to take the old man home and then come back here in, say, an hour. Everyone will have gone by then."

Georgia presses her lips together and says nothing for a moment.

"Would it be too presumptuous of me to ask what this is all about?"

"Yes it would. But you and presumptuous are old friends, aren't you, Georgia, dear? No, you just be here, that's all."

"And if I refuse?"

I give a short laugh.

"You see this delightful gathering? You wouldn't want it all mash up, as you Jump Ups say, now would you? Wouldn't want to upset Old Man James by letting him see you in a brawl. Right now, they..." My arm encompasses all the people in the room. "They think they know. But I'm willing to give them chapter and verse. They already think I'm a fishwife. What have I got to lose? I'll show them your dirty underwear tonight, Georgia, if you don't agree to come back!"

Her eyes narrow as she scrutinises me for any hint of bluffing.

"All right," she says with an indulgent sigh that sounds fake, "I'll be back in an hour."

As she walks away, I grab her by the arm. There is a violence in the gesture that surprises even me.

"When you come, the front door will be open. I'll be waiting in the Sun Room. You know where that is, of course. I've been away enough times in the past five years for you to know this house like it was your own. And," I say, lowering my voice, "Not a word to our husband."

Miss Haughty-Ass swings herself away. I can see from the set of her shoulders that she is furious, frightened and intrigued all at once. I feel a little proud of myself. The coffee is clearing away the fog. All I have to do is to think of what exactly I want to say to Georgia.

Voice Three:

I have to ask myself what I'm doing, driving back to Philip's house after depositing C.J.. It's the depths of night and starting to rain. Summoned to the boudoir of the Lady Wife. To the web of the black widow spider. Will she stun me and eat me alive? She'd like nothing better, I'm sure. However, she and I both know that none of her poisons work against me... So what am I doing, driving through the rain to meet a woman, one half crazed with jealousy, the other half with drink. To meet her while my lover sleeps in blissful ignorance in his room upstairs. It makes no sense. I should have looked her coolly in the eye, agreed to come, then gone home to bed. What could she have done? Ranted and raved in that hole-in-the-wall she calls the Sun Room.

But here I am, going back to her. Why? Why won't this rain stop falling and why won't my knees stop shaking? I'm so good at analysing other people's motives. Why can't I read my own? Got the kind of mind that sees straight lines intersecting, forming patterns, cause and effect, motivation and consequence. It's why I'm so good at my job. I know what makes people tick. I study them, observe them and then a moment arrives when they become known to me. But me? I don't seem so straightforward anymore. Predictable old me, treading the path of rationality. But for the past five years, what have I done? Felt things, done things that have no justification in reason. None! I've been like a ship without a rudder. I have to be in control again. This aimless drifting has gone on long enough. If Philip loves me – which he does – and if I love him – which I do, then something's

25

got to be done... This love business crept up on me unawares. Even when I was very young, it wasn't on my agenda. Only work and achievement. But – like a blow to the brain – I discovered something else.

So is this why I'm going back? Perhaps there's a logic in my actions after all. Can't take this constant turning on and turning off of my life just to keep the Lady Wife on an even keel. It's got to be faced. Tonight, I felt relaxed, among friends, at home, even. Then, when I bumped into her at the door, all those lovely feelings drained out of me. She reclaimed her territory, pushed me back to my life without him. Well, I won't have it! She has something to say to me? Not as much as I have to say to her!

Nearly there. In more ways than one. I must have him. I will have him. She thinks she knows him so well but she doesn't. There are demons prowling around Philip. The strangest is this thing he has for his dead mother. What it's all about I don't know. Philip keeps her shrouded in mystery or shining with the light of many halos. You can be sure of one thing, Lady Wife. It's me he needs to help wrestle with his demons, not you. You can't help him. You're one of them.

Voice One:

Footsteps! I knew Georgia would come. The woman beneath the white cloth whispers to me, gives me the courage to look into those eyes the colour of river water. I feel like a warrior, clothed in bright armour, ready to die.

There you are. To any one else, she'd look full of self-assurance, despite the splatters of rain on her dress and hair. But I know better. We have the deadly intimacy of enemies and I can see her collapsing inside, blinded by my bright armour and my towering strength.

"Come over here, Georgia, I've something to show you."

She doesn't budge but arranges her features so they take on a defiant look.

"What's this all about, Eve? Insisting that I come here at this time of night is more than a little bizarre. Even for you."

It sounds nice and tough but I'm not fooled. I am alert and hear beyond her words the language of her body. Her ram-rod back has weakened into a curve, a slump. There is tension in her fingers and where is that celebrated eyebrow raised in contempt? I glory in my artist's eye. It allows me to see the truth. She's afraid of me.

"I want you to see this."

I unveil the portrait and move towards Georgia. I follow the line of her eyes and see that she is looking above it. A flare of anger blooms in my chest. For the second time tonight, I touch her – how easily taboos are broken – her arm feels clammy against the dry scales of my hand.

"Look at it, damn you!"

My hand closes around her wrist and I can feel the resistance of her bones. As my left hand increases its pressure on her wrist, my right hand grasps her shoulder and Georgia exhales the stench of fear. They may have taught her many things at the Inns of Court but physical courage was not one of them. I never thought I had any either but now, at this dark hour of my life, it comes to me like a lover.

"What do you think I call this painting?" My words are light and jaunty but my hands are still tight around Georgia's wrist. Her eyes are empty when they eventually come to rest on the painting. She clears her throat, playing for time.

"Eh…"

"Well?" My sense of theatre is fed by Georgia's poor quaking body. I am brimming over with the desire to inflict pain on this flesh which has raised so many welts on mine. I squeeze her shoulder hard and words come pouring from her mouth.

"Woman. Woman in a bar." Hers is a child's voice,

buckling with fear. "Old woman. In a bar. Drunk. Drunk woman. Prostitute. Old whore in a bar..."

"Wrong!" I yell.

I start to laugh. It's a laugh which has nothing to do with laughter. It is hard and dry and loud. While I laugh, I keep my grip on Georgia's shoulder. She looks away from me. And the painting. My nostrils fill with her fear. As suddenly as the harsh noise starts, it stops.

I take in a great gulp of air and say with dignity. "The name of the painting is 'Mother'."

Terror gives way to incredulity on Georgia's face.

"What? Mother? My heavens, you really need help."

"You're the one who needs help! Yes, you. You want to know why?" I let her go and walk towards the canvas, which is directly under the light. "You're completely illiterate. Your eyes are so blind; they could only see things like old and drunk and whore. What about the tenderness? And the love and the caring? I know they're there because I put them there!" I straighten my spine and raise my eyebrow in contempt.

"But even more to the point, the reason why you need help, is because I am a mother! I am THE mother, of Philip's children. And had it come to your notice..." I'm singing inside. My mind is clear – the coffee has done its work – as I lash the river water eyes and the mulatto hair and the light, light skin and all the black man fantasies and the younger woman delusions and the stuck-up-bitch arrogance – I lash them all. "Has it come to your notice that Philip worships the notion of motherhood? He lies down at its altar. Brings flowers to it every day. Yes, Georgia dear, you're the one who needs help. To get him away from me, you'll have to get him away from 'Mother'." I thrust my arm out towards the painting. "And even if I get to look like that, you'll still never get him away from his ideal of mother."

Georgia's shoulders slump. She sits, pale and shaking. This should be the moment for the kill, when the matador plunges the sword into the neck of the beast. But strangely, sadly, I feel a weakening in myself. I keep on talking but with every word, I feel my strength retreating.

"Yes, I'm bound to him by the blood of his children. The ones I carried in *my* belly. Two together! The ones I pushed out into the world twenty-two years ago. I know him. He won't leave me to go to a woman who can maybe give him smart talk and good times but who's as barren as a stone." Georgia is holding her head in her hands. I know it without even looking.

The woman in the bar watches us and waits. Outside, the rain overwhelms the night.

Voice Three:

I underestimated Eve. She may be many things but she's not stupid. How could she see the fear that I thought was so well camouflaged? One chink in my armour and that gin-soaked matron, the bake-sale organiser, the collector of atrocious art, exposes me and reduces me to this humiliating silence. How did she know? I thought that I'd kept my eyes bright and clear whenever Philip talked about David and Nicola – I can see him puffing up at the mention of their names – or when he talked about his mother whose canonisation is imminent, if one is to believe him. And that word "we". "When we went to Mexico", "When we had to rush Nicola to hospital", "When we were building the house". It wasn't the royal "we". It was an instinctive, rock-bottom "we", that put me in my place, outside the charmed circle. That "we" has gnawed at me these past five years, but I thought nothing would give me away. But even in her alcoholic haze, the Lady Wife saw it.

What she's put me through tonight! I hate the night rain and she made me drive through it, alone, to come to listen to this. And look at her! She seems deranged, sitting there on a stool right next to the painting. Hasn't moved a single muscle for the past five minutes. She's so still she doesn't appear to be breathing.

"Eve?" I'm shocked at the quivering sound. I call her name again. She turns. Her eyes are as blind as those of a fish on a market stall. Something's happening. Her tongue has become thick and she is slurring.

"I want you to see her as she really was... not the way he ..."

I can't believe what I'm hearing. Only a few minutes ago, she was clever enough to silence me. Now she's barely coherent. Can alcohol really play cat and mouse with a person like that? An escape door is opening.

"Eve!"

"Huh?" Fish eyes stare at me.

"Eve, I'm going. It's over. Your little party. It's over."

Not moving from her stool, she covers up the portrait. Her movements confirm the message sent by her words. No control, no defences. *When you see the soft underbelly, strike!* I walk towards her, my confidence returning with each step. I stop in front of the portrait and right next to her. Her head and shoulders are curled over like a foetus.

"What you said was right, but only partially so." I look down at her hair which shows signs that it was once thick but now is an odd mixture of fragile reddish wisps and grey roots. This is truly oppressed hair. I'm glad I never had to mutilate mine.

"Yes, Philip has a sense of family. To be honest, that's one of the things I love about him." It's amazing how easily that lie came out. Even in her defeated, helpless state, Eve lets out a disparaging grunt.

"But you've got it all mixed up, Eve. He loves his children. That's as it should be. He loves his mother – also true and, I would agree, almost to the point of obsession. However," – I'm getting the warm rush of anticipated victory that

I feel in court – "You're not his mother. You, his mother – separate people, separate feelings. His feelings for his children are also separate from his feelings for you." I strut about in front of her. I can't help myself. "And let's talk about the children. First of all, they're not children. They're grown-up, independent adults who are interested in their careers, their love affairs, their dazzling futures. Of course they're still children for you. But you can't use them the way you might have when they were younger. They can't mend what's broken between you and Philip."

I have delivered my closing speech to a bowed, two-toned head. I wait for that silent response I get in court, the one that says that the jury has truly heard. She raises her fish eyes to me. There is life flickering in them.

"Have you finished?"

"Not quite. You've got to face facts. Philip needs an equal and a challenge. Not someone who requires his assistance through life. Face it! He needs me."

My lips are dry as I hurl the truth at her. She begins to laugh, a demented gurgling that starts in the pit of her stomach.

"Please don't do that! Spare me that horrible laugh!"

She eventually obliges but when she does, the Eve who had earlier bullied me into silence has returned. She rises from her stool and runs her fingers through her conquered hair. She looks at me. Is it my imagination or does she give me a look of pity?

"Georgia, I remember when I first met you. I didn't like you but I envied you. Tough and in charge, that was you. Now look at you! You're no better off than me. Gave your whole self to that man, same as I did. Only I called it 'Family, Marriage and Home'. You called it 'Work'."

She's making me angry with her spurious comparisons! I can't stand a person who doesn't argue rationally. She won't stop.

"So when I hear you say he needs you, what you're really saying is that you need him. So bad it's a shame." Eve passes a weary hand across her brow. Where has the fight gone? It's as though the Viet Cong have laid down their arms.

"The frightening thing about this is that he doesn't need either of us. Somewhere inside him there's a walled city. You've never been inside it and neither have I. Maybe nobody has. Except..." She walks towards the picture in the centre of the room. Something snaps in me.

I'm right up in her face. The muscles in my cheek jump and writhe. A blazing heat flashes up and down my limbs.

"You're talking pure crap! Walled city! To you maybe. But I know him, I mean, I really know him. Why should I listen to a crazy person like you? Everybody knows you're crazy..." Even as I say it, my courtroom self, hovering over my head, poses the question about who is acting crazy. Some instinct tells me to look around.

There, wearing crumpled pyjamas and a look of anguish stands Philip. The words pouring from my mouth dry up in mid-air.

Voice Two:

In the instant before Eve and Georgia become aware of me watching them, a memory assaults me. It's a memory of noise followed by silence. I'm fourteen and waiting for Mother to come back to our room in Till's Hill. It's dark and she should've been home. I eventually go down to my Granny's house on Angle Street to see if she's there. She isn't and Granny sucks her teeth and says bad things about Mother. She tells me to wait while she goes looking for her. I follow Granny in the shadows of the dark streets as she enters one smoky dive after another, calling her daughter's name. Then she goes into a big house with boarded-up windows. I stand outside in the dark, shivering, hearing shouting from within – women's voices, men's voices, Granny's, Mother's – all clashing and crying and cursing. I'm scared but I go inside anyway. There's a corridor I have to walk down, with doors on either side. People with strange eyes watch me pass. I see someone and know it's Mother. I run to her. Mother is on a dirty mattress and is kicking and biting Granny who's trying to drag her up. Every now and then, a man, also on the mattress, makes a grab for Granny and then slumps back down. I stop in my tracks and take in the whole room. There are bottles and old food everywhere and in the corner, there is a second mattress on the floor with a couple lying on their elbows, staring as though at a TV screen. I look at Mother again. Her hair is standing out, her clothes are half open and her legs are splayed wide. But worst of all is the noise she's making. The screams and sobs and the words without meaning as she wrestles with Granny curdle my blood. Suddenly, she sees me, standing at the door with my school uniform on. The silence which falls is more awful than the noise.

And now, here I am again, at the doorway of a room, caught between the silence and the noise. They face me, the two women, looking guilty and afraid. The screaming sobs of my memory continue in my head but this time they seem to be coming from both Georgia and Eve. They are chanting one single word – love! love! love! The word flies in my direction in the form of a ravenous mouth that tries to consume me. I dodge and weave and close my eyes. But all over my body I feel the wounds left by its sharp teeth. Breathe! Breathe, Philip! That's all that can save you. You must learn to breathe in order to live. Serenity returns and I can look at the two women again. It's obvious to me which one I love.

Georgia cries out and runs to me. I enfold her in my arms and feel her inhaling the comfort of my body. I concentrate

33

on making her feel safe but it takes several minutes for her trembling to abate. At last I acknowledge my wife. There is devastation in her face but no madness.

"What's going on?" The question is quite ridiculous – maybe why I've made it in this business. Deadpan in the face of murder and mayhem. Eve mumbles a reply.

"I can't hear you, Eve. Speak up!"

"I said I just wanted to show her something."

"Well what is it? This thing that has made Georgia come here in the middle of the night. The thing that has her so terrorised!"

Eve doesn't answer but just stares blankly.

"Well?"

"It's between me and Georgia. It's got nothing to do with you." Her face is working, flitting from one set of emotions to another. It settles into a grim hardness around the mouth. Georgia has stopped crying and has become tense in my arms.

"It's the painting, Philip." There's a beautiful coolness about Georgia's voice. I fall in love with her all over again. "Show it to him, Eve."

I notice the covered canvas for the first time and remember the days when art was a part of our lives. The art that we collected and the little paintings that she did. That's all in the past now. When I'm just in front of it, Eve steps between me and the painting.

"Don't look at it, Philip!"

I pull my lips back and show my bottom teeth. After twenty-five years, she knows what that means.

"I'm warning you. Don't look at it!" There's almost a pleading in her voice.

"Eve, there's nothing you can do, in this room or anywhere else, that can bother me. Your reign of terror is over."

I draw back the cloth.

The shock strikes clean behind the knees, deals two

heavy blows to the temples. I stagger back, reeling... The screams of wailing women rage in my ears and my eyes are on fire. From a long way off, someone is calling. "What's wrong, darling? What's happened?" An arm clothed in burgundy holds me up and guides me to a chair. A milk-coloured hand slaps my face and wipes the sweat from my forehead. I sit. I can do no more.

I become aware of my abdomen, my lungs, my throat, my mouth, my nostrils. I snatch oxygen from the air and gulp it down. I teach myself to breathe. It is very hard but eventually I succeed. I teach myself to breathe. But the person who gets up from the chair is not the person who sat down in it. The new person has ice where blood used to be.

"Why would you do it?" I ask in a flat unbroken tone. "Why would you sully the memory of the dead?"

"Philip ..."

"If you hate me so much, stab me, claw at my eyes, abuse me in any way you wish. I at least can try to protect myself." I look for the last time at the obscenity. "But she ... she has no defences. She's been in her grave for twenty-three years."

"Let's go, sweetheart," Georgia says. Her voice is so warm and concerned, but I can't look at her. I don't want her to see the darkness inside me. She takes my hand and we walk towards the door.

"Georgia!" the she-wolf cries. "I want you to be a witness to what I say."

I want to get away from that voice but Georgia holds me back.

"I knew Daisy," the she-wolf continues. "She was far from perfect but there was a lot of good in her. She drank and she swore and she went to bars. And your life with her was sometimes – maybe even often – a bumpy ride."

She's panting, this devil, with the effort of all the lies.

"But! She loved you, Philip. You were the one good

thing in her life. And she worked like a slave to give you a chance. But that wasn't enough for you."

She turns her mad eyes to Georgia.

"Did he ever tell you that he once caught his mother in a house of ill repute and drunk out of her head?"

I stand and listen to this, amazed that my hands are still at my sides and not squeezing the life out of that vicious throat. But she has not finished. She's looking straight at me again.

"Yes! I knew about that night. Daisy told me herself. How your grandmother refused to let you see your mother for over a year after that, how Daisy moved heaven and hell to get you back. And how, when she did, you could not forgive her, even though, for the rest of her life, she never took another drink and was as virtuous as a nun. You could not forgive her and it broke her heart."

The voice saying these words detaches itself from the woman's body and fills the room like a towering wave, ready to drown every living soul with its venom.

"But her love was not enough for you. She had to be without human flaw – all your women have to be! When they don't measure up, you discard them. And every day since Daisy died, you've worked to rewrite her. To reinvent her. Inventions you can love. Flesh and blood women – never!"

The infernal voice is slowing down, running out of gas.

"Let me tell you one last thing. That painting is beautiful because it tells the truth..." She hesitates. "Isn't that what we should all want?"

"What I want is a divorce. Come along, Georgia."

As we walk through the house in the dark, Georgia puts her head on my shoulder. She is trembling again. The house seems like one long corridor, very long, very dark with strange eyes blinking at me. But if I concentrate on my

36

breathing, just breathe and block all other things, I'm going to be just fine.

Voice One:

Their footfalls vanish and are gone, leaving nothing but silence and the night. The one with the eyes like river water has achieved the prize. Will it be a golden apple or a tainted one? Who knows? As I sit here in the dark, all I know is we are on a floodtide, all of us, swiftly moving towards the empty caverns where Daisy lives.

But until then, I have something to do. I place my chair to face the huge window watching for the first signs of night retreating. I must rest my fingers and my eyes and my heart so that when the sun rises up over the ocean, I can pick up my brush and go to work.

WHERE THE REMOTE BERMUDAS RIDE

WHERE THE REMOTE BERMUDAS RIDE

The staff of the Nursing Home had whipped the old people into a near frenzy. At the far end of the room, someone pounded out a rousing version of "Onward Christian Soldiers" on the upright piano while the two rows of seated octogenarians facing each other warbled and gurgled to the tune, their snowy heads nodding, their slippered feet slapping the floor in time. But the star of the show was Nurse Cumberbatch who had snatched up a cane and was prancing with it, majorette-style, between the rows of chairs. An old man, the only one in the room, set off in hot pursuit of the nurse's ample bottom, his arm outstretched, heedless of the straps that bound him to the chair. Hopping along steadfastly, he finally made contact with the object of his desire and was rewarded with a teasing smack, first on the hand, then on the lips.

The old women loved this, their wizened faces breaking into toothless smiles, their raucous cackles overwhelming the Christian Soldiers and causing the pianist to give up in confusion. Esther noticed how the mid-afternoon sun streamed in through the windows, how it touched the grizzled heads with light, how laughter was now the music which filled the air. Giving a wistful sigh, she made her way towards her sister.

Quiet lay over the room like a fine mist. Pearl's bed had been positioned at an angle facing the garden on the other side of the sliding glass door so that Esther could only see the bed, the vanity with its bevelled mirrors, the potted plants, the family photographs. There was an acrid smell in the air.

"What! They haven't given you your bath yet and it's after four?" As she always did, Esther took Pearl's face in her hands. There was a brief quickening in the huge dark eyes, otherwise the face was still. More than anyone else, Esther could detect differences in Pearl's expression – sometimes it was as sadly serene as the Buddha; sometimes it was passive, as it was today; occasionally, on those fearful days, her face wore the contours of a primal scream pitched too high for human ears. Esther kissed her forehead, smooth and dark as bitter chocolate, and set to work.

Pearl's eyes did not follow Esther's movements as she ranged her equipment on the bedside table: brush and comb, hair dressing, hair pins, nail clippers, emery boards, nail varnish. Pearl did not react to this bright display, just gazed out at the bed of purple and white petunias dozing in the slanting sunshine. At last Esther stood ready with a wide-toothed comb in her hand. She loosened the two ineffectual plaits and began to comb Pearl's dense profusion of black hair. Esther's rhythmic easing of the comb through the strong, thick mass, her care not to cause pain by tugging at the roots, her systematic parting and clearing of the hair like the felling of a great forest, her applying of oils to the translucent scalp like the anointing of the prophets – the power of this ancient female ritual lured Pearl away from the sunny garden and soon she was staring at the mirror, watching her older sister with eloquent eyes.

Esther's monologue ran on unbroken.

"Look! A few more grey hairs. I thought you'd never get them. Not like me..." Esther patted her smooth jet black bob. "Maybe she's born that way. Maybe it's Maybelline," she sang, then stopped. For a moment, she too looked at the mirror and instead of seeing an immaculate full-bodied woman in her early fifties, she saw a gawky, raw-boned teenager with "picky" hair, seated on a stool, giving thick braids to a beautiful child with slow black eyes, a ready smile and skin like bitter chocolate. Where did we go? Esther whispered to herself.

"Speaking of grey hairs," she said, smoothing the skirt of her church dress, "even the wonders of science couldn't prevent me from getting some more of them last night...That Azaria! If things carry on as they're going, one of us will go crazy. I can't take much more of it!" Esther's voice had lost the brittle cheerfulness of the professional care-giver and had lurched into the husky tones of the confessional.

"We had a terrible fight last night," said Esther. "We'd just finished the dishes and were talking. You know, no problem. Then she says she's going out and I ask her where. A session down Number One Shed, she tells me. I tell her to be careful – all that loud, mindless reggae music and drugs. But you know her!" Esther shrugged. "Doesn't like to be told anything. So she makes a speech about reggae music. What was it again? 'When we want to dance, we listen to dancehall; when we want to think, we listen to Robert Nesta. And we don't all get high.' Something like that, to be understood only if you're under twenty. I'd heard it all before. What came next though was new. Now she drops the bombshell. You know what she told me?"

Esther cleared one side of Pearl's hair, thinking about the thousands of dollars she and her husband Slim would save if Azaria won the scholarship she'd applied for. She thought about how it would feel to tell her friends about her brilliant daughter. Pearl watched with unblinking eyes as the white comb plunged into the darkness of her hair, making ripples as it went.

"She told me she's not going to the interview for the scholarship tomorrow. Just like that! This is the second interview. There are only two other candidates and she has better grades than them. She's almost a sure thing. But My Lady is not going. And why not?"

Esther waited, as though for a reply.

"Because she's too full of herself that's why!"

Esther passed a hand across her forehead, grasped the comb, traced two lines on Pearl's scalp and, with the intervening hair, began to braid, flat on the head, making it look like a perfect sheaf of grain. As she worked, a single tear escaped her eye, fell into the hair and was woven in. Pearl never felt a thing.

"I don't know what I'm going to do with her. She's too rude. You should've heard the way she spoke to me. Not to mention what she actually said. How I forced her to apply for the scholarship. How she wasn't going to sell out the way our generation did. How she wouldn't take their dirty money if they paid her. On and on she went, running her mouth like a freight train. I just can't take it when she's rude like that!"

Esther glanced up at the mirror and saw that Pearl's eyes had stolen away to the petunias.

"Pearl?" she whispered. There was no response. Once again she was grateful for this sister, the perfect listener, to whom she could pour out all her troubles, without fear of disturbance or judgement.

"You know I had a saucy mouth when I was young. Say the wrong word and I'd go off like a sky-rocket. But can you imagine me being rude to Sammy? I wasn't that stupid..."

Esther fell silent as her deft fingers continued to cornrow Pearl's hair. The image of her father rose up before her, trampling over the carefully-erected barriers of adulthood, exposing her once more to the childlike love and fear of him she had always known. She tried to remember Sammy as he had been before her mother had died. But all she could recall was the man who had visited her waking and night-time hours with glowing eyes and reeking breath. Even then, she had known he was a broken man, exhausted by mourning his beloved wife who had died in childbirth, broken by a lifetime's physical labour, worn out by the struggle not to abandon his two daughters and retreat to the mouth of a rum bottle. She remembered how she had waited up for him that night over thirty years ago and how he'd looked, swaying slightly in the doorway.

"Deddy, can I ask you something?"

Despite his condition, he'd turned and looked at her in surprise. Normally, their topics of conversation were restricted to food, clean shirts and swept floors. Esther had braced herself to talk to him about the subject of the hour – the impending theatre boycott.

"I want to go town tomorrow night." Sammy Dill sat on the rickety chair and peered at her through half-closed eyes.

"I know you don't let me go out but this is different. You know why, don't you? The boycott. That's all we been talkin about at school. Things are really goin to change around here." Taking his silence as a sign of interest, Esther had continued in a breathless rush. "Why shouldn't we be able to sit where we like when we go movies? We're just as good as them. Those whites've had it their way too long! Don't tell me those fellas hav'n been talkin about it down the docks."

Sammy got up.

"Ya not goin! Ya got to stay home and see to ya sister."

"But Deddy!"

He faced her and filled the room with his drunken menace. "Ya stayin home!" The left corner of his mouth had started to twitch, a sign, as Esther knew, of approaching danger. But he turned to go, muttering as he went. "Dat's what I get sendin you to dat worfless school. Fillin ya head with trash."

Esther was incensed. She had wanted to defend her school. She had wanted to say it was one of the very few things coloured people could call their own. And though Sammy felt a grudging pride in Esther's achievements there, he feared it would turn her into a dreamer.

"But Deddy!" she pleaded, "I want to be there! This boycott is important. For you too."

Sammy swung around, his mouth twitching again.

"For me! I'm out dere in de hot sun, bustin my ass to put food in ya belly and what you come home talkin about? Movies! It's a lot a talk for children and fools! Ya sister's not right in de head and it's ya job to see to her. So you keep ya tail in dis house or I'll knock ya teeth out!" With that he had reeled out of the room.

The memory was so vivid that Esther could almost smell Sammy's toxic breath on her skin.

"But we both went, didn't we Pearl," she said out loud. "On June 15, we were there!" She had dragged Pearl through the Back-of-Town's darkening streets to the Island Theatre, where they had joined the crowd's attempts to dissuade their less enlightened brethren from entering. The thought of that night with its promise of an altered universe could still move Esther profoundly. That's why her daughter's taunts hurt her so much. She had defied her father. She had literally risked her life to be there. The events of that summer so long ago had put an indelible mark on her. But her daughter would not be impressed.

Esther's fingers continued to work mechanically on Pearl's hair.

"Maybe I should have been more like Sammy and beat some respect into her. But I vowed I would never do that. And I don't even think it would've worked. I never met anyone so hard-headed." Esther finished the last braid and was just weaving them together at the nape of Pearl's neck when she was suddenly aware of another presence in the room.

"Oh! You scared me!"

Azaria stood only inches away from her mother, wearing that composed expression that Esther found so unnerving.

46

Around the girl's neck hung the headset of a walkman.

"How long you been standing there?"

"Long enough to hear you unload on poor Pearl about the good old days when you were a radical."

Esther did not rise to the bait but instead stared into the mirror and marvelled once again at how much Azaria looked like Pearl. The same fine limbs, the same delicate features, the same huge dark eyes. But there were differences. Azaria had taken the colour of her father's people, those light-skinned Nelsons, with the "good" hair. And where Pearl's eyes usually reflected stillness and patience, Azaria had the unflinching stare of a street tough. Esther looked at her daughter's eyes and couldn't decide what she saw in them – stupidity or courage.

"So what brings you here? Shouldn't you be out burning down Government House or something?"

"I came to see my aunt. Is there anything wrong with that?" she answered coolly. "And to let you know there's no hard feelings about last night..."

"Ha! That's a good one!"

Azaria gave a sigh. "Whatever I do, it's always the same. You never show me any respect."

Esther had to laugh. Azaria was actually serious.

"Excuse me for being so dense – I'm afraid my education ended at high school – but don't you have this the wrong way around? Aren't I the one who puts food in your mouth, clothes on your back and books in your hand? You're the one who should respect me!"

"Respect is a two-way street. If you give it, you'll get it."

"Always some smart answer!" Anger flared in Esther's face. "And anyway, since when are you so interested in your aunt?"

Azaria did not respond but did a circuit of the bed, glancing for the briefest moment at Pearl, then letting her eyes come to rest on the flowers outside. But it was impossible to still all of that restless energy; she took to turning and twisting the ring on her right hand. "Let's not quarrel, Mum."

The words damped Esther down and she looked at her daughter once more: the clean profile, the unruly curls, the slender body, the drab, shapeless Bob Marley T-shirt camouflaging a surprising fullness of the breasts. She shook her head and turned back to Pearl, whose eyes were soft and attentive. Esther smiled and took Pearl's hand.

"It's manicure time, sweetheart. What I wouldn't give for nails like yours, so long and shapely. Now what shall we go for today, Montego Blaze or Spicy Red? What do you think, Azaria?" The girl's shoulders moved in a barely visible shrug. "Let's try Spicy Red. Bright is in this summer. All the girls in the office are wearing reds and yellows. But you look good in any colour, don't you, Pearl? When he was sober, Sammy used to call you his Brown Sugar. Yes, you can wear..."

"Is there anything I can do to help?" Azaria interrupted, with an edge in her voice. "I mean with Aunt Pearl. Does she need a drink or is it time for her to be fed?" Azaria was pacing about the room, twisting the ring viciously.

"It's too early for that. But if you want to make yourself useful, go to the nurse's station and bring me some cotton wool so I can take this old polish off." Azaria plugged the headset into her ears and walked out of the room, all of her pent-up energy immediately swallowed up by the music pounding out its message for her alone.

"She thinks I'm an idiot," said Esther after her daughter had left. "It's written all over her. And maybe she's right. When I'm around her, I'm always walking on eggs. Pearlie, having a child today is no joke. I can never relax with her. She takes all my time."

That old-fashioned phrase hurled Esther down a tunnel of time which opened out once again in the year 1959, in a classroom, with her history teacher, Mr. Smith.

"You people take all my time," he used to say. "Especially you, Esther Dill. Always wanting to know why."

And then he'd smile that broad, heart-stopping smile and Esther and her friends would thank the Fates for sending them such a man. The word "teacher" was woefully inadequate in describing what Stephen Smith was to the fifth form class. This son of the soil had recently graduated from Wilberforce and had returned home bringing tidings from other worlds which broke through the confines of the Cambridge School Certificate with his talk of W.E.B. Du Bois, Marcus Garvey, Rosa Parks, Kwame Nkrumah. With Stephen Smith, history was the shattering of the glass in which Clive of India and the imperial banditry beheld themselves. The more Stephen Smith gave to his students, the more they hungered for what he gave, the more they turned their eyes on the piece of rock beneath their feet and made it tremble with their questions.

He had told his students that the winds of change were blowing over the entire planet, including each and every one of them. He had said to Esther that a way would be found to persuade her father to allow her to stay in school so that she could eventually go away to college. This idea was so alien yet so thrilling that it kept her awake at night and would always be her first thought when she opened her eyes in the morning. College was for others, not for people like her. But Stephen Smith had made her believe that this was a new day and that all things were possible.

When in the spring of that same year, the first leaflets had appeared, signed by an anonymous band called "A Progressive Group" and when the leaflets had called for a boycott of segregated theatres in a segregated land, his students had surrounded him and said, "You're one of them, aren't you? Aren't you, sir?" He'd neither confirmed nor denied, had only given them an enigmatic smile which lifted their throbbing hearts.

"On the threshold of a dream," thought Esther. "That's where we were..."

Footsteps behind her failed to rouse Esther from the trance into which she had slipped. Even Azaria's words could not pull her back into the present.

"Here it is, Mum."

As she reached for the cotton wool in Azaria's hand, she searched her daughter's face for something in it that would rekindle the hope of those heady days so long ago. Nothing.

"You O.K.?" Azaria's voice had lost its sharpness and there was a look of concern in her eyes.

"Of course, of course." Esther took the cotton wool and started on Pearl's nails. Pearl's eyes lay flat and unseeing on the flowers outside. Esther swabbed the nails with the pungent cotton wool and tossed the red-stained debris into the bin. At the sliding door, Azaria tugged at a thread from the bottom of the wrinkled grey-green T-shirt that enveloped her. From Esther's vantage point, it looked as if Azaria was pulling on one of Marley's dreadlocks.

Before she could stop herself Esther said, "I wish you would wear some decent clothes. You look like a..."

"Like a what?"

"Nothing. Forget it."

"No! Say it. Tell me what you think I look like!" Azaria's eyes were bright, her body very still as she concentrated on meeting her mother's challenge.

Esther remembered when she had first gone to New York and had boarded the express train instead of the local. She had desperately wanted to get off but had to stay on until the end of the line. She felt like that now.

"All right. You want to know?" Esther asked, looking at Pearl rather than Azaria. "You think I'm going to say you look like a tramp, a female Tommy Tucker? Well you don't. But you do look like someone who takes no pride in herself, who doesn't care how she looks and what other people think. You look like that and sometimes when I'm in town with you, it makes me feel..."

"Ashamed? At last we're getting somewhere." Azaria's words threw off an intense heat, which sent trembling waves of light bouncing from the glass door against which she pressed herself, as though anxious to join the sleepy flowers on the other side.

"What you want is for me to look like a nineteen year old version of you. Colour coordinated down to my under-wear, face painted in Spicy Red and the hairs on my head Kentucky-fried!"

"Nobody asked you to look like me. I just wish you looked like you'd had a bath." Esther reined herself in and tried to sound mild.

Azaria moved away from the door and approached the bed. Her mother's head was bent over Pearl's hand which she was holding as though it were a life raft on a stormy sea.

"In this island, you have to look the part, like you just stepped out of a magazine. And if you don't, they think you're on coke," snorted Azaria. Her words whipped above Esther's head, who sat there holding Pearl's hand, ducking.

"But I'm telling you once and for all, Mum, I'm not living up to anyone's stereotype!"

On hearing this familiar tirade, Esther's heart regained some sense of equilibrium. "How does the rest of the speech go? 'Conformity is the rescue of the weak.' The only thing you seem to have learned at the College. Good thing it's so cheap. Otherwise I'd demand my money back!" She chuck-led, hoping that this would be the end of it.

"You see, you won't take me seriously."

"Why should I? You're serious enough for all of us. Sometimes I think you were born old."

Esther addressed Pearl's extended hand. "One thing we can say, Pearlie. At least we can say we were young once. We know what it means to be young."

51

"Stop talking to Pearl, Mum. Why don't you talk to me for once!" Azaria's flashing eyes raked over the unmoving figure in the bed. "I don't know how to make you understand. I cannot and will not be that person you want me to be. I won't do it! And I won't go to the Somers Isle Bank tomorrow and beg them for their money. You and your generation think that everything that comes in a pretty package is clean. But I ask you this, do you know who was a major investor in Bermudian banks before 1994?"

"No, but I have a feeling I'm about to find out," Esther replied wearily.

"South Africa! And not Mandela's South Africa either. Apartheid South Africa! That's blood money, Mum. And..." Azaria was breathing heavily and tiny beads of sweat had broken out on her brow. "You're so concerned about drugs in Bermuda. You should be. They're killing us all in one way or the other. So... Who launders the drug money coming into this country and makes it look respectable? The banks, that's who. No! No! I won't take that kind of money. I won't soil my hands with it."

Esther placed her sister's hand on the bed and looked straight at Azaria. Esther's movements were slow and deliberate as though giving her daughter time to understand that it was now her turn to crack the whip. As she fixed Azaria with an unwavering gaze, she recalled the day a few months ago when she had been handed the application form from the Somers Isle Bank. Although she had been a customer for many years, it was the first time she had felt any real connection between herself and her country's ultimate source of power. As she clutched the form, her fingers had burned from the intimate touch of prestige, influence and wealth. The burning was not pain but pleasure, one that she wished to give to her daughter.

"Azaria, why don't you grow up? All that so-called 'dirty' money can make life easier for me and your dad. You think university's cheap? And... and..." Esther's index finger jabbed the dangerous space which separated her from her daughter. "Instead of getting a degree from a place no-one has ever heard of you could have the best. The best education money can buy!"

"Like it's a bag of sugar! Education happens up here, Mum," she said, tapping her head. "It can't be bought."

"With that under your belt, you wouldn't have to take orders from anybody. You could beat them at their own game."

"That's just it. I don't want to play their game. As long as you play their game, they win."

"Keep talking! You youngsters make me laugh, always inventing the wheel. You don't want to believe this but thirty years ago when I was your age, they thought I was a hothead. I was there, you know. Because of us, they desegregated the theatres..." Esther paused momentarily and grimaced, seeing the impenetrable look on Azaria's face. There had been no breakthrough. "And the restaurants and hotels. And every other thing that had a 'Whites Only' sign. You wouldn't know... This place was just like Mississippi! And we changed it." While Esther was speaking, Azaria examined her scruffy white socks. Despite evidence to the contrary, she was listening.

"Mum, I know all that. You've told me a thousand times. But what I'm saying is..." She gave the leg of the chair an impatient little kick. "It hasn't changed. The people who owned the Island Theatre back then are the same ones running the Somers Isle Bank today. What they gave away with one hand, they took back with the other. Nothing's really changed from those days."

"That's just not true," said Esther with a deep sigh. "You have to use everything you can, including the Somers Isle Bank, to get where you want to go. There's no other way." Esther ran her hand over the sheet of Pearl's bed with a

53

disconsolate air. "So what are you going to do, phone up tomorrow and say you won't be coming?"

"No, I just won't show."

"What! Did you hear that, Pearl?" Esther exploded, looking from one pair of huge dark eyes to the other. "They'll not only think you're a fool but have no home training either!"

Azaria's face broke into a smile.

"Oh God!" Esther continued. "What's wrong with you? Do you know what they'll do? Your name will go down in a book!"

Even with her hand over her mouth, Azaria's laughter escaped at the thought of her name being inscribed in the Book of Deeds.

"You laugh! I've worked in Government long enough to know that these things are real!"

Esther glared at her but was greeted with nothing but infuriating smiles.

"You know what they'll say? They'll say; 'Azaria Nelson; bright, very bright, but we hear she's into this Black thing...' Your name will go down." The gravity of her own prediction struck Esther with a sudden and awesome intensity. She crossed her arms around her waist and, without knowing it, started to rock to and fro.

The smile vanished from Azaria's face as she felt herself drawn into the vortex sucking in her mother's spirit.

"I don't care what they think. I just don't care."

"But you should care! People like those have your life in their hands."

"The only hands holding my life are these," and she stretched her long olive fingers wide, with the uncompromising assurance of the very young.

Esther looked at her daughter's hands, remembering them as they were as she had first seen them, just as they were when Azaria was born, wrinkled, white, with the fine brown of pigment outlining every tiny nail. She could see the ring on Azaria's hand, the ring with the luminous black stone, that had belonged to her mother whom she hardly remembered. She had died giving birth to Pearl. Esther saw Azaria's hands and struggled to fix in her mind the stranger who owned them.

All of a sudden, there was a slight movement in the bed and Esther noticed that Pearl was gripping the sheets. Her mouth was twisted and her eyes were clouded by a look of fear. Ester turned on Azaria, rage leaping from her black eyes.

"Now look what you've done!" she said, her voice harsh and loud. "You've gone and upset your aunt."

"Oh sure, everything's always my fault," Azaria growled.

"Selfish!" Esther retorted. "Always have been. It's all right for you to rant and rave and abuse me. I'm used to it. But I forbid you to upset Pearl!"

Azaria's body began to shake.

"Pearl! Precious Pearl!" she cried. "That's all I've heard my entire life. She's an obsession with you. Precious Pearl and the sacred year of 1959!" Azaria made a gigantic sign of the cross and pressed her palms together. "Everybody has to take a back seat. Look at Daddy!"

Even in the midst of her anger, the mere mention of her husband Slim had a calming effect on Esther. Although seen by many as one of life's doormats, to Esther he was the glue that kept her life together. A man with feet firmly planted on the good earth who provided the perfect foil for Esther's flights into heaven or the abyss.

"Sometimes I wonder if I have a father." Words flew from Azaria's lips at great speed. "He clocks in for meals and sleep. The rest of the time he's out driving taxi. Working, working. Anything to get out of the house. What do you call that?"

"I call it a decent man." Esther's voice was low and ominous.

"I call it a dead man!" came Azaria's swift reply. "If you gave Daddy and me a fraction of what you gave her, we'd be happy. But oh no! Not you, you and your precious Pearl! And what about me? Why do I always have to play second fiddle to... to... her." And her finger was a spear that she aimed at Pearl.

"What kills me is the way you talk to her, like if she understands."

Azaria saw her mother begin to rise from the chair but she too was on the express train hurtling into the unknown. "You see that limestone wall out there?" Azaria pointed out to the garden. "You'll get as much understanding from that as you do from her. Only it doesn't drool or stink up the place with pee or..."

Azaria did not see her mother marshal her strength and put her full weight behind her hand as it travelled in a slow arc towards her. But she did feel the shivering air in the dangerous space that separated them and the thunder of blood as it raced down her face where the stunning blow had landed. Azaria crumpled where she stood. Esther sobbed as though a fountain had burst from her.

The door of Pearl's room was flung open. Nurse Cumberbatch, looking startled and unsure, took one step forward.

"What's going on here?"

As her eyes swept over the scene, the nurse became transformed, no longer the figure of fun in the Day Room. Her eyes bulged, her hands were planted on her hips and her large breasts seemed to be trained on the combatants like twin cannons.

"I said, what the hell's going on?"

Holding the side of her face, Azaria stumbled past the nurse out of the room.

Hunched over, weeping, Esther heard Nurse Cumberbatch attempt to soothe Pearl. She could not bring herself to look at her sister, but she could not block out the whimpering sound that bored into the centre of her brain.

"It's all right, darling. Don't upset yourself," the nurse said to Pearl. With a sudden hardening of her voice, she said to Esther. "I think you'd better leave. I'm going to have to report this."

Esther opened the sliding glass door and looked back at her sister. Pearl's eyes were two black points of terror, her mouth a broken line, her body a tight corkscrew. The way she'd looked that June night so long ago.

Esther's tears blinded her as she staggered across the garden, leaving, as she went, a trail of crushed blossoms, purple, mauve and white. She half-walked, half-ran, only dimly aware that she was leaving the Nursing Home behind. At last she stopped and looked about her. The graceful old building was no longer in sight, obscured by a curtain of oleander and cedar. She heard the lapping of water and headed towards the source of that sound and soon was sitting on the gray-brown sun-warmed rock, made smooth by wind and tide. She felt the heat from the limestone radiate through her flesh into the very marrow of her bones. She heard the music of the shore and it was a blessing to her spirit. And although her eyes were closed, through her eyelids she could see the scarlet outline of the sun as it began its descent into the western ocean. She sat motionless, fused to that remote rock riding the Atlantic waves, adrift on the breath of the late afternoon.

The sound of approaching footsteps made a gradual impression on Esther's mind. She continued to watch the setting sun work its magic.

"Mum?"

Esther turned with regret from the peaceful horizon and looked at her daughter. Azaria's eyes were red and swollen, her step hesitant. Her face was tear-stained, pale, with red blotches scattered from her forehead to her throat. Her left cheek bore the distinct outline of her mother's hand. Her eyes could not seem to focus on any one thing. She seemed completely lost. Esther wished only to resume her contemplation of the sunset and the sea but was moved to pity at the sight of Azaria so helpless and confused.

"Come," said Esther, beckoning and patting the gray-brown rock. "Sit down here beside me."

Azaria lowered herself down next to her mother, gingerly. They sat in silence, neither looking at nor touching one another.

"I'm sorry," mumbled the girl. "I didn't mean..."

Esther placed her fingers against Azaria's trembling lips. "Don't!" she said and gently touched the blazing left cheek. "Whatever happened back there was my fault. Has always been my fault."

"What do you mean?"

"They stole her from me then and they're stealing you from me now and it's all my fault."

"You're not making any sense, Mummy. Tell me what you mean!"

Esther's glassy eyes slid over Azaria. Her voice was flat and dead as she began to lift the veil that had enthralled her daughter's life from the day she was born.

Azaria had been so right when she had said that the events of the summer of 1959 were an obsession. Historians now say that boycott signalled the awakening of a people's consciousness. For Esther, it was about being young and daring to rattle the bars of her personal prison. She had managed to outsmart her father for eight straight nights. She and Pearl would slip into town, join the crowds outside the Island Theatre and Playhouse and be back home before Sammy returned from drinking with the boys.

"In some ways, it was the happiest time of my life," Esther said.

"The summer of '59?"

"Yes." Esther shifted her position on the rocks. A small smile played about her lips. "I felt so alive! The banners, the

58

crowds, the speeches. Once I even got up on a box and said a few words!"

Then the Bermuda General Theatres shut down all operations, Esther recounted. The boycott was hotly debated in Parliament and in the press.

"When they closed down the theatres, we could smell victory and it smelled sweet," Esther continued, bringing her hand to her breast, holding on to the memory. Within a week, the big hotels and restaurants desegregated and a few days after that, the theatres reopened.

"Now we could sit where we liked. They couldn't spit down on us from the balcony any more. We weren't shadows any more. But," and she waved her hand in a limp, defeated gesture, "it came too late for me, for us."

Azaria received her mother's words like a pilgrim, weary and footsore, seeing the gates of the holy city partially open.

"I understand about the boycott, Mum," she said. "But there must be something more!" Azaria could not fathom the tides of emotion washing over her mother's face.

"They stole her from me."

"Mum! You're driving me crazy. Will you tell me what this has to do with Pearl?" Her words vibrated with bewilderment and, despite herself, a creeping irritation.

Esther glanced about her as though noticing her surroundings for the first time. The little point of straggling crab grass and rock was littered with bits of rubbish, a discarded fishing net, some rusty hooks. In a land of pristine beauty, it was a dishevelled backwater, tucked away, as if not to offend the fastidious eyes of the tourists. Esther felt a sudden affection for this place; it was rugged, ragged, exposed, beaten but not quite destroyed.

"We never knew who did it. No-one was ever brought to trial."

"Trial?" echoed Azaria.

"Some people said it was a sailor. It could have been more

than one. We'll never know." Esther seemed frozen where she sat, the soft sea breeze unable to stir the light material of her dress, or lift a single strand of her hair.

"Pearl couldn't tell us, wouldn't tell us, didn't want to tell us another thing after that night." Esther's voice had dropped so low that the brushing of wave against stone all but drowned what she was saying. Azaria leaned closer, silence enfolding her like a robe.

"It was the one night that Pearl didn't come to town with me," Esther whispered. "Island and Playhouse had already closed down and we knew we were going to win. We were strong. We were celebrating already. We had this motorcade that drove all the way down to St. George's." Esther clasped her hands together.

"I hadn't been in a car before," she went on, a sad smile briefly lighting her face. "I thought I was in heaven, sitting there next to Stephen Smith, feeling different about myself, about the world."

"Stephen Smith, that was your teacher, right?"

Esther nodded. For a moment she seemed incapable of another word. She took a deep breath.

"It was a magical night. I felt for the first time that the whole sky belonged to me." Esther pressed her lips into a hard, tight line. "What I didn't realise was while I was out enjoying myself in the name of the people, the person I was really responsible for was having her life taken away from her."

Azaria's eyes widened as she watched her mother bow her head.

"When I got home, I found Pearl beaten and raped. She went away from me that night and she never came back." Esther paused. "All these years I've been trying to bring her back but she never came."

There was nothing Azaria could say. Tears rolled down her cheeks, over the spot bearing the imprint of her mother's hand. The dark blue evening waters rubbed themselves against the rocks, sighing in an endless rhythm.

"She never talked much, you know. She was slow, couldn't learn much. But after that night she decided there was nothing she wanted to learn or talk about. And little by little, she's drawn into herself. Now all that's left is a person in a bed. In a place where people come to die."

"Oh poor Pearl! Poor Aunt Pearl! Why didn't you tell me before?"

Esther appeared not to hear. "The part that hurts most," she said, "is that she was looking for me when it happened. Wandered out in the dark, looking for me. Sammy found her not too far from the house." Esther heaved herself up and dusted off her dress. She looked down at Azaria's shock of untidy curls. She recalled how she had taken the beautiful black forest of Pearl's hair and made it into a work of art.

Azaria stood up. The sun was stretching its arms out over the earth and sea in farewell. Azaria looked into the sun's golden eye before it slipped behind the waves. When she faced her mother, something in her had changed.

"So all these years you've been blaming yourself..." The muscles in Azaria's face worked as she strove to find the right words. "But you've got to stop, Mum. It wasn't your fault. You love Pearl! You've loved her all your life." Azaria paused, trying to get her mother to look at her. "If you're to blame, so was Sammy, the neighbours. Not to mention that animal who did it. Mum, everyone has to take the blame, not just you!"

"Azaria," Esther said, taking her daughter's hand, "I know you're trying to make me feel better." The dark hollows beneath Esther's eyes seemed to fill with unshed tears. "But nothing you say can convince me of that. It was my job to look after Pearl and I failed." Esther's voice lost its tremor and was now matter-of-fact. "Why? Because I was out having fun, trying to save the world. So after that I said,

Let someone else go out there and get involved. I did and look what happened. Pearl paid the price." Esther turned to go. "I decided to just look after my own."

"You know what," said Azaria as they started to walk slowly back. "Pearl's not the only one. We've all paid; you, Daddy, me. All of us." They walked along together in the fading light.

"Mum, what ever happened to Stephen Smith?"

"Oh, he left. He went to study law in England and never came back."

Azaria frowned and shook her head but her mother did not see. As they walked away in the gathering twilight, Azaria put a protective arm around Esther's shoulder.

The sun rose the next morning, like a young girl flaunting her beauty. At ten o'clock precisely, Azaria entered the Board Room of the Somers Isle Bank. Opulence furnished the room with its Chinese carpets, heavy bronze fittings, its oil paintings in gilt frames, its polished cherry oak table. Seated behind this was a panel of six smiling men. There was an air of celebration as the men surveyed their prize. In her white linen and with hair swept back and bag slung over her shoulder, schoolgirl style, Azaria perfectly fitted the profile: she was bright, hungry and black. Just right. Her choice as recipient of the major award would go down well in the community. It was people such as her that they wanted in their corporate pocket.

"Won't you sit down, Miss Nelson?" The next twenty minutes flowed seamlessly, with the rubber-stamp questions and answers moving back and forth like the motion of the tides. It was so painless that Azaria found her thoughts slipping away to the Nursing Home and the ragged point of rock that jutted into the sea. When all was done, the chairman of the panel smiled and said, "Is there anything you wish to ask us?"

Azaria took the large bag from her shoulder, opened it and for a moment seemed to fumble with a metallic box which the panel members could only partially see. Then she turned a serene face to them.

"No, gentlemen, I don't have anything to ask you. But there is something I'd like you to hear."

There was a click and before the six suited men around the table could draw breath, a song descended from on high, casting a net over them.

"*Old pirates yes they rob I,*" sang the shaman's voice, an ethereal voice filled with courage and with tears. A solitary guitar accompanied him.

"*Sold I to the merchant ships...*"

Azaria sat straight-backed as the astonished interviewers all started babbling at once.

"What's the meaning of this, young woman?"

"Are you trying to make some sort of statement here?"

"I don't understand..."

"You can't help some people..."

Azaria sat in a pool of stillness, her eyes fixed on the world outside the window, as the consternation of the panel members muffled the words of the song which nonetheless continued to glow in the air of the Board Room like burning coals. From that well of quiet in which she was submerged, Azaria drew the strength she needed to lower her gaze from the window, sweep her eyes over her interrogators and raise her right hand. That gesture was a command to the men to cease their outraged prattling. To listen to the song.

"*Won't you help to sing*
These songs of freedom
Cause all I ever had
Redemption songs..."

Azaria was on her feet handing out copies of the lyrics, all the while stilling the puffed-up men in suits, with her upraised hand, forcing them by her presence, by the shining armour of her youth, to flee into a cowed and smouldering silence.

"Emancipate yourself from mental slavery
None but ourselves can free our minds
Have no fear..."

The shaman was without mercy as he sang the pleasures of liberation. The panel members would take it no longer. As a body, they took the decision to refuse to be intimidated – in the heart of their terrain, in their bronze and gilt-edged bunker – by this slip of a girl and her wild-haired wailing prophet. They started protesting again, spitting out half-thoughts clothed in windy rhetoric. Their eyes were hard and ugly as they blustered, unable still to look at her, this danger, this enemy, this serpent who had slithered into their midst.

Azaria leaned over to switch off the tape recorder, singing along when the voice proclaimed, *"We've got to fulfil the book..."* Slowly, with all the dignity she could muster, she walked to the door. She felt their inflamed eyes upon her. When she turned, silence fell once more. "I find no redemption here," she said in a steady voice. "No possibility of freedom. Just an upmarket prison." Then her face broke into a smile. "Thanks for the offer of all that money, but I think I'll pass."

The interview was over.

Azaria rushed past the secretaries, jumped into the elevator and ran across the main banking hall. Everything was a blur. It wasn't until she was out in the hot sunshine of the street that she became aware of the loud thumping in her chest and the shivering that had taken hold of her. In a few moments, though, the heat of the sun reached into her pores, drove out the cold and began to still her racing heart. She straightened her spine and prepared to face her parents and the struggle that would be her life.

Esther and Slim had not gone to work that morning. They sat in the living room of their home, waiting. On the floor next to them lay an envelope with the words "To be discussed with the Somers Isle Bank at 10:00 a.m." written in bold print. Esther was holding the text of the song that Azaria had just played in the board room. Two lines of the song had been highlighted in red.

"We forward in this generation
Triumphantly"

On the bottom of the paper, Azaria had scrawled, "Mum, I'm taking up where you left off. Don't be too angry."

A heavy silence hung in the air. Slim took the paper from Esther's hand and held it close to his face as though trying to decipher a script from some lost civilisation. His breathing seemed to shake his slender frame. At last, he looked across at Esther. Her attention had shifted to the sunshine flooding through the bay window.

"It doesn't make sense," he said in a choked voice. "It just doesn't make any sense."

Esther said nothing. She continued to stare at the dust particles trapped in the shafts of sunlight. Slim shook the sheet. His anger made the paper give a sharp crackling sound.

"What's she trying to prove, Esther?" he cried. "This won't hurt them. Only her." He put his head in his hands. "All our work, all our hopes for her – gone!"

The whispered despair in that last word wrenched Esther away from the window. She moved closer to Slim and kissed him.

"I don't really understand," she said. "Maybe it's just something she felt she had to do."

Slim raised his eyes and looked straight at Esther for a moment, long enough for her to see the full extent of his pain. Then, without a word, he got to his feet, slammed out of the house and into his taxi. The roar of the taxi's engine filled Esther's head for what seemed like hours afterwards.

When silence eventually returned, Esther glanced around her and saw the comforts that she and Slim had carefully

accumulated over the years. They had thought these familiar objects would provide them with some security in this,
the afternoon of their lives. But as the sun poured in, the
most solid thing in the room seemed to be the sheet of white
paper, lying in an attitude of defiance, in the middle of the
floor. Esther went over, almost fearfully, and picked it up.
Thoughts of that distant summer, that defining moment of
her youth, engulfed her like a balm, easing the strained
muscles of her neck and back.

"It's her turn to try," she whispered to the hushed room.
"Maybe it won't be just a dream any more."

Esther looked up at the window again and saw how the
sun made the particles of dust shine and how they moved
and floated free.

At the western tip of the island, Nurse Cumberbatch
pulled back the curtain drawn across the sliding glass door.
Sunshine streamed in.

"How's my sweetheart this morning?" the nurse asked
beaming. "Good? You're the lucky one today."

She bustled over to the bed and touched her favourite
patient's smooth cheek.

"Somebody came early this morning and left something
for you. Here it is. You want me to open it for you?"

Nurse Cumberbatch opened a small white envelope.

"Look, Pearl. It's beautiful."

She slipped the ring on Pearl's finger and they both
watched as its dark fires danced in the heart of the stone.

For the first time in a very long time, Pearl smiled.

THE CEREMONY OF INNOCENCE

"Come now, *Chéri,* just close your eyes, make a wish and blow out the candles. If you blow them out all at once, your wish will come true."

The child looked first at the speaker, to be precise at the tiny pearls of sweat on her top lip, then at the five flickering candles on the blue and white cake, and finally at the swirl of expectant faces watching him. He shut his eyes tightly and blew with all his might. The cheers which followed confirmed his worst suspicions. He snapped his eyes back open and found that, yes, the faces were still there. Another grownup lie! He opened his mouth into a loud, indignant howl.

Marie-Ange's elegant hand flew to her mouth, blending the pearly moustache into the blood-red paint on her lips. She could not move. A gaggle of aunts, nieces and cousins rose as a body and swooped down on Marie-Ange and her wailing child. The pair was quickly obscured by a knot of designer suits, sleek chignons and tinkling silver bracelets. But clearly the victim of this assault was not taking things lying down and his tears were now accompanied with flailing arms and legs.

Amid the overpowering splendour of the room at the Hotel Trianon, sharp little comments could be heard coming from the luncheon guests:

"Spoilt! A little brat, that's what he is. We give these children too much."

"I blame Marie-Ange. She gives in to his every whim."

"And the father is just too busy…"

"But they're all like that, children nowadays."

No assessment could have appeared less accurate than this last one on the evidence of the thunderstruck expressions of the dozen or so small children seated near to where the skirmish was taking place. They were frozen in a watchful stillness, letting Didier speak for them. But for the thirty or more adults at the polished tables, there was no such restriction and the idle chatter of a few minutes before was replaced by a rumbling ground swell of discontent which rose to the ceiling like a storm cloud where it met the lightning cries of the protesting birthday boy.

"Enough!"

Attention shifted to a tall young woman with an exasperated expression on her face. Joelle cut a reckless path towards the boy, nearly toppling sweating bottles of Chablis as she went. In one sweeping gesture, she pushed aside the designer suits and snatched up the struggling child. He felt her arms around him, fixed his eyes on her livid face, stopped screaming and started to sob, *"Tanti! Tanti!"*

She ran with him to the long, plate-glass window which made up one complete side of the room. The opposite side was panelled with gilt-edged mirrors (reminiscent of the Hall of Mirrors at Versailles, the hotel brochure said). The overall impression was one of space and fractured light. The backs of Joelle and Didier, dark silhouettes amid the flood of sunshine, were the meeting point of every eye in the room.

"See how high up we are, *petit.* And look! See the fishing boats coming in over there. Don't they look small?"

The *pirogues* slipping through the lagoon below looked like toys on dark blue satin.

Everything seemed unreal from the top of this luxury hotel overlooking this city where Europe and Africa were locked in a mortal embrace. Skyscrapers rubbed shoulders with shanty-towns; crowded motorways left the city and cut into the dense green forest. Abidjan, city of illusion.

"Didier, don't the boats look small?"

The child nodded, swiping at the tears on his face, craning his neck and trying to control the heaving of his chest.

"And look, all the way over there. Look where I'm pointing. There. That's Grand Bassam. We're going there for a picnic this weekend. Want to come with us?"

"Yes, *Tanti*." A smile broke through as Didier absorbed the tall buildings of the city, the vivid blue of the lagoon and the rest of the coast as it curled out of sight in a crooked line of rocky inlets and bays.

Marie-Ange came over, high heels clicking, and took Didier by the hand.

"Well then, *Chéri*, now that that's all over with, shall we cut the cake? Your guests are waiting." She lifted her head and looked at her younger sister, that permanent thorn in her flesh. "I would have thought that you might have found something more, eh, appropriate to wear."

Marie-Ange's critical eyes raked over Joelle's body. In her striped T-shirt and short denim skirt, Joelle did not flinch, not even for an instant.

"And I would have thought," Joelle's tone mimicked Marie-Ange's to perfection, "that you might have found something more, eh, appropriate to do on your son's birthday than to inflict this torture on him, not to mention on his father's bank account."

"So you're telling me how to bring up my child now!" The sweaty pearls bulged.

"No! I'm saying that all that interests you is showing off and throwing around darling Pascal's money," retorted Joelle. "Didier would have been much happier rolling around in the dust in Sinabre than being part of this circus!"

The rumblings started again. Marie-Ange caught their muffled message and seized the opportunity to put this upstart in her place. Years of unsuccessful combat with Joelle had not blunted Marie-Ange's appetite for battle. She knew she won hands down in the beauty department. She was a classic beauty, pure in line and contour, whereas there was a kind of subversive asymmetry in the startling attractiveness of Joelle. But Marie-Ange had enough wit to know that brains and personality were what gave dominance. The grumblings of her family members gave her a chance she would exploit publicly.

"Your problem is you lack respect. Our father wasted his money on you. Sent you to France to do all kinds of useless studies and what did you learn? To be no better than that white shopkeeper's son you've dragged home with you!" The one white face in the room flushed brick red. Marie-Ange continued undeterred. "These things have to be said. She gets away with too much. *Merde!*"

Someone had appeared next to Joelle, had taken her arm and was talking softly. It was Maryse, the sister who had always seen it as her duty to keep Joelle out of trouble.

"Calm down. Is this really something to get worked up about?" Maryse, a stocky young woman, looked into the face of first one sister, then the other and saw herself reflected in both. Yet the differing beauties of Marie-Ange and Joelle added up, in her, to an emphatic plainness. This was her lot, which she bore with a sullen grace.

"You're right, Maryse," said Joelle, bestowing on her a gap-toothed smile. "Why am I wasting my time?" She made for the door in a few long-legged strides, giving the nod as she went to the hapless youth from the Alpes Maritimes who was only too anxious to leave. Nervously flicking back the lock of the dark hair from his forehead, Jean-Luc rose and followed Joelle.

But she was not quite finished with Marie-Ange yet.

"I don't get it," said Joelle, turning back from the door. "So what's new?"

"Here you are telling me how to be a real African..."

"Of course, you know everything there is to know about that – you and your French boyfriend!"

"Yet," continued Joelle, undaunted, "you're the one who has to spend each August in France because it's too hot here." Joelle was visibly warming to her subject. "Your children are not allowed to speak any other language but French..."

"When they can write their *Bac* in Baoule, then I'll let them speak it!" Marie-Ange had her back to Joelle, tossing these one-liners over her shoulders.

"And when they have a birthday – a very un-African thing, by the way   they have to get all dolled up and sweat through a six-course meal." Joelle moved to face this child-abuser. "Worst of all, you insult an invited guest. Our ancestors should have sent down a thunderbolt for that alone! Come on, Jean-Luc, let's get out of here!"

With great aplomb, Joelle flung open the door, let Jean-Luc pass, then made her exit.

Suddenly the French language vanished and Baoule broke out like automatic weapon fire. Most of the outraged exclamations were directed at the empty space at the door-way where Joelle and Jean-Luc had stood a few moments before. A small group consoled Marie-Ange who sniffed daintily into a handkerchief. They urged her to ignore her sister and the catastrophic end of the birthday party. When there was a lull, she said in voice as silken as her garments, "I don't know how she could even look at such a pale, uncircumcised thing."

Gusts of laughter blew through the private dining room of the Hotel Trianon. With the laughter came forgetfulness.

At the far end of the room, Didier and his friends ripped off their bow-ties, ribbons and choking laces and started wrestling on the floor, happy that the party had begun at last.

In amongst the heedless grownups, yet visibly alone, Maryse filled her glass from a bottle of vintage Burgundy, put

it to her lips and slowly drained it dry. Then she took out of
her bag a small leather-bound book and started to scribble:

*Joelle and Marie-Ange have been at it again. In grand
style, in the private dining room of the Trianon. As usual,
Joelle won. But not completely. Mother and Father won't
like hearing that their daughters have been trading insults in
public. Still, Marie-Ange deserves to be put down and
Joelle is the only one to do it. It will all blow over. It always
does. Joelle will be forgiven. She always is.*

Joelle and Jean-Luc came out of the Trianon laughing.
All the way down from the fifteenth floor, Joelle had teased
Jean-Luc so much that he had discarded the look of angst
that had invaded his face at Didier's party.

"I did warn you about my family, Jean-Luc. Especially
Marie-Ange. Such a show-off!" Joelle said, grabbing his arm
and steering him across the anarchic traffic. "But she and I have
a long history. She never forgave me for being a cute baby."
She threw her head back in infectious laughter and Jean-Luc
joined in, glad to have fallen victim to this particular illness.

They threaded their way through the crowded street,
jostling men in dark suits, clutching attaché cases and
beautifully-dressed women, sauntering along in their fin-
ery, stopping frequently to plant four red kisses on the
cheeks of their friends.

"It's not her fault," Jean-Luc said as they passed shops with
names like 'Quartier Latin' and 'Au Printemps'. It's the fault
of History. She resents me because of our colonial past."

"You think Marie-Ange is capable of something as com-
plicated as that? She resents you because you came to the
Ivory Coast with me. That's all!"

They turned down a side street and found themselves in
front of a small sidewalk cafe, its circular tables overhung by
a red and white stripped awning. The deep shade looked

tempting. It was off the beaten track. They decided to "take five" before facing the crowded Air France office where Jean-Luc had to confirm his ticket. As they sipped icy drinks, they continued to rehash the events at the Trianon, with Joelle ragging her friend without mercy when he attempted to place them in some earnest socio-economico-politico-historico context. He eventually gave up.

"You know, Joelle, I really love your country."

She gave him a sharp look. "After only three days? *Mon Dieu,* do you always fall in love so quickly?"

Jean-Luc reddened. His discomfiture with Joelle's words was replaced with annoyance at being cursed with skin that revealed his emotions like a scarlet flag. He hoped Joelle had not noticed.

"Although I've been here only three days, I feel like I've been here forever." Jean-Luc ignored Joelle's raised eyebrow. "I know you think that theories of economics and history are all that interest me..."

"The most brilliant student in our year. Not to mention dedicated and gorgeous," Joelle added with glee.

"Be nice," he implored, feeling the heater in his cheeks switch on again. "It's true. As soon as I touched down here on Sunday, I could see all theories in action. The exploitation of the South by the North. The IMF's heavy hand. The money-grabbing middle class – no offence, Jo." The teasing look left Joelle's face. She was listening. "Everything is so out in the open here. Not like in Europe where the corruption that goes on here exists too, but is much more carefully hidden."

Jean-Luc was encouraged by Joelle's attentiveness and, flicking hair out of his eyes, pressed his point home.

"But what has intrigued me is not that at all. And it's certainly not the skyscrapers!"

"Well what then?" A tiny grain of irritation had crept into Joelle's tone.

"It's what I call the African dimension."

"The what?"

"The African dimension! I felt it as soon as my feet touched the Ivorian soil. There's a timelessness about the place. A mystery..."

"But, Jean-Luc, who would have taken you for a hopeless romantic!" Joelle started to chuckle. "Timelessness. Mystery. All that in three days? Next you'll be telling me you've seen spirits flying over Abidjan!"

"Anything is possible." Jean-Luc's voice was quiet but his shoulders stiffened into a defensive posture. When Joelle spoke, there was an aggression in the way her lean limbs inclined towards him.

"Let's get one thing straight. In the unlikely event that there is an 'African dimension', it belongs to us. And not to someone born in the South of France!" A fraught and nervous silence hung between them, broken only by the clinking of ice cubes swirled by Joelle's finger. Jean-Luc cleared his throat.

"Another thing I love is that everyone here looks beautiful. Not just people like your family and friends. When it comes to chic, they fall off the scale! No, it's everyone. The market vendors, the men who work on the docks. Even if they're in rags, they still have unlined skin, perfect white teeth – things you have to pay a fortune for in Europe! I find the Ivorian women particularly lovely..."

"I hope you're not suggesting," said Joelle, her laughter returning, "that you have found someone here who is more beautiful than me. Because if that is the case..."

"Don't make fun," he murmured, miserably aware of the furnace doing its work from neck to crown. "You know how much I..."

"May I join you?" Both Joelle and Jean-Luc jumped.

"Oh, M! How did you know about this place?" Joelle gave a broad grin, then glared at Jean-Luc. "Dear sister, will you please save me from the amorous advances of this Lothario?"

Jean-Luc got up, trying hard to appear calm.

"Please sit down, Maryse. But you must excuse me. I've got to go to the airline office. See you later, Joelle." He walked away, without turning back.

"He looks upset. What have you done to your little Frenchman?"

"Maryse, how many times do I have to tell you? Men are tiresome. If it's not one set of confusion, it's another."

"Nevertheless, I don't think it's fair. He's your university classmate. You invited him here. It's bad enough that Marie-Ange gives him a hard time. But then you go and do the same thing. Only it's a different type of hard time. You've got to learn to be a bit more kind, Joelle."

"You are right, oh wise one. From this day forward, I will be kind to those unfortunate creatures of the male persuasion."

"You're impossible."

"And you are possibly a saint." Joelle sighed. "Why can't I be more like you?"

"The day you become like me, Marie-Ange will have to find a new sparring partner; Mother and Father will have to find someone else to alternately rebuke and indulge; little children will have to find a new champion and scores of men world-wide will have to find a new reason to get up in the morning. In short, the world will go mad, if such a day dawns."

"Hmmm. You may have a point there." Joelle squeezed her sister's hand. "But I do worry about you, M. You're almost invisible in the family. Always on your own. You know what our lot's like. If you let them, they'll roll right over you. And – what about creatures of the male persuasion?"

"Look," Maryse said, wishing to change the subject. "I'm fine. I've got my dissertation..."

"Can a dissertation keep you warm at night?"

"This is Africa. I don't want to be any warmer than I already am."

"Well, suit yourself." Joelle jumped up and rummaged around in her large bag for some change. "Would you believe it? I don't have a 'sou'! Would you mind awfully, awfully paying for the drinks?" She bent and kissed Maryse. "I'd better catch up with my *chéri-coco* and apologise to him for being as big a bitch as Marie-Ange. You see, Saint M, I'm trying to put your good counsel into practice." Snapping her bag shut, she added, "I'll see you later. But not till after dinner." She paused. "Once I get Jean-Luc sorted out, there's someone I have to see."

Joelle set off at a run, leaving Maryse sitting alone. She ordered black coffee, took out the leather-bound book and wrote:

> *Someone very special? I wonder who that can be? You can never tell with Joelle. It could be the President of the Republic or the filthiest beggar in Treichville. That's what extraordinary about her. Alpha and Omega waging constant war inside her head. She who will flaunt a white man in front of our parents is the same person who has this strange bond with our grandmother who's halfway in the spirit world already. She's beautiful and she's brave – but I don't envy her a bit. Her life's going to be a lot stormier than mine. I've got my thesis that I will spin out as long as I can. I've always been a plodder. Why stop now? And my topic is so obscure, a tiny piece of St. Augustine's writings, no one will be bothered either way. Which is why I steered clear of African literature. What's the purpose of a book if it's not to escape from your daily pain?*

Joelle hesitated outside Adjua's door, as she always did. It was dusk and the house was quiet. In some distant part of the city, a muezzin called the faithful to prayer. She knocked and went in.

An intricate web of light and shadow stretched across the

room, robbing all objects of discrete substance, texture and form. In the fading colours of twilight, the room appeared to Joelle as a single unit, devoid of particular parts, a single throbbing thing, as ancient and as powerful as the earth itself. It seemed a million miles from the Hotel Trianon.

"Grandmother, it is I." As always, the Twi language fell from her lips with difficulty at first. But she knew that within a few moments she would feel as though she knew no other.

"Ama, my child!"

Joelle could not be sure where the voice was coming from, so suffused was the room with muffled shadows and the muted evening light. White curtains fluttered at the window and in a darkened corner, a flame glowed. And then, there she was, her tiny frame gaining definition against the obscurity.

Joelle crossed the space between them and, when she could see Adjua's face clearly, bowed her head and made a slight genuflexion. Adjua too bent an arthritic knee before her granddaughter and raised Joelle's head with a gnarled, henna-tinted hand. A moment of eternity seemed to envelope them, a tear of glowing amber round a tiny flower. The room appeared to observe the two women, separated by years but joined by blood and heart. Neat stacks of calabashes, large baskets full of folded cloth, leather pouches suspended from the ceiling, straw mats on the floor, a single wooden stool, a plain narrow bed: all watched as Joelle and Adjua faced each other in an instant beyond time.

"I come to present my greetings, Grandmother."

"And you too must receive mine. How is your health?"

"I am well, Grandmother."

"And that of your father, my son and your mother?"

"They are well, Grandmother."

"And that of your brothers, sisters, their husbands, wives and their children?"

"They are well, Grandmother."

79

"Then peace be with you all."

"For that we give thanks, Grandmother."

The formalities over, they sat on one of the mats. In front of them were a covered enamel dish, a large mug, a basin of water and a towel.

"You are in good time. Kwantema has just brought food. Eat with me, child."

They washed their hands with water and a chunk of brown home-made soap and set about the plate of steaming foo-foo. Adjua had this dish every night no matter what filet mignon was going on in the rest of the house. She insisted that the soft mush of palm oil, okra and pounded banana was well suited to her gums and stomach, as was the hot pepper to her soul. She and Joelle dipped their right hands into the hot food and ate until they were full. They covered the dish, drank from the mug, washed their hands again and sat facing in different directions in the gathering darkness. Adjua began polishing her few teeth with a small resinous stick.

"It is a long time since we were truly together, Ama," said Adjua.

"Grandmother, I came to see you this morning, as I've done every day since coming from France."

"Yes but you came as a duty. They all do. Morning and evening they come through the door and my dim eyes can see they are eager to be gone." She paused. "With you it is different. And tonight some disturbance brings you here."

Joelle closed her eyes and listened to her grandmother's voice, its authority belying the fragile body in which it was housed. Behind her eyelids, she saw the room and knew it could be found in every remote corner of this western coast of the continent. The room was Joelle's buffer against the bedlam of her father's house, that sprawling white villa that was the envy of all Abidjan. But for Joelle, it was a place of difficulty. At any given moment, she had to strive to maintain a balance on the dizzying see-saw of her family: the rhythmic "squish squish" of a servant washing clothes in a galvanised tub versus the "ping" of the microwave; the stern voice of the teacher of the Koranic school on the pavement outside versus the stern voice of Buju Banton within; the straw mats spread out under the stars by relatives up from the country versus the four-poster monstrosity in the air-conditioned master bed-room; prominently placed portraits of blue-eyed Jesus versus amulets, talismans and gris-gris, stored under beds, in drawers, worn beneath clothing, next to the skin. Only in Adjua's room was Village Africa triumphant, routing the tongues of Europe, its ways, its names, its Gods. Unlike her sisters and brothers, Joelle acknowledged this place as a sanctuary, giving her special access to her grand-mother's heart. But Joelle was also a child of her own times and sometimes preferred the maelstrom to the uncom promising purity of Adjua and her world.

"There is no disturbance, Grandmother. Only it grieves me that you are so apart from the rest of us. So alone in this room. It wasn't always like this."

"Do you come on a mission from your mother?" Adjua's tone was robust.

"Grandmother! What a question!"

"Your father, then."

"No," Joelle said.

"Well, why do you speak to me of such things?"

"Grandmother, I'm concerned about you. You're be-coming distant from us. I guess because I'm away most of the time, I notice it more when I come home. Whoever wants to see you outside your room will have to get up before sunrise to catch sight of you and Kwantema walking around the courtyard."

"Ama, Ama! I spent years in the other rooms of this house – the house of the one child given to me by God. During that time, I tried and tried to remind them all of our ways, the old ways. But they did not wish to hear and I grew old and tired." She sighed. "But here, there is peace. And I am content. I ask for nothing more."

Joelle took one of the old woman's hands and massaged it lightly.

"But I worry about you, here all alone..."

"I am not alone. Kwantema cares for me well."

"Yes, but she's..."

"She is what we in Sinabre call 'blessed'. Her quietness should be a lesson for us all."

Joelle stood up and retied the *pagne* about her waist, saw it fall in straight, clean lines down to her ankles, felt the familiar stretch of the waxed cotton across her hips. The room was dark now, the stealthy invasion from the window complete.

"Grandmother, you are wise and generous and because of this, you are a problem in this house."

"That problem is theirs, not mine. My duty is to sit and await the pleasure of God." Adjua paused. "But I do have a request. Of you, child."

Joelle turned up the flame of the lamp and waited.

"Do you remember when you were children and your father, my son, had a mother he would still listen to?" Adjua's mouth tightened into a bitter line. "Do you remember at this time of year, when your schools were closed for holidays, how we would all go, every one of us, to spend two months in our village? And how you would romp and play and learn. About the stars and the blades of grass moving in the wind and the spirits living in the great trees of the forest?"

Joelle stared into the flame and remembered.

"And every year we went and I still believed then you could all be safe because of that journey." Adjua stopped and gazed at the stick she had been chewing on even in the midst of her monologue. "And then it happened. Your elder brother caught the fever and nearly went to join his ancestors. Do you remember? How your mother refused our medicine and fled with him back to the city among her own Baoule people, where he was cured. I know she is your mother, Ama," Adjua's tone softened, "but she is a Baoule woman whose soul is offended by the ways of the Twi. Complete victory was all she could tolerate." There was a pause. "Your brother's fever was the gift she was waiting for." Joelle heard her mother's voice ringing across the years. "Etienne, will you allow your mother to sacrifice our only son?" As the years rolled back, Joelle recalled how, little by little, the journeys to the village had dwindled until Adjua became the sole pilgrim. Adjua drank again from the mug. "As you know, my child, tomorrow I will go back to the village for my visit. I would like you to come with me."

"But Grandmother, I..."

A raised hand stopped Joelle short. She trembled a little at the force behind that wrinkled hand.

"Every ten years there is a ceremony that takes place in Sinabre." Adjua straightened her back and looked upwards with a strange light in her eyes.

"It involves only the old women of the village. We who with our old wombs have spent our lives engendering and nurturing the race."

Joelle leaned forward, her ears straining to understand the unfamiliar Twi words. Even ordinarily, her grandmother's speech had a lofty tone; but now her language had the heightened rhetoric of a sage.

"No one but the old women can participate in it..." Adjua intoned. Her words flew high in the air on the wings of poetry. She told Joelle how the old women would enter the sacred forest and prostrate themselves before God who, in his mercy, would cleanse them and make them as spotless as maidens, as blameless as newborn infants. And the cleansing would strengthen the people and let them walk more closely with God.

"Only the old can take part," Adjua repeated, "but just to be in the village when it happens confers its blessing." Adjua looked directly at Joelle. "Of all my son's children, I have chosen you to come with me."

Panic struck Joelle a body blow but, summoning her courage, she went and sat at the old woman's feet. When she spoke, it was with the merest whisper.

"Grandmother, I can't."

Adjua's position altered slightly as she once again began polishing her teeth.

"You do me great honour and I would dearly love to come with you but..."

"There is an obstacle?"

"I have a friend here this week. The stranger I brought to see you on Monday. I can't take him to Sinabre and I can't leave him here on his own. I'll come and join you as soon as he goes back next Monday."

"It will be too late. The rites will already have begun. And," said Adjua, anticipating Joelle's next point, "when the next one comes around, I will no longer even be a memory."

Joelle was on the verge of tears. "What can I do about the stranger?"

"Ama, is he your husband?"

"Excuse me, Grandmother?"

"It is a simple question."

"Of course he isn't. It hurts that you could think that!"

"My old eyes saw his eyes upon you. He seemed to be your husband."

"He's just a friend, a *copain*." This was the first foreign sound to be uttered in the conversation. It ricocheted off the walls.

"For us, there is the man who is your husband and the men who are not. For you, it is all one." The old woman sighed deep and long, then she got up. The audience was at an end.

84

"Grandmother, forgive me. I..."

"Ama, my child, each of us guides her own destiny." She clutched Joelle's hand. "Although I feel you walking a path so different from mine, I will pray for you. Now wipe your eyes. Go. Pass the night in peace."

Joelle walked through the door and down the corridor of her father's house like a phantom. Lights blazed from every room and from every room leapt activity and noise. Here, youngest sister Sylvie, clad in a leotard, was trying to burn up her puppy fat with the aid of an aerobics video. There, her brother Remy, the one who'd caught the fever so many years ago, was asking his parents for money to fund one of his "projects". Further along, sister Christiane was weeping – husband Charles had been caught out again, a school girl this time. In another room, youngest brother Simon held Jean-Luc captive in an urgent exchange about African Socialism. A tower of Babel in the African night. Down the hall, Maryse was humming, nursing a nightcap. She saw Joelle glide past her door without stopping.

All Joelle could see and hear was the black silence of Adjua's room.

The next few days spun by in a blur as Joelle continued to show Jean-Luc Abidjan. Lunches, dinners, parties, *boîte de nuits* were all crammed into the insufficient hours. The debacle at the Trianon was forgotten in the fever of activity. By Friday evening, Jean-Luc, who was unused to the hectic social schedule of the African urban dweller, showed signs of flagging only to be told that he had to be up at five the next morning to go to Grand Bassam, eighty kilometres along the coast. This was to be the high point of the whole visit with twenty-five or so of Joelle's assorted relatives and friends accompanying him, jumping at the chance to spend the weekend at this favourite seaside haunt of the French in colonial times.

Just before eight on Sunday morning, a convoy of six cars – four Peugeots, one Citroen and Joelle's father's Mercedes – rolled out of the city. Naturally, Joelle and her party were in the splendour of the air-conditioned Mercedes. Little Didier was there with two of his friends, all delighted to be leaving their mothers behind in this adventure. Maryse looked content and smug at having manoeuvred to be with Joelle, knowing that she would claim her place at the top of the totem. Jean-Luc had recovered from his initial shock at the numbers involved in this trip. (As the week progressed, he saw this as a major element of his cultural adjustment to Africa. Was there always a throng? Could one ever be alone or with only one person?) He was quite animated in the coolness of the car, commenting with his customary zeal on the scenery as it changed from the jangling metropolis to the rich greens and browns of the countryside. Only Joelle did not seem to be herself. She scarcely spoke a word during the journey, except when the road first became a ribbon cutting through the dense forest. Then she surprised everyone by saying, "I wonder how our grandmother is," knowing full well that Adjua was by now ensconced in her beloved village near the border with Ghana. She did not say another word until they arrived at Grand Bassam.

The town was not as Jean-Luc had imagined it – all those crumbling walls and rusty roofs. "Your people left it like this when they went back to France," Joelle said but seeing his pained look, pulled him along by the arm towards the beach. Here everyone's spirits rose. A long curve of golden sand; bold blue water; lines of thatched shops and restaurants. Picturesque and exotic, it was a tourist's dream of Africa. All that was needed to complete the picture was a bare breasted girl and a drum.

As soon as the bags had been deposited at the beach-front hotel, the party started and it went on all day. There was an endless round of eating, drinking, dancing, game-playing of all kinds. At one point, the favourite game was berating absent relatives and friends. Marie-Ange, high society's high priestess and Remy, would-be film maker and accomplished womaniser and layabout, came in for particular flogging from Joelle's cousin Delphine, who raised the custom of ritualised insult to an art form. Poor Jean-Luc! He watched as the others fell to the ground, crying with laughter, incomprehension written all over him, the door of their culture slammed in his face once more. Maryse started to tell him that this sharp teasing was more a mental exercise than something done in malice. However, her explanations failed to keep his interest as the focus of attention shifted to Joelle, who was giving a demonstration of a particularly provocative Baoule dance. All eyes were on her as she raised her arms to the heavens and cried, "Our ancestors knew about life! We know by the dances they gave us." The sun streamed down on her as her body twisted and turned in delight. Maryse watched Jean-Luc looking at her sister. His yearning eyes were almost indecent. She vowed to leave him to his fate.

There was another awkward moment later in the day. The sun was high and everyone was watching the water. Jean-Luc asked why no one had gone into the sea. "If God had wanted us to swim, he would have given us fins," said Delphine. Someone else said that in these parts people tended to avoid going into the sea because it was treacherous, with dangerous and unexpected tides and currents. The incorrigible Delphine pounced again. "And Mamy Wata is as greedy as ever. She feeds off the flesh of beautiful young men and women." Jean-Luc's eyes lit up.

"Tell me more." A ripple of astonishment mixed with disapproval moved through the party. Once again, Delphine took the initiative. She led Jean-Luc by the hand to the water's edge. She pointed to a place along the coast.

"You see over there?" Jean-Luc followed the line of her finger to a cove a few kilometres away, almost entirely

87

surrounded by rocks. "You see that place? It is a place of taboo. There is the sea and there is the sacred wood behind it. Only a chosen few can set foot in that place and live to tell the tale." Her finger continued to point. "That, Jean-Luc, is the Africa of our forefathers and it is ours. We would be fools to think your science would protect us from it."

"Stop scaring him, Delphine!" Joelle snapped. "I've already told him all this has nothing to do with him."

Jean-Luc was silent but all through the long afternoon, Maryse caught him stealing glances at the rocky cove along the coast.

Later, most of the group hit the local night spots. Jean-Luc complained of a headache and said he preferred to sleep it off in his room. Joelle volunteered to look after Didier and his two friends. Maryse insisted on keeping her sister's company. At first Joelle chastised Maryse for being such a wallflower.

"You should go out and enjoy yourself for a change," Joelle said, wagging her finger.

"I hardly call it enjoyment to be trapped in a cramped smoky room, being deafened by loud music, and jammed up against people I don't even like. I think I'd rather a night out with Houphouet's secret police." The sisters looked at each other and with one voice said, "Well, maybe not!" They both laughed but then Maryse caught herself. "Hey! I'm not spoiling anything, am I? Any appointment. Between you and Jean-Luc, I mean?"

"*Mais non!*" Joelle said with sudden vehemence. "He really is in a mood tonight and, to be honest, I'm glad to have a break from him." She put an affectionate arm around Maryse. "Come to think of it, it could be fun. Just the two of us. Like the old days at school!" She broke into her brilliant, gap-toothed smile. "Let's get rid of the kids!"

So began an evening of gaiety which far outstripped anything experienced by the cousins sweating and grinding to the strains of Youssou N'Dour and Alpha Blondy. Didier and his friends did the decent thing and went to sleep at once, the early rising and salt sea air proving an irresistible combination. From then on the sisters were free. First they raided the kitchen and in so doing recalled their days at boarding school in France. As they loaded up with fruit and cakes and cheese and wine, they blessed their father for owning shares in the hotel. The steady consumption of their booty stretched over the hours, as did the snores of the three little children ranged across Joelle's bed, as did the music of innumerable tiny creatures singing in the darkness. But most of all there was talk which bubbled like a mountain stream, breaking round boulders and diverting into tangents and tributaries. Therein lay the fun.

"Did you know that our dear brother-in-law is going to be a daddy again? Another little bastard. Poor Christiane! She is seeking solace in the church. With the Monsignor in particular. Hear he's going to be a daddy too! Have you ever seen him in his full get-up for High Mass? He looks pretty stunning. I'd love an outfit like that. Saw one like it on the Champs Elysées..."

On it went, the flow of words and the worlds they shared. Despite the frequent diversions, certain themes recurred: the family, a never ending source of material for farce; Maryse and what Joelle saw as her aggressive refusal to participate in "normal" life; Jean-Luc and what Maryse saw as Joelle's aggressive refusal to answer the question, "Who is this man?". The sisters talked and ate and laughed and cried. Sometimes they quivered on that exquisite point between laughter and tears. They spread out the tapestries of their lives in the space between them. Some parts of the tapestries interlocked; others were very different. Didier and his friends slept on while Joelle and Maryse lived in a moment of sharing.

Eventually wine and weariness began to weigh down their spirits. It was coming up to two o'clock. There were more and more pauses and the occasional yawn. Maryse looked over at Joelle and knew that sleep would soon overtake her. She would make one last try.

"Joelle," she said, her voice low and serious, "Who is this Jean-Luc?"

"I told you. He's just a friend."

"Some friend!"

Joelle stretched then sighed. "I know what everybody thinks. But it's not true. We're not lovers." She sat on the bed with her legs folded. "You want to know the truth? It's not pretty. I brought him home on a whim, a last minute whim. Because I knew he liked me and it would cause confusion. I told you it wasn't pretty." Joelle spoke in a whisper and Maryse could feel all the joy of the preceding hours trickle away. Joelle shifted the bodies of the little sleepers and climbed in bed beside them. She sat upright and looked Maryse fully in the face.

"If only I could meet a man who would make me pay attention! Does that sound crazy? All the men I've ever known – they're all the same. They simper, they babble, they groan." Her body was very still but there was a slight movement of her head. "I need someone who's not a push-over. Who will ask something of me that is hard to deliver."

She fell silent, lay down in a curled position and pulled the sheet over her head. As Maryse got into her bed, she tried to make sense of what had just happened, this strange full-stop that had ended a sentence of joy. They had been so close during the long night but now Maryse was left wondering about the corners of Joelle's mind still not revealed to her.

The night was not over yet.

Maryse was tossing on her bed when there was a knock at the door. While Maryse considered what to do, Joelle went from sleep to full wakefulness and was at the door asking who was there. A low voice replied and Joelle went out into the dark. She returned about ten minutes later and without saying a word, went straight back to her bed and very soon her rhythmic breathing indicated the return of sleep. Maryse, on the other hand, looked about her with sleepless eyes. Her bewilderment would not go away. In the end, she sat up and pulled out her book:

Tonight has been a night of wonder. A sister revealed only to be hidden again. She leaps from Alpha to Omega in the time it takes me to blink my eye. I feel like a slow heavy thing in comparison to her. It's the middle of the night and instead of sleeping, I'm here studying her as though she were an examination paper. Anger and resentment are my birth-right. I'm angry that she's robbed me of this happy night. I'm angry that she plays with people the way a cat does a mouse. And I bitterly resent that there's no one knocking at the door for me.

The car came to a halt and its two occupants sat without moving. Although only a few hours ago they had been locked in feverish conversation outside a hotel room, they now seemed like strangers. Around them, leaves, still dark and wet from night-time, rubbed noiselessly against each other and the eastern corner of the sky welcomed the first light of morning.

They got out of the car and started down the sandy path between the trees. Joelle went first, her body taut and aware, ducking beneath the overhanging branches, feeling the dew-drenched trees reach out to touch her bare legs. Behind her came Jean-Luc, furtive, hesitant, stumbling over roots and stones, his hand groping before him like a blind man. Apart from the crowing of some distant cock, all was silence. The wood became more dense, the sandy track was swallowed up by the hungry ferns and grasses. Thin threads of light snaked through the twisting musculature of the great trees and fell on the forest floor, impotent and in disarray. The two people stopped, surrounded. They felt the forest's dark breath upon them. It smelled of earth and rain and golden flecks of sunshine. It smelled of immense heat steaming above swirling, flooding rivers. Its odour suggested the travail of birth mingled with the stench of death. In the dappled darkness of the forest, the flesh of the woman and flesh of the man rose up in terror at the breath of this creature into whose belly they had strayed. They set off again, almost at a run, crashing into tree trunks, kicking aside rocks, creating noise on a planet of silence. Suddenly, before them stood a curtain of stout vines covered in thick shining leaves. They stood panting before it, wondering. Then they tore back the curtain and stepped through it, leaving behind them a whirl of shredded leaves, their glossy fragmented flesh floating slowly to earth. Within moments the deep obscurity lifted and they found themselves on the threshold of a fine white beach.

Minutes passed before they spoke. They busied themselves laying out their belongings on the sand. When Joelle passed Jean-Luc a towel, she noticed that his hand was shaking.

"Well, are you satisfied now?" she said with studied flippancy.

"About what?"

"About your famous African dimension, of course." The words sounded loud in her own ears. She made an effort to modulate them but it was difficult. Her voice seemed to have detached itself from her, to have flown off like a falcon breaking free of its trainer. But she had to retrieve her voice because some force within compelled her to speak.

"You want proof – empirical, sociological, anthropological proof – that it exists. And now, *mon dieu*, you have it!" Joelle's voice rang out with the clang of tempered metal over the soft hiss of the surf. They both watched as the clean, calm water heaved itself over the rocky barrier which provided an almost perfect wall against the sea.

Joelle sat down and leaned her head onto her knees. The

sound which came from her throat fluttered in erratic syncopation.

"I just hope you're satisfied. Bringing me here against my better judgement... to Akima!... My God!... against my will..." Her words dropped away into incoherence. Jean-Luc stared at her sitting there, blubbering, all of her brittle knowingness stripped away. A swell of tenderness rose within him. He edged nearer.

"It was never a scientific experiment for me, Jo," he said. "I just wanted to know. I wanted to... to experience it for myself."

"So you can write about it in some French journal and become famous?"

Jean-Luc flinched but did not rise to the bait. "What I felt in there," he said, glancing behind him, "what we both felt was real. There's no word for it – but it was something. Something as palpable as you and me sitting on this beach on this July day. But..." Jean-Luc once more inched closer to the forbidding figure of Joelle, hunched over, head bowed to her knees. "But you know, when all is said and done, no damage was done. We're here. We're safe. No harm done except a little fright." He laid a tentative hand on her shoulder.

Her first instinct was to shake off this unwelcome touch but she let the hand stay there and, to her surprise, discovered that it brought her a little comfort. She concentrated on the hand on her shoulder. She felt the slight roughness of it. In her mind's eye, she could see its pallor against the blackness of her skin. As the hand continued resting there, she could feel the gathering up of miniature pools of sweat sandwiched between his skin and hers. These things seemed so real. And they could not hurt her.

She raised her head and looked towards the sea. The endless cycle of wave against rock and sand appeared gentle enough. She twisted around and stared at the entrance to the wood. The trees were still rooted to the ground; they were still mute. The forces of Nature continued to enslave them and render them incapable of giving vent to their fury. They were just trees, dumb and unconscious. That was just water, locked into place in the natural chain of command, doomed forever to just ebb and flow, ebb and flow.

These were Joelle's thoughts as she finally allowed her body to loosen and let some of its fear melt away. She smiled and saw lights blaze in Jean-Luc's brown eyes.

He coughed and shifted on the sand. It was his turn to be tense and fearful.

"Joelle," he said feeling the scarlet tide flooding his face. "Why do you think I asked you to bring me here?"

"To see Akima. To feel Akima. To prove beyond a shadow of a doubt, that our gods are as dead as yours." The metallic clang had started to creep into her voice again and she ended by putting her hand over her mouth as though to make it hush.

"Is that why you came?" he asked.

"I came because you threatened – in the middle of the night – to have some sort of breakdown if I didn't bring you. To have the ultimate African adventure, the one not mentioned in the tourist books." Joelle's hands began to clench and unclench as though in spasm.

"If I'd known it would be so upsetting for you, I'd have asked you to take me somewhere else..."

"Somewhere else?" Joelle jumped up and glared at him. "You asked me to bring you here! Right here! To this spot on earth!"

Jean-Luc also got to his feet. They were the same height and so looked each other directly in the eyes. He could see the anger and the fear. She could see the confusion and... there was something else. She looked again and saw this other thing in Jean-Luc's eyes. It was getting clearer and clearer until it was as visible as the red flag flaming across his face.

"Oh God!"

"What?"

"Oh my God!" she repeated, turning away. "How could I have been so stupid?" She started to laugh, a hard clanging laugh. "All the while I thought you wanted to come here – to Akima. To this special place." She snorted. "When all you wanted..."

"Was to be alone with you."

Jean-Luc's naked eyes flared up again. Joelle could not stand it. She turned her back on him in a clumsy, abrupt movement. His hand shot out to within a whisper of that shining expanse of skin, divided in two by the thin bright line of her bikini top. Courage failed him. His hand dropped to his side. He began to speak as though to himself.

"Before I came here, I thought there was only one colour black. But now I know there are many. Black with undertones of brown and red. Blue black, intense and unbelievable. Matte black, the one that absorbs all light. Then there's the most beautiful, the one that shimmers like ripe aubergines. The colour of Joelle..."

Joelle stiffened her spine and squinted up at the sky, which was by this time awash with light. As she tried to enumerate all the scenes like this that she had already lived through, she was aware of a great emptiness within. What was wrong with her? Why had she never felt what Jean-Luc was feeling right now?

"I'm sorry, Jean-Luc. I didn't realise you felt this way." Joelle winced as she saw the effect of these words which struck him like sharp hammer blows.

"Why can't I believe you?" he said at last with an edge. "The whole of Abidjan knows so why wouldn't you?"

"I didn't think it was so serious..."

"Just because you don't take anything seriously, that doesn't mean that the rest of us don't."

A light breeze stirred the leaves in the forest and ruffled the satin of the waves. Joelle and Jean-Luc didn't feel it.

Jean-Luc's breathing had become erratic and the light in his eyes was changing.

"So you've been stringing me along all this time! Ever since Paris. I've been nothing more than a Christmas toy to you!"

"That's not true," she said without conviction. Her dull gaze swept across the beach, the sombre trees at the edge of the sand and the rigid form of the man standing so close to her. She did not seem to see him. The words that took shape came as from beyond the frontiers of a dream.

"I thought you were asking something of me that was hard to deliver. To bring you here. To challenge the only thing greater than me... Do you know what it's like to live a life where everything is easy?" There was a plaintive note in Joelle's question but it failed to move Jean-Luc who was set hard against her. "I live in two worlds and I've seen many different ways of being. But," she added with a small gasp, "I chose the wrong one to challenge." She rubbed her arms up and down as though suddenly cold.

There was a coldness too about Jean-Luc. Only his lips moved.

"I would have expected more from an intelligent girl like you. All this Akima business is just hocus-pocus. Some self-induced collective hysteria that will always keep this continent in chains." The coldness vanished to be replaced by a white heat which consumed him and drained every drop of colour from his face. "Bah! It's all an excuse! A way of explaining what you've been doing with this poor naive white boy." Neither of them moved but the weight of a great weariness pressed down on Joelle's shoulders.

"I didn't mean any harm," she said feebly. "I really didn't."

She turned away but he caught her arm.

"Show me, Joelle. Show me this was not all a game to you, that you have some feelings for me."

When she faced him, she also faced the sun so she

96

couldn't be sure whether the look in his eyes was of supplication or menace. She felt steely fingers close around her arms; he did not increase the pressure of that grip. Neither did he release her. Still blinded by the glare, she felt him draw her closer. His voice was low and glutted with emotion.

"Show me. Here. In this place. Sacred, is it? Just this once. You owe me that much. Then I'll leave you to your Africa."

She looked straight into the equatorial sun, mesmerised by its golden fires. The heat of the man's breath was no more than that of a dying candle to her, the awkward fumbling of his hands was like the fretting of a breeze and the undulations of his back were like the tremors of a wave on the lagoon. She watched the sun in its power and glory through tearless eyes. When all was over, she plunged into the sea, silently beseeching the waters to make her clean. Then, on the wet sand, where the lacy surf could caress her, she lay, face upturned, feeling the sun burn into a scarlet mist. Through sealed lids, she saw a throng of women, old and wrinkled, prostrate beneath the great trees of the forest, their voices crying out to God.

Jean-Luc also slept, a heavy dreamless sleep. He awoke, disoriented. The sun was overhead, bearing down on him. He looked at the water and found it altered. Profoundly altered. The tide was inexplicably high, the beach reduced to half its size and the placid water of an hour ago had been replaced by curling waves and a boisterous surf. Where was she? He called her name again and again. He scrambled up on the jagged rocks; he braved the water. To no avail. At last, he turned his back to the sea and there, between him and the car, the highway, the city, Air France with its destination of Paris Charles De Gaulle, stood the dark, sighing wood.

Grief has broken out like a contagion in my father's house. Over twenty-four hours have passed since Jean-Luc came screaming into my hotel room like a crazy man. The drive back to the city was wild and fearful with him huddled in one corner of the car like an animal, endlessly touching the long scratches on his limbs. Then there was the scene when he reached home and told the family. A deep silence was followed by the clamour of grief. Woye! Jean-Luc faced our father and talked as though he was under the influence of a truth serum. He and Joelle had gone early in the morning to the beach at Akima. Woye! They had crossed the sacred wood. Woye! They had made love on the beach. A silence that deafened. When he awoke, the tide was high and Joelle was gone. Woye! Woye! Woye! The police came and took him away for interrogation.

As soon as Jean-Luc had pronounced the name Akima, we all knew what he could not know − that our daughter, our sister was worse than dead. She was beyond our reach, where we could not say farewell or commit her to the earth with full rites and honours. Joelle was lost to us for all time...

So wrote Maryse in her little book in a moment of stillness snatched as the whirlwind spun around her. The house was inundated with people coming to say *Yako*. Some came to slake their curiosity, others to see how the great had fallen, others were drawn by the horror, others still were brought by love. They came for many reasons but it was the family's duty to offer them food, drink and hospitality. Both Joelle's mother and Marie-Ange were in a state of collapse, so the task of receiving the scores of people fell to Maryse. Her clear-headed efficiency forced order out of chaos as she bore the burden of those who faltered. She was glad to be too busy to think and when something pulled her in the direction of tears − such as a photograph of Joelle laughing, or the swollen face of Didier, or the sight of her father surrounded by police chiefs – there was perhaps an involuntary intake of breath. But she did not cry.

For the first time in her life, Maryse was a support to her father. She was there when he learned that although police boats were combing the area (the police refused to set foot on the beach itself) there was little hope because of the riptides. She was by his side when he heard that sharks had been sighted. *Yako, papa,* she whispered under her breath. He came and told her about each desperate conference with the police and the unfolding diplomatic dimension of Joelle's disappearance. First the Ministry of State Security had informed the French Embassy of the possibility of murder charges being laid against Jean-Luc Sarazin. The French Embassy protested, suggesting that Sarazin could not get a fair trial. The Ministry sent a note denouncing this outrageous slur on the Ivorian judiciary. There was deadlock.

"Then everything changed," Maryse's father told her in a tired voice. The French ambassador went to interview Jean-Luc and after that, things became much more low key. The French requested that Sarazin be repatriated due to his unstable state of health. The Ivorian Ministry agreed that as soon as the search was called off, Jean-Luc would be put on the first plane back to France. After all, the young woman clearly drowned in a notoriously treacherous stretch of sea.

"Why the change of tune, Papa?" Maryse wanted to know.

"Because the French Embassy suggested that the Ivory Coast, as one of the most advanced and progressive countries in Africa, would surely not wish to become embroiled in an international incident in which a French citizen was accused of being a participant in some sort of witchcraft."

Maryse watched as her father absorbed all this through a mask. A lifetime of training in African manhood held him together – just.

After dinner, the house cleared. The Monsignor and lesser ranking priests had left, all prayers said, every candle in the house lit. The family was in the living room, Marie-Ange, Remy, Christiane, their spouses and children, Sylvie, Simon, Maryse and the parents. They sat without speaking in the descending darkness. Somewhere there was a soft flurry of noise - they took no notice – but within a few moments they were faced with the tall silent figure of Kwantema, followed by Adjua. She was swathed in royal Kente cloth and stood before them in the darkness, burning with a pure bright flame.

"Mother!" The word broke through the mask, revealing the anguish beneath. Joelle's father took a few steps towards Adjua and collapsed at her feet.

She reached down to him. "Get up, my son. This is unseemly." She led him back to his chair with gentle hands. Adjua waited as he struggled to compose himself.

"You received the message then." He was not yet in control of his voice. "Communications with Sinabre were so difficult, because of the observances this weekend."

"Yes, my son, I received your message." There was something immensely buoyant about Adjua, something almost like ecstasy. "My sisters and I were in the forest, in the presence of our ancestors and the earth, our mother. While we were there stretched out beneath the silk cottonwood trees, I felt a sharp stabbing in my breast and I knew that a great catastrophe had befallen us. I emptied myself until I became nothing, emptied out even the stabbing pain so that our Gods could fill me up with their wisdom and blessing." Her pause was electric. "And they did. They washed me clean and made me as innocent as a newborn." She stopped again, as though for breath.

"When my sisters and I stepped out of the wood, I was met by your messenger who told me that Ama had been taken."

"Mother, we cannot find her body. We cannot bury our child."

Adjua and her son appeared to be the only ones in the room, the others mere shadows.

"What will we do?"

"We will ask forgiveness. That is all we can do."

"But why did she have to die? She was so young, just a child!"

"Even a child knows not to transgress the laws of her elders. Ama's spirit was so troubled. There was longing, there was confusion. There was a great void. In that moment of madness, she lacked the wisdom even of a child."

"Mother, I beg you, no more. Do you not think I have been sufficiently punished?"

Joelle's father sank back into his chair, head in his hands. Joelle's mother looked away, trembling. Adjua continued to stand before them, bright, pure, unbending.

"I will bring Ama back. I will go to the waters of Akima and retrieve her earthly remains. I will give them back to you, my son." In a whisper, she added. "I will fetch back the child of my heart."

"Oh, Joelle!" her mother cried.

"Call her Ama!" Adjua snapped. "It is her name."

The old woman let her anger die away before going on.

"Tomorrow, when the sun has risen and the dew is no longer on the grasses, Kwantema and I will cross the sacred wood at Akima until we reach the water's edge. I will need one other person to come. We must be three."

"I will go!"

Adjua silenced Joelle's father with her hand.

"It is not for you to offer but for me to select. The one I choose must not fear, for you will be protected by the power I received at Sinabre. But you must have courage. And you must have love for our lost daughter." She paused again. "I choose Esi."

Maryse jumped from her chair and went straight to Adjua, finding the courage to look her in the eye.

101

"Grandmother, I am not worthy."

Adjua stared at Maryse with unblinking eyes. No one in the room dared to even breathe.

"I choose you, Esi, for the love Ama had for you..." She bent an arthritic knee to her granddaughter. "Come with me now. The rest of this night we'll spend together in prayer and preparation."

Sometime during that long night, Maryse wrote:

My grandmother commanded me to come. When I declared I was not worthy, she took me captive in the field of her eyes. They stripped me bare and showed my imperfect love for Joelle. How it was often envy. How it was sometimes hate. But there is no hiding from Adjua. So I have let myself be led away to partake of things I've heard about only in whispers, the invoking of the spirits, the anointing of the body with holy oils. I walk in fear but it does not overwhelm me. For I have been chosen. Esi. It is my name.

The sun beat down on the two cars parked on the side of the road. From one emerged an elegantly dressed couple. Joelle's mother dabbed her eyes with a handkerchief; her father looked beyond the treetops. From the other car, three women got out. They exchanged a few words with the couple and set off down the sandy track between the trees. A cool darkness enveloped them. The tall, powerfully-built woman led the way, walking without haste or hesitation, her sure feet not bruising the roots or stones scattered along the path. The second woman, old and frail, seemed to glide, her small feet making scant contact with the sand and the soil and the long grasses. The young woman came last. Her face was contorted into a grimace of concentration as she studied the movements of the other two and tried to imitate them, to show veneration in the very tread of her feet. Apart from the crowing of some distant cock, all was silence. The overarching branches became more impenetrable, the darkness deepened and the sandy track was no more. The old woman gestured to the others to stop and from the folds of her clothing, she withdrew a handful of rosy kola nuts and a vial of newly tapped palm wine. Supported on each side by the other two, she bent her stiff limbs to the earth and placed her gifts at the base of the largest tree. She drew back the curtain of stout vines and allowed first the tall woman then the young woman to pass. The curtain swung back into place, each leaf shining and intact. The obscurity lifted and within moments, they were on the threshold of a fine white beach. The old woman continued to walk right to the water's edge. The other two lingered in the shade of the coconut palms. They watched and waited. The sea heaved itself in smooth rhythmic waves over the rocky barrier into the clear blue crescent pool that the beach had become. A cloud moved across the sun and the water darkened. The sun broke through again but in the water, a darkness remained, moving towards the shore.

The two women saw the moving shadow at the same time and came running from the shade into the brilliant sunshine. They reached the water's edge just as the darkness was deposited on the sand. They gazed down at her. She who had once been Joelle who was now truly Ama. She seemed to be smiling; they could see the gap between her teeth. The long fingers, the clean limbs, the skin the colour of ripe aubergines. She lay on the sands as perfect as on the day of her birth.

Something in Adjua seem to break, all fires within her forever extinguished. She took the cloth from her shoulders and draped it across Ama's body. The tall woman bent to pick her up but before she did, she opened her mouth into a ululation which rent the water and the wood. It was the first sound anyone had heard Kwantema make.

The young woman put her arm around her grandmother's shoulders to stop them from shaking as they prepared to re-enter the sacred wood. When Esi spoke, her voice was as bright as flame. "Now the burial rites can begin," she said.

Overhead, an Air France Airbus scurried across the African sky towards its destination of Paris Charles de Gaulle.

DOUDOU'S WIFE

DOUDOU'S WIFE

Women did not become a problem for Doudou Camara until he entered his sixty-first year. Until then they had been a diversion, an escape, sometimes an irritant and occasionally even a joy. But he had taken them, as he had taken most things, lightly and with a grain of salt. On his sixtieth birthday, however, Doudou felt a strange tightness in the pit of his stomach. There was no doubt about it. Time was passing. Liaisons with the daughters of England had taken up the better part of the last forty years but their reproductive efforts had come up with nothing but girls. As the sun rose feebly on another Ilford morning, Doudou experienced the urgency of his need to leave behind a son, as evidence of his passage in the world, and in order to do this, he required an African wife.

The clink of an opening gate aroused Doudou from his musings and made him look out of the window of his ground floor flat in time to see the dun-coloured sack of the postman disappearing into the back section of this block of flats, formerly owned by the Council, now by Margaret Thatcher's new property-owning working class. Moments later, he heard the tinny report of the aluminium letter-box against the door. The noise gave Doudou a sinking feeling. He knew what awaited him on the bright patterned carpet. Four cards from his children who, no matter what chaos swirled around their colourful lives, remained dogged in their determination to make him celebrate his birthday, Christmas and, more recently, Father's Day. He had long since given up trying to convince them, without hurting their feelings, that these "days" were of no importance to him – that he was a Muslim so Christmas was a non-starter, that he had very much enjoyed making his children and then had enjoyed his loose, somewhat carefree connection with them during their growing up years. He did not need to be congratulated about being a father now. In the debate about these two "days", he sometimes won his point, usually by leaving town the night before. But somehow he always lost the battle of his birthday and had to face up to the cards, the phone calls and the "do" in the evening at his oldest daughter Naba's house.

The birthday was the most ludicrous "day" of all because Doudou Camara had no idea of the day, month or even year of his birth. He was of the generation of Gambians whose official documents contained the famous phrase "born approximately". In the silent hours before dawn, when his bones cried out in protest at the thought of another day on the factory floor at Dagenham, Doudou was sure he was sixty-three, even sixty four. But now, as he contemplated the image of a nubile, ebony-skinned bride, the promise of a new life flared up in him and his mind skittered about like a youth of forty-five. When he had stepped off that boat in Liverpool all those years ago, he'd had to fix a day and a month and a year to prove that he existed. He had written them down in a beautiful slow hand and in so doing, had laid down the foundation of this yearly trial with his daughters.

With an exasperated sigh, Doudou stooped to pick up the four cards, with a sudden awareness of the stiffening of his joints which always accompanied the approach of winter. As his squat fingers fumbled with the envelopes, Doudou's inner eye saw the plump black child who would know, without having to be told, that these foreign rituals served only to remind him of the distance between himself and Africa – and should be avoided. He also saw, with a clarity that both excited and disturbed him, the child's mother who, with long, tender fingers, would stroke out the cold locked into his bones with the secret oils of home. Standing there in the middle of his neat living-room, with the timid November sunshine nosing its way through the net curtains, Doudou was overwhelmed with the vision of the life that awaited him, the moment when be would at last join the ranks of responsible men, by marrying and bringing forth sons. He would write to his older brother Ibou, who would arrange it all. With the birthday cards in his hand forgotten, Doudou breathed a few words of thanks – *Yalla bahana* – God is good.

Thoughts of the letter to his brother and the life beyond enabled Doudou to remain serenely detached from the goings-on at Naba's house that night. Confusion reigned as Doudou's daughters assembled en masse. Mary was overnighting from Manchester, Josephine had driven across from Barkingside and Katy had come from her flat two doors down the road. Each had her personal entourage of lovers, would-be lovers and children. The honeyed voice of Maxi Priest flowed from Naba's impressive stereo system while the sharp little cries of the under-fives provided a high-pitched descant. All of Doudou's grandchildren – there must have been about a dozen of them – were decked out in smart outfits, their faces chubby and well-scrubbed. They were all, without exception, badly behaved, due in part to the fact that their mothers were ignoring them. Josephine was in the midst of a risqué joke. When the punchline came, the four sisters screamed their delight and fell helpless into each other's arms. From his chair in the corner, Doudou observed with a quiet eye. Jonsaba, Mariama, Khatidja and Jeynaba. Why had the girls' mothers insisted on giving them those awful English names? Only Naba stayed close to the original source. Only Naba.

As if on cue, Naba saw him watching her and, in the middle of the wild laughter, smiled at him. It was an extraordinary thing, to be able to change gear like that, to hear the quiet amidst the noise. But then she was like her mother, that wise, wisecracking bus conductress, with her hourglass figure and her merry blue eyes, who had eased his pain in the early years. Josephine had inherited her looks but it was Naba, the first-born, who had been bequeathed her mother's temperament. Sometimes Doudou wondered whether he shouldn't have married Annie but he had known then, even as he knew now, that the prohibition was too great. Marriage was a grave undertaking and despite the two babies and ten years spent together, Doudou had not been able to declare before the world that this was his soul's choice, a person who did not know how to winnow rice or carry a baby on her back or balance a bucket on her head, a person to whom he could express his heart's yearnings only in a broken travesty of her language, a person who was born not knowing Allah by his true name.

"Come on, our Dad! This party's supposed to be for you." Naba still sounded like a Liverpudlian despite more than a decade in London.

"What?" guffawed Josephine, still under the influence of her own wit. "Oh yeah. Dad!" Although in her teens when she and Naba had come to live with Doudou after Annie's death, Josephine sounded as if she had been born directly beneath Bow bells. Cockney to the core. "Ere, Naba! Change that bleedin' music. Put somethin' on that Dad can shake to!"

Doudou shook his head imperceptibly. Josephine spoke fast and raw, just like Mick, her almost-husband, the almost-mini-cab driver, who had given her stylish clothes, three bonny children, a big house which he'd paid cash for before having to excuse himself to do a stretch of porridge at Her Majesty's Prison at Brixton. Josephine was Annie on a bad day.

"Shush everybody," Naba called, once more giving her father that special smile. "Dad, this present is from all of us. We hope you like it." She watched the gleaming disc disappear into the CD player and then glanced expectantly at Doudou. The music leaped into the room with an almost visible force with the violins, flutes, horns and drums merging into a throbbing tissue of sound. The music of Cuba, that tree with the African root transplanted in the New World, whose fruit had crossed the Atlantic again, spilling its bounty across the whole of West Africa, making monarchs of the likes of Johnny Pacheco, Tito Puente and Celia Cruz... It was the last sound ringing in Doudou's ears as he'd boarded the steamer for Liverpool, that and the soft noise of plastic Bata shoes sliding against a concrete floor as the energetic youth of Bathurst – it had not yet become Banjul – had put on spectacular displays of the Patchanga. This music had remained Doudou's intimate friend across the span of years, its melodies so joyous, its polyrhythms as familiar as a mother's heartbeat. As long as they'd known him, his daughters had heard what they'd considered this strange music, rendered more strange by the scratched and aging LP's from which it issued. Imagine Doudou's pleasure at hearing his music, made clean and clear, through the magic of the Sony Corporation. And imagine his surprise that his personal joy had been noticed by his daughters, these sometime strangers whom he had fed and housed and bailed out as, one by one, they'd come to the big city to seek fame and fortune. What they'd mostly found was pregnancy – four girls, ten years, eleven children. But in amongst all of that, they'd noticed his music. For a moment he stopped composing the letter to Ibou in his head and looked at the four girls again as they advanced towards him to pull him up to dance.

Doudou took a mental snapshot of them as he rose to his feet. They were unalike in so many ways. Naba's body was soft and spreading, Josephine's had proportionate curves,

111

Mary's was slight to the point of seeming airborne, Katy had his hard lean lines. Their complexions were like cream in its various stages towards becoming butter, from almost white to a kind of dark gold. But these young women could not escape Africa which surged in them without their permission. Their hair was African. Plaited, cropped, straightened into lankiness, there it was – a fact. (Doudou remembered how Annie would exclaim in dismay at the bushy profusion which faced her every morning.) And their bottoms were African – high and round or falling in a dizzy slope, each one capturing a corner of black male fantasy. So Doudou would laugh when his daughters complained about their frizzy hair and their fat bums, pitying them for being unaware of their true beauty.

Now everyone was on the dance floor, Doudou, Naba and her four kids, Josephine and her three, Mary and her three, Katy and her baby, plus a few bemused young men. An exuberant, good-natured disorder seemed to be the guiding principle of their lives. Touching the head of one of Naba's little girls, he forgave his children for forcing him into this yearly performance. He appreciated them giving him the music of his youth. But as his noisy offspring cavorted around him, Doudou suddenly no longer felt like keeping up with Johnny Pacheco and the gang. He longed for the dignity and rigour of African life where a man carried out his duties and received due honour, in a manner laid down by ancient custom. He was sixty years old. It was time for him to stop dancing.

He waited until the piece had finished then went over and switched off the stereo. "Oi!" boomed Josephine. "What's goin' on?"

The dancers stopped, gaping like fish suddenly taken out of water. A few of the smallest children continued jumping to their own music. Eventually they too stopped. All eyes were on Doudou.

"What's wrong, Dad? Don't you like it?" Naba's voice sounded hurt.

Doudou cleared his throat.

"Yes. It's... er... it's... fine. Very fine." He felt his tongue swell in his mouth and turn the crisp English sounds into sludge. "I want you to know," he paused, looking around him. "I go get married."

"Am I bleedin' hearing things?"

Doudou put his hand up, quelling Josephine's strident question. He waited for silence to fall once more.

"I letting you know I go get married. Next year sometime, I go take the plane to Gambia and I go get married. Bring my wife back here to Ilford. We go live right up here in my flat."

"But Dad..." Katy wailed as she felt a carpet being snatched from under her.

"It's all settle. You big women now and I getting on. I need some peace. *Djaama, rek!* So I go get married." He paused again. "You understand." It was not a question.

Doudou looked with compassion as emotion curdled the creamy complexions but the decision was not negotiable.

"Naba, I go come see you tomorrow and you go help me write a letter. Now put back the music on. I go sit here and watch you dance."

As the silence of consternation continued, Doudou looked out of the window and saw the rain falling in heavy sheets. It fell all night and the next day, as Doudou sat with a dull-eyed Naba, composing the letter. Cold and drenching, the rain persisted for the next several months, making it the wettest winter in years. It met Doudou every morning as he prepared for work. It was his sole companion at the end of the day as he painted and refurbished his flat for the new bride. At night, as he lay in bed, he remembered the sound of African rain as it rampaged across the zinc rooftops on the hooves of stampeding horses. He remembered his childish terror of those rains - how he longed for them now! He recalled that in the Diola language (the language of his grandmother), sky, God and rain were the same word *emitai*. Oh Africa! But over England, a drizzling, soaking, godless rain hovered like a sullen bird and would not budge. It was raining still on that April morning at Gatwick Airport when Doudou waved goodbye to Naba, Katy and their brood. But in Doudou's heart, there was pure sunshine.

This inner light lingered throughout the flight and smoothed over the rougher edges of his arrival at Sir Dawda Jawara Airport where he was greeted by ravening customs officers, porters, taxi drivers and assorted beggars whose practised eye identified him as a returnee, with suitcases crammed with presents, wallet overflowing with pounds sterling (or US dollars and other strong currency that they could favourably convert into dallassi) and a heart crying out to be relieved of its worldly goods and its guilt. Doudou took them all on, with neither naivety nor arrogance. He understood them. Being poor was no joke, especially in the face of seeming wealth. He allowed himself to become engaged in exchanges with some of them, parting with money here, still more there, enjoying the banter, the quick-fire repartee, dodging the clever verbal traps, soaking up the eloquent flattery, easing himself home. When his nephew arrived, late and perspiring, he wasted no time in rescuing Doudou and scattering the vultures with his sharp bark and the waving threat of his arms.

"But Uncle," he said, picking up Doudou's huge suit-cases, "why do you bother with those people?"

"The Koran tells us it is our duty to give alms," Doudou replied, his tone a little defensive. They made their way towards the nephew's battered car and the hot night closed in around them.

"Yes, but it does not tell us to reward thieves and scoundrels!" The nephew turned and spat, drenching the dusty earth with his contempt. He looked up and, seeing himself teetering towards disrespect, he hurried over to where Doudou was standing. "Forgive me, Uncle," he said opening the car door, "but times are hard." Doudou eased himself in, glancing at the back seat which was laden with dog-eared papers and yellowing files. His nephew's office.

"Here, we have to deal with our African realities. Not like you back in jolly old England!" He threw back his head and made a sound that as little resembled laughter as anything Doudou had ever heard.

His nephew's barking voice returned to Doudou's consciousness later that night when he lay, caught somewhere between wakefulness and dream, listening to the murmur of the crowded, sleeping house. There was a harshness in the air that had taken Doudou by surprise. His nephew's household had gone through the formalities of welcome but the warmth of the true *teranga* was missing, with the bare bones of statutory obligation clearly visible. Doudou sighed as he remembered how the eagerness in his nephew's eyes had drained away as he saw that the clothing and the money his uncle had brought him were insufficient. It had come as a moment of illumination for them both. Those who escaped into the outside world could never bring enough back home to solve the problems of their family members. With the vivid expectations on each side, it was never and could never be enough. Doudou consoled himself with the thought that this was the town. City living did strange things to people. Up country, where his brothers and most of his family still lived, it was different. The way of life had not changed for a thousand years. It certainly would not have changed since he'd taken the boat to Liverpool as a young man. As he drifted off to sleep, he felt the heat of his internal sun burning with a renewed intensity.

Before daybreak the next morning, Doudou arose and said his prayers. After the first few years in England, his religious observance had been spasmodic, but this journey necessitated a renewed engagement with his faith. He would pray, he would fast, he would perform acts of charity... he would be a good Muslim. Renewed, he would become a good husband... He shared bread and sweet bush tea with his nephew who, on their way to the centre of town, outlined some of the intricate financial manoeuvres he would have to accomplish between now and sun set. By the time they reached the taxi stand, Doudou felt torn between pity for this young man's burdened life and impatience with his jangling presence. He wished more than anything to set his face in the direction of his true country home. They bade each other farewell and before long, Doudou was on his way.

The black Peugeot had seen better days and Doudou and the four other travellers had to accustom themselves to its shuddering and the occasional grinding of its gears. Otherwise it was quiet as they sped out of the city. Doudou's fellow travellers – two women, a small child and an elderly man – resumed their sleep. Only Doudou was alert, drinking in the freshness of the air and secretly urging the driver on. He wished that the half-day journey was already over but looking out of the window, he was almost glad that it wasn't.

The land, dewy from sleep, seemed to exhale a fine mist, pungent with the mingled scents of hidden waters, moist dark soil and the endless tangle of virgin bush.

"The earth in the morning is as beautiful as a new bride."

Doudou turned around in surprise and discovered that the old man was no longer asleep but was watching him. The old man extended a bony black hand, introduced himself, required the same of Doudou, then leaned over with a conspiratorial air.

"You've lived on the outside a long time, haven't you?" Doudou nodded. "I can tell by the way you look at everything. As though for the first time."

116

"I've been away a long time." Doudou sighed. "Perhaps too long."

The old man raised a quizzical eyebrow.

"Everything changes..." Doudou went on, almost to himself.

"A mother's love for her child doesn't change," the old man said. "A husband's love for his wife doesn't change, although she no longer be young and lovely." He settled back in his seat, comfortable, his thoughts easily translating into words. "A man may go to the outside, even into the land of the toubab, but it does not change his blood. It is like a bird that flies off the earth and lands on an ant-hill. It is still a bird and its feet are still on the ground." He stopped a moment and looked fully at Doudou who was drinking in the music and the meaning of every word. "It's the same as the love you feel for your country. All may seem to change, but that which is essential – like our life's blood –" Here the old man grasped one of his thin wrists, pushing into prominence ribbons of veins and arteries. "That does not change." The old man looked away.

Doudou suddenly felt very young, as though his development as a man had been arrested by the forty-year absence of the wise counsel of his elders. He studied the face of the old man. The surface of the skin was a tapestry of lines, but beneath there was a discernible sheen. His head was clean-shaven and was partially covered by an embroidered white prayer cap. A plain Moroccan-style boubou covered his frame. An old man, Doudou thought. But old in the African sense where old is good, an objective one works towards, where old means becoming a seasoned traveller on a tortuous road. In years we are probably not very different, thought Doudou. But in experience and reflection, he has been moving forward while I... I am as I was when I got off that boat.

"I have come home to get a wife," Doudou said.

"Ah!"

The old man said nothing more for a few moments.

"You do not have one on the outside?"

"No, older brother. Children, but no wife."

"Ah!"

The driver changed gears with maximum flourish, leaving Doudou and the old man separated first by a wall of noise then by a resonant silence. Doudou stole a glance at his companion. His face was closed, as though he were communing with a higher power. Fearing that he had been abandoned, Doudou cleared his throat and said, "Older brother, life on the outside is not as it is here. There are no rules about how to do things. Every man makes up his own rules." The old man clicked his tongue at this but Doudou pressed on. "But now that I've returned home, I need to be reminded of many things." Doudou took a deep breath. "Today, Allah has put in my path a heart that is full of wisdom. As I approach the home of my new wife, I ask you to guide me as though I were your own kin."

"I am listening, Doudou Camara."

The next four hours were a virtual monologue as Doudou recounted his life. The years at the Liverpool docks – the work had been back-breaking but then he'd been young; his introduction to dark bitter ale and the flesh of the pig (here, there had been a sharp intake of breath by the old man but Doudou was not deterred); the time with Annie during which she'd tried to convince him that black and white, Gambian and English, Muslim and Christian were all possible; the years he'd spent with Annie, Naba and Josephine in a version of family life which had rocked like a boat with a slow leak, inexorably taking in water; the way all arguments ended with Doudou telling Annie in a quiet voice how things were done back home where women knew the art of being truly women; Annie's stricken eyes when he'd left; work in Manchester, work in London; the discovery of a few Gambian families with whom to eat, laugh and bathe in momentary forgetfulness; encounters with women, all brief, all casual, two producing babies; four years in the Iraqi oil fields – no ale, no pig, no women, but plenty of money; the return to England and the purchase of his Council flat; the gradual arrival of his daughters, fleeing from the loss or neglect of their mothers; the years as "Dad", provider of shelter, food but not of anything which might quieten the bedlam of his children's lives.

He spoke of his uninterrupted longing for home. And his need for a wife.

The old man's response was only the occasional grunt as they traversed the country and the hours. Quite early on, they had lost the other three travellers and picked up no new ones, much to the irritation of the driver but much to the relief of Doudou for whom the clattering Peugeot had been transformed into a place of confession. So when he came to the end of his story, Doudou felt elated at having been able to shed so many burdens carried for so long. And he revelled in the freeing of his tongue in the language of his youth. He looked expectantly at the old man.

"Well, older brother, I have told you all of this in order to ask you about marriage." The old man was very still and continued to say nothing. Doudou cleared his throat and leaned forward.

"How many wives do you have?"

"One."

"Good! The thought of one wife is frightening enough, let alone more than one. My brother Ibou has three. I don't know how he manages. Anyway, what qualities did you look for in a wife?"

"She was chosen for me by my parents."

"Oh!" Doudou hesitated. "And how do you maintain discipline in the marriage? I haven't waited this long for my home to be a place of noise!" Doudou moved closer. "I mean, how do you ensure that she is happy and yet let her know who is wearing the trousers?"

"Doudou Camara, the questions that you ask are not those of a man of mature years. You are in the season of reaping not planting!" Sounding almost exasperated, he added, "Only the other day my grandson came asking me questions such as these!"

Anxiety and determination fought for control of Doudou's face. "But that's just it, older brother. My years on the outside are as nothing. Like the chaff that the breeze blows away. I have, Allah be praised, reached this age in good health but I am yet in the season of planting. So it falls on you to tell me..." As he leaned forward, there was entreaty in Doudou's eyes. "Tell me what to do with a real wife, an African wife!"

The old man sighed and shifted in his seat. Advising his glossy-skinned grandson on the duties of a husband was one thing but advising someone with a head full of white hairs was something quite different. He sighed again.

"I have never been on the outside but here there is no mystery about making a marriage work. And I will tell it as my father told me as I entered the wood of circumcision. Man and woman are two parts of one whole. If man is the head of the body, woman is the neck that enables the head to turn to the left and to the right. If man is meat in the stew, woman is the salt that robs the meat of its rank animal flavour and the fire that makes it tender. If she wishes you to protect and provide for her, she must respect you; if you wish her to honour and obey you, you must respect her."

Doudou was motionless as the old man intoned these words which stirred up the dust of ancient memory. He felt sure that the exact same words had been said to him by his father a whole life time ago. Doudou smiled to himself as the deep security of the old man's formula seeped into his bones.

"What is the worst part of marriage?" This question seemed to throw the old man somewhat. It did not feature in the normal litany. After a moment's pause he said, "Waking up in the morning knowing forty people depend on you to eat."

Doudou nodded, the back of his eyes pricking at the selfishness of his life.

The old man twisted in his seat as though wishing to terminate the conversation. But Doudou was relentless. He had one more question.

"And what is the best part of marriage?"

A startled look flashed across the old man's face and then he smiled, showing two rows of straight teeth, irredeemably stained by years of chewing kola nuts.

"The intimacy."

The word stood there between them so naked and exposed that Doudou felt ashamed. He had gone too far with his questioning and yet he was thrilled with the old man's reply. Later when they parted with lavish wishes for Allah's misericord and grace, Doudou's eyes thanked the old man for pinpointing the one thing missing in his soul, that unconditional sharing of his life with that of another.

"But now," Doudou said, looking out as the Peugeot coughed back into life, "all of that awaits me at the end of this road."

A young woman sitting in a sunbaked yard raised her head and stared at the road which passed by her house.

"Penda! Keep still or you'll go to meet your new husband looking like this!" The *coiffeuse* seated on a low stool tugged at her client's head. It was still a work in progress, with three-quarters of the hair dragooned into battalions of thread-thin shoulder-length braids while the other quarter dozed, un-troubled, like a dark spongy skull cap. It was still a far cry from the masterpiece it would become – when the remaining part had been plaited, the tiny beads positioned, the artificial hair precision-cut, the ends oiled and burned into hardness. Give or take a few hours for sleep and other bodily functions, the *coiffeuse* had been at it for over thirty-six hours and would require at least twelve more before completion. But she was a professional, a cousin from Casamance brought over especially for the occasion and, with a certain pride, she noted that her fingers hardly hurt at all.

This freedom from pain was not shared by Penda, Doudou's intended, who had to look forward to another half day in the sweltering heat of April with her hair pulled by the root, her shoulders clamped between the hairdresser's sturdy thighs and her bottom pinned to the hard ground. As if that weren't enough, they had been joined by Badjene, the universal aunt, whose tongue was the terror of all of the men and most of the women of the village.

Fortunately, Badjene was in a mellow mood.

"Ah, my daughter. Soon Doudou Camara will arrive. Fate has smiled upon you, Penda, for it is a good man who has come from the outside to take you to wife."

"Yes, Badjene." Penda's voice stopped just short of being totally devoid of expression.

"Not to mention a rich one!" the old woman added. This raised contented smiles all round.

"And by tomorrow noon," Badjene continued, "you will have taken the rice, which you yourself will have prepared, to your uncle's house where Doudou Camara will be the honoured guest. He will see you for the first time. You know what you must do?" The old woman threw a sharp look in Penda's direction.

"Yes, Badjene. I have been instructed in what I must do." Penda lowered her head and murmured, "About a hundred times."

"What's that?" Badjene cupped her good ear with her hand.

"I said, I'm grateful to those who have given me instruction." Badjene's watery eyes contemplated the veil of braids around Penda's head.

"We are joyful for you, Penda. The next days will be full of feasting. For you, the orphan of the village, will have found a husband."

Penda said nothing but continued to watch the road that emerged from a deep pocket of green and then twisted by, swerving out of sight. His car would come out of the forest, right there. She vowed not to let her eyes stray from that spot until she saw the dust from his wheels disappearing from view. Badjene's voice, especially in this rare mood of nostalgia, would provide a background for her gazing.

"Yes, poor Penda. Both mother and father dead before you could pronounce their names."

"In my uncle's house, there has been a home for me." There was a subdued, almost automatic quality to Penda's response. All intensity centred on her eyes which never left the road.

"Your uncle! You call that a man? No order in his family! Too many problems and too, too many wives. It's a miracle he can walk unassisted!" Badjene warmed to her subject – a favourite of hers – but almost as quickly returned to the pool of quiet reflection into which Penda's approaching marriage kept pulling her.

"It is by Allah's grace alone that you have turned out as well as you have. You know how to work and you are respectful. Much better than that basketful of useless daughters your uncle has!" Badjene's lip curled at the thought of them. She fixed her cloudy eyes on Penda again. Her look was intent and scrutinising. "But look at you! As succulent as a ripe mango! I hope too much of your sweetness does not cause Doudou Camara's belly to ache!"

Penda did not react as both Badjene and the *coiffeuse* squawked loudly. She was tired of all of this talk of fruit. Wherever she went in the village, all the married women would stop whatever they were doing to give descriptions of her person that made her feel like a walking orchard.

There was guava to indicate the smoothness of her cheeks, sugar-apple for the savour of her mouth, mango and paw-paw for the contour of her breasts, melon for the firmness of her buttocks. Then there was the best fruit of all, the essence of all the others, the one that would eventually grow inside her body. Penda flicked a phalanx of braids from her eyes and shook her head.

Badjene and the *coiffeuse* were still at it.

"Poor Doudou Camara," Badjene sniggered, wiping her eyes. "I remember him. He used to play with my small brothers many rains ago. But does he think all of the money from the land of the toubab will give him the courage to contend with a firm juicy fruit the likes of our daughter?" Again, Badjene and the *coiffeuse* were submerged in the waves of laughter that washed over them.

Penda gave an irritable sigh. She knew this was all part of the build-up to the ceremony. On the one hand, the solemn recitation of a wife's duties and responsibilities. On the other, the ribald innuendo about sower and soil and seed and fruit. As Badjene continued her rampage across the bridegroom's manhood, Penda lowered her head. But it was not in embarrassment. Fear and shame were not part of Penda's make-up. What was to take place between her and her husband, under the cover of darkness, would take place, as inevitably as the sun rising in the heavens. But this fruit, the secret fruit of marriage, was one that she had decided not to relish, whose sweetness would not flood her soul. It was a fruit that would never cause her belly to ache.

In a lull in the cackling of her two companions, Penda said mildly, "At this rate, I will see my husband for the first time looking just like this." She touched the unadorned section of her hair. "And I will say it was that *coiffeuse* from Senegal who is responsible."

Calm returned to both to the *coiffeuse* and to Badjene

who rearranged the folds of her boubou, momentarily revealing a long breast flattened against her thin rib cage. When she started to speak again, her voice moved on the unruffled tide of ancient liturgy.

"Penda, if your mother had lived, she would have spoken these words to you. Marriage is not a palace of pleasure. No, my daughter..." Badjene adjusted her seating position to give some ease to her old bones. "It is the pot in which a wife cooks the soup of patience. A lifetime of forbearance, of restraint, of generosity, of forgiveness. These are the ingredients needed. And you must never let your eye wander from that simmering pot, for from it will emerge the sons and daughters who will be your crown. Either of thorns or of stars."

The fingers of the *coiffeuse* found their rhythm again as Badjene's words rose and fell on the notes of their ageless music. Penda was glad to be released from the tyranny of fruit. There was strange comfort to be found in these recipes of behaviour, laid down by antiquity.

"The road ahead will not be easy. When I was married to El Hajji Abdou, may Allah have mercy on his soul..." Badjene was becoming lost in her oratory, oblivious of her audience. Penda, whose mind had started to drift, heard only the word "road" and turned her attention once more to the spot where the forest gave way to the dusty dirt track.

"I went down that road once before," Penda said to herself, "But it brought me back."

The day that Penda had left the village rose up before her. She was eleven years old and was being taken to the capital by Sister Gabriella of the Sacred Heart, from Donegal. Why the young Irish nun had loved her Penda never knew, but after a year in the village vainly preaching the Good News of Jesus Christ to the Infidel, Gabriella had persuaded Penda's uncle to let the child accompany her to Banjul so that she could attend the convent school. It had not been difficult despite the problem of religion – one less mouth to feed – and even when Sister Gabriella had told him, with regret, that Penda would not be able to board at the school, a hasty scheme had been cobbled together whereby she would live in the house of a distant relative of distant relatives. It was, by all reports, a highly respectable house and the family noted for its kindness. So early one morning, Sister Gabriella and Penda had set off down that same dust track.

"No one cried for me that morning," Penda thought, wrapped in a cocoon of memory that blocked out the pulling fingers of the *coiffeuse* and Badjene's droning voice. "Not my aunts or my cousins. Not my uncle. Nobody." Then she gave a small smile. "But then I didn't cry either!"

In fact, the thrill of that day's journey had had all the qualities of a dream. With its cars and electric lights, Banjul had seemed like a fairyland as had the Convent itself where she and the Sister had spent their first night. The halls had been cool and quiet and the school room large and inviting. But the crowning moment had come when Sister Gabriella had presented her with her uniform, a navy pleated pinafore with a navy and white sash and a pair of brown buckled sandals. In her whole life, Penda had never seen anything more beautiful.

Penda's eyes filled at the thought of the wonder of that first night. A single tear rolled down her cheek. She brushed it away with a stealthy hand. But she needn't have worried. Badjene, spirit guide of young virgin brides, was in full cry and her dim eyes saw nothing.

"The labour of a wife is never done. She must afford a true welcome to her husband's family, her husband's friends. Her door is always open, her bounty is always endless for it is on these things that she will be judged."

Penda returned to the memory of ten years before. On the day after her arrival in the capital, the Sister had taken Penda to meet her new guardians. There, in the sprawling

126

stone and zinc compound, the head of the household had extended a warm greeting to them both. As she'd left, Sister Gabriella had told him, in Penda's presence, that the little girl would be expected at the convent in a week's time, when the school reopened. She had bent down and kissed Penda on her forehead. Penda remembered the coarse touch of the nun's habit on her cheek

This was the last time Penda had seen Sister Gabriella, or the convent school for that matter. She had been put straight to work somewhere in the bowels of the compound. The beginning of term had come and gone but Penda's guardians all seemed to suffer from a collective loss of memory and never quite got around to sending her to school. Instead, they'd found that hers were just the extra hands they needed to sweep, to wash, to iron, to mind the several infants recently born into the family. It was not that the work was harder than what she was accustomed to in the village. It was just that now there existed the navy dress and the buckled shoes and the new world they embodied. Every night, before she curled up to sleep, she would finger the pleats of the navy dress, dust off the shoes and use the sash to wipe her eyes. But in that respected house known for its kindness, there was no witness to her mute tears.

The first time Penda had plucked up the courage to ask when she was going to be allowed to go to school, she had been sharply scolded; the next time slapped. The next time she had been denied food for a day. The following morning, when someone came with a bowl of sombi, Penda had refused it and continued to refuse all nourishment until, a few days later, she'd collapsed. After some hurried ministrations, she had been despatched back home, amidst outraged protestations that "there's something wrong with that ungrateful child". So Penda, the orphaned niece of a distant relative of distant relatives of a great family in Banjul, had returned to the village, thin, ailing, with nothing to show for her six month ordeal except a navy blue and white sash which she clutched in her grimy little hand.

Penda remembered how she'd felt when the road had returned her. It had seemed to resemble a potent spirit, serpentine, coiling and vicious. When she had left home with Sister Gabriella, she had not cried because she was too full; when she'd returned, alone, she had not cried because she was too empty. Years after her return, she had found out that Sister Gabriella had gone back to the stone and zinc compound to plead for Penda but to no avail. Eventually the Mother House, wishing to head off a potentially troublesome situation, had sent her back to Ireland. But for Penda, the damage had been done. Not only had she been denied the dreamworld promised by school, something in her heart had been so badly bruised that it had become tough and wary. And now, with the coming of the car out of the forest, she would once again have to entrust her life into the hands of another. How could she do this, and do it with joy?

"Penda! Penda! Answer when your Badjene speaks to you!" Penda's eyes were wide when she turned to find Badjene sitting straight-backed and with a look of displeasure on her face.

"Badjene, I'm sorry... Didn't I answer..." Penda's voice was full of contrition but Badjene was not appeased. For the past few minutes, she had been trying to elicit a response from Penda but the old woman's words had fallen on ears deafer even than her own.

"Forgive me, Badjene... I was just thinking..."

"Obviously, you prefer your 'thinking' to the counsel of your elders. And, as that is the case," Badjene said, rising to her feet, anger making her suddenly agile, "I will leave you to your thoughts." She started to walk off then turned and said, "Doudou Camara had better be careful. When his mouth sinks into the flesh of the mango, he'd better watch out for that hard seed inside. Huh! He could break his teeth on it."

128

Penda made a move to go after her but the *coiffeuse* sat her back down again. "Don't you know better than to bother with Badjene? Can't you remember when her dear El Hajji Abdou died, there was not one unbroken tooth left in his head?"

Penda turned to smile at this when a sound like thunder jolted them. Out of the green forest roared a black car that ground its gears and hurtled along the dirt track, throwing up whirlwinds of dust as it passed. It took several minutes before the sunbaked yard returned to its afternoon stillness.

The *coiffeuse* resumed her labours and for a long time said nothing. Then in a tender voice, she said, "The road has delivered your husband. And soon it will take you both away."

Half a kilometre away, in the village centre, under the giant arms of the silk-cotton tree, Doudou Camara was received into the bosom of his family with due ceremony and the true spirit of *teranga*. The multitude that gathered stayed flocked around him all of the evening and most of the night, watching him closely, listening to tales of the outside. It was not until the middle of the next morning, when people had set about their habitual tasks again, that Doudou was able to have a few moments of quiet contemplation. Two emotions vied for pre-eminence. Gladness at being on this special spot on earth, feted at last as a returning brother; and worry as he faced the moment when he would see the one who would become his new wife. He recalled the letter that he, via his daughter Naba, had written to his brother Ibou outlining the qualities he hoped for in his wife. He wanted her to be easy on the eye. But not beautiful. A beautiful wife was trouble. Everyone knew that. She must be an excellent cook and be able to keep an immaculate house. The years Doudou had spent living alone had taught him to cook and clean. He knew he would be an exacting judge but he vowed to try not to be too harsh. In addition, he wanted her to be pleasant and submissive (Annie would argue for days about something if she thought she was right); considerate and thrifty (Katy's mother was always asking for money); placid and gentle (Mary's mother used to throw things). It had seemed a sensible list and Ibou and all of the others he had spoken to assured him that the chosen one more than met the criteria. But now, as he prepared himself to see her for the first time, he thought of the tranquil spirit of his companion in the taxi. What would he have said? Some wise old saying, no doubt. Doudou reached back to a time when the rich symbols of his language were at the tips of his fingers. His search was interrupted by Ibou, whom the planning of these nuptials had cast into a state of profound agitation, announcing that it was time to go. It would be improper to arrive late at the home of the future in-laws. As Doudou mopped his brow, an old riddle came to him, stilling the tremor of his hands.

"My brother," he said, "when does the lion fear the gazelle?"

Ibou grinned and retorted, "When God forgets to put the morning sun in the sky!"

In buoyant mood, the two brothers strode off in the direction of Penda's uncle's house and Doudou Camara's destiny.

Everything went according to plan. All the brothers, joined by other male relatives were met with great cordiality. There was some introductory talk and then the meal was brought. Penda placed a huge bowl in the middle of the circle made up of her uncle, Doudou and the other members of the delegation.

"Penda, bring us water," her uncle said casually. This she did and then, bowing slightly, disappeared as the men washed their hands.

They ate with gusto, emptying the bowl of its cargo of rice, fish, okra and palm oil. With the sun high in the sky, they "killed the ant" with more talk, all wholly unrelated to the marriage and when enough time had passed for it not to appear rude to leave, Doudou and his party stood up. But it was the eldest brother who spoke.

"Tell those who prepared the food," Ibou said to Penda's uncle in a ringing voice, "that their toil was pleasing to our palate." The heads of the two families shook hands and in the touch of those two palms, the marriage contract was sealed.

From that moment on, Ibou Camara's life was not his own as he set out to arrange the biggest wedding the village had seen in years. As Penda's uncle was notoriously unreliable and as he, Ibou, was born to organise, the burden fell on him. Great sacks of rice had to be purchased in Farafenni as well as bolts of cloth to outfit the entire village. Nearer to home, Ibou's wives clamoured to have their jewellery melted down by the Mauritanian silversmith and reworked into something more elaborate. Then there were three bulls to be slaughtered. Details! Details! Ibou's head buzzed with them so he failed to notice the silence which had enveloped Doudou since the first official meal with his in-laws.

Doudou's silence was like the silence of palm wine in ferment, like the silence of coals aglow with their inner heat. He had gone to the home of his intended a little nervous, perhaps, but armed with all the protective wisdom of the sages. But when he had laid eyes on Penda for the first time – with her eyes, hooded and black, and her limbs that flowed like water – all was consumed by the fire which leapt from his loins in one sharp and brilliant flame.

Doudou Camara, who had toyed with love in the world outside, was now faced with a game infinitely subtler, more complex and powerful. He thought again of the old man in the taxi. This couldn't have been what he'd meant by intimacy. This was torture. After a few days, he shook off his silence and sought out his brother for advice. He found him surrounded by a group of children who were being sent to points throughout the village and beyond.

"Omar, take these knives to Mustafa Keita. Tell him I need them to be as sharp as a razor. What are you doing? Are you mad? Walk, child, walk!"

"Moussa, tell your father to meet me here at noon. Go! Amadou, pump up the tyre on my bike. I'm going to have to ride to Djana this afternoon. Hurry, child, hurry!"

While Ibou commanded his troops, Doudou looked on, fascinated by the magisterial air that his brother had acquired over the years. Seeing that it would be impossible to divert his attention during the issuing of orders, Doudou waited for the last child to go scurrying off before making his approach.

"Ah, Doudou, it's you." Ibou's preoccupied eyes swept over to his brother, rested for the briefest second before travelling again until they halted at the shade tree in the corner of his courtyard.

"The heat is already upon us and it's not yet noon! Come, Doudou, we will sit in the cool for a while and then discuss arrangements for the ceremonies tomorrow."

"Before we do that," Doudou said, marvelling at the way whatever Ibou said sounded like a directive. "Before we do that," Doudou repeated, hearing his own voice melt into apology, "there is something I wish to ask you."

If Ibou had been paying attention, he would have seen the earnest appeal in his brother's face. But he was still distracted, by the trials of wedding management, by the heat and by the noise of argument coming from the back of his house.

"Anything you wish to know," Ibou sighed. Then in a gesture of magnanimity, he decided to elaborate. "Everything has been taken care of. For instance..."

"Not about that," Doudou cut in, fearing slow death in a swamp of protocol. "No," Doudou's voice lowered. "It's about marriage. The nature of marriage itself."

"The nature of...?" Ibou looked blank for a moment and turned his head in the direction of the raised voices. "Hey, you back there! Does the simple cooking of a meal require such noise?" Silence fell but Ibou continued to glare at the house as though he could see through it to the kitchen behind. "What's wrong with you women? Don't you see it's hot? Must my brother and I die of thirst? Aida! Water!" Ibou could now relax and turn his head and his attention towards Doudou.

"Now what were you saying?" he asked, gathering his dignity about him.

Doudou gave a slight cough and wished for a different setting for this kind of talk, one without heat, dust and quarrelling to oppress them. Nonetheless, something impelled him to make one last effort.

"Older brother..." the noise from the back broke out again. Ibou's head snapped around.

"Water! Water, I say!" Ibou's voice boomed, blotting out all others. For a long moment, an unearthly silence prevailed.

Doudou dared not wait an instant longer.

"Older brother, can a husband desire his wife too much?"

For the second time since they'd sat beneath the shade tree, Ibou appeared to struggle to grasp his brother's meaning. "Can a husband..." He seemed to be looking down a long corridor of time trying to retrieve some notion called desire. Finally he smiled and his body assumed a posture that located him somewhere between general and godhead. "No," Ibou said, "there is never too much desire." His smile broadened as, in his mind, he surveyed the beauteous gifts rendered to the lion by the gazelle. "It is, after all, a man's birthright."

A look of pure contentment had just settled on Ibou's face when all of a sudden, there was a terrific clatter of cooking pots being hurled followed by a series of piercing screams. All those pleasurable thoughts of lions and gazelles drained from Ibou's face and it was an old man with

133

drooping shoulders who stumbled to his feet. "Aida, didn't I tell you to bring water? Water, I say!" Even his voice had been diminished by this sudden aging.

A tight knot of women erupted onto the courtyard, rolling along like a ball, but within striking distance of the shade tree, it broke apart, revealing the two principal pugilists, two of Ibou's wives, one of them dripping wet and weeping. For an instant, everyone seemed to freeze. The born administrator, wedding planner extraordinaire, husband of three wives, father of many children, Ibou Camara stood there like a doomed saint, incapable of utterance.

Aida, the dry wife, her eyes aflame and her head-tie askew, showed not the least concern for the tribulations of her spouse.

"Here is your water, Doudou Camara." Pointing to the wet wife, she continued, "I gave it to my co-wife instead of you. Her thirst was greater."

A babble of voices rose skywards. Doudou experienced a great need to be gone and, bending over to within earshot of his beleaguered brother, he whispered, "Older brother, we will talk again later."

It was all Ibou needed to find his voice and, turning a blazing face to Doudou, the locked door of his rage flew open.

"Doudou Camara, do not burden me with these childish matters! You have been spoiled on the outside! I have seen the photographs of your house with the carpet on the floor, the flush toilet and all the toys of the toubab. And now Allah has given you a ripe young wife. As your older brother, I forbid you..." Ibou's voice was increasing in volume, because of his anger but also because the wives had recommenced their free and frank exchange of views. "I forbid you to question me any further about marriage!"

Doudou lost no time in quitting Ibou's turbulent courtyard and, heedless of the noonday sun, walked fast and hard, putting distance between him and the fracas, seeking out the shadows and the stillness. After a while, he found himself by a stream, low at the moment as the earth waited for the rains, but just deep enough for washing. A young woman was kneeling there, placing her completed laundry in a basin, standing and balancing it on her head. Her movements were fluid and oddly familiar.

It was Penda.

She was momentarily startled when she saw him but then started to walk. As she passed him she said, "Go in peace, Doudou Camara."

"And you also, Penda Seydi."

He watched her as she slid between the trees and out of sight. And as he watched her, knowing that she would be taking the road back to the village, that same road that would take them both away, he felt his heart fill as surely as would the stream with the coming of the rains. And when it was his turn to go, he went in peace.

That peace accompanied Doudou over the next hours during which he returned to pacify his martyred brother and his peevish wives; over the next few days during which he was wed amid a celebration of epic proportions; over the next weeks during which he prepared his bride for departure from the village, country and continent of her birth; over the next months during which he and Penda adjusted to their new life together in the land of the toubab. Amidst these upheavals, Doudou's serenity held, sometimes waxing, sometimes waning but always there like a spring that one day murmurs beneath the surface and the next flows strongly in the sunlight. There were some moments when Doudou dared to believe that the peace that passeth all understanding would be his, now that he had a real home and a real wife.

Inside this new home, all was warmth and order. From the kitchen came the smells and sound of yet another sumptuous dinner. *Domada, bene chin, yassa.* Which would it be tonight? Doudou patted his flat tummy with affection and made a leap into the future when he and Penda would contemplate the roundness of their bellies and know that love was swelling them both.

"*Nidiaye.*"

Doudou started. He was still not used to being called this. All the years that Annie and the others had called him darling, lovey or sweetheart, he had remained unmoved. But hearing this young woman, his wife, call him a word that literally meant "Uncle" did not fail to unhinge him.

"*Nidiaye, caye lek.*"

All Doudou could do was grunt as Penda made ready for the meal. She moved the low coffee table aside and unrolled a straw mat, placing it on the carpet. The dining room table languished, dejected, in the corner. Penda had been keen to put it to good use. But as soon as Penda had arrived, Doudou had been firm. From this day forward, we eat like Africans.

Doudou appeared to be adjusting his watch but in reality he was watching his wife, studying her every movement, in detail. She moved neither slowly nor with precipitation, setting down the enamel bowl piled high with steaming groundnut stew and rice. She placed two large spoons at the rim of the bowl and arranged a small mound of orange peppers in the centre. She rose to her feet, the movement accentuating the curve of her breasts. She walked away from Doudou towards the kitchen door in that same unhurried way, pulling her wrapper tightly across her hips and buttocks, making her silver bracelets tinkle.

By the time Penda disappeared behind the door, Doudou had broken out in a sweat. Eh Allah! Am I to be tormented at this age with desire?

There was the sound of footsteps.

"*Nidiaye.*"

Doudou flinched and fervently wished for the day when his yearning for his wife no longer afflicted him like a pestilence. It was so unseemly.

Feigning nonchalance, he went and squatted beside Penda in front of the bowl of food. The *domada* was delicious, its reddish-brown sauce unctuous and piquant with limes and hot peppers. Penda's spoon sought out the choicest cuts of meat and placed them by Doudou's. They ate in silence and when the bowl moved slightly, their fingers clutched its rim, warding off any malicious forces which might wish to harm their marriage. They did not speak. Once or twice Doudou stole a glance at Penda, memorising the closely-cropped head, now bereft of the serried ranks of braids, the smooth line of her shoulders, the flawless black satin of her skin. Once she caught him and for a fragment of a second their eyes held. Yet again, Doudou was confounded by the contradictions of Penda's eyes – the dutiful, wifely affection and training that had produced this meal, which kept the house like a shiny new pin, which gave itself to him, without passion perhaps, but without reluctance either. But there was something else, something that was mainly hidden but now and then made sudden startling appearances. Something like a hunger. He saw it when they went out shopping on the high street and her eyes devoured all of those heaped-up things – the videos, the steam irons and washing machines, the microwaves, the stereo sets – the "toys of the toubab", as Ibou had called them. He saw it as she watched television, her face tight with concentration as she tried to make the connection between the images and the sounds. At times such as these, he felt the spring of his serenity dwindle to its lowest ebb. After only a few months of connubial bliss, during which Penda had not put one foot wrong, Doudou had started to worry about that look and what it might mean.

The doorbell rang. It was Naba.

"*Nangen def...*"

"*Mangi fi, rek,* our Dad."

"Jeynaba, *caye lek.*"

"No, it's all right. I've just now had my tea."

Naba settled herself on the sofa as Doudou and Penda finished their meal. Her eyes flitted about, taking note of the polished table tops, the pristine floor spaces, the almost austere sense of order that prevailed. She thought of the toy-strewn mayhem of the place that she called home. And yet her father's house was no longer the refuge that it had long been for her. Things were different now. She found herself staring at the couple. Penda felt the heat of her eyes.

"Naba, *caye lek.*"

"I said..." Naba caught herself. This would not do. She would not be like Josephine and the others. "It's all right, Penda, but no. *Dedet.*"

Penda gave a small smile and resumed eating. Smug, are we, Naba asked herself. Well you have every reason to be. Everything's going your way. Got our Dad eating from mats on the floor. Got him eating out of your hand. Got me speaking African. That's why your "daughters" – had you noticed that we're all bloody older than you – none of your daughters except me comes to see you.

"Why should I have to learn a foreign language just to speak to me own Dad!" Josephine said. Naba tried to push back these sour thoughts. After all, she had come to give her father some good news.

She waited until the meal was cleared away. When she heard the sound of dishes being washed in the kitchen, Naba seized the opportunity.

"Dad," she said to him, leaning close. "I've got something to tell you."

As though by magic, Penda reappeared, wiping her soapy hands, kneeling down to pick up microscopic food particles from the floor. Naba's face fell and Doudou did not fail to see it.

138

"What you can tell me, you can tell my wife." Doudou spoke in a mild tone but there was a solid feel to what he said, as though the edges of his words were made of hardening concrete.

Naba felt her cheeks grow hot as she fled from the displeasure in her father's eyes. In her flight, she stumbled once again upon Penda, still absorbed in the seemingly endless task of extracting minutiae from the fibres of the carpet. Naba took a deep breath.

"Dad. Penda..." Penda looked up, very calm. "I wanted you to be the first to know." There was a dramatic pause. "I'm getting married."

Doudou created a diversion by giving a resounding belch, while in his mind he quickly passed in review the cavalcade of amiable young men he had found in Naba's house over the years, drinking cups of tea, playing with the kids, lounging about like pashas. All their faces merged into a featureless blank.

Naba was not amused by her father's evident confusion.

"You see what honeymooning does to you. You don't notice anything but... Dad! It's Cliffie. You know, the bloke from Liverpool, the one with the cheeky laugh. He's been coming down every weekend for the last four months..."

Naba was on a rising tide of agitation midway between anxiety and anger. "I can't believe this! Only a couple of weeks ago, you talked to him in my living room. He told you about how his business was going. Plumbing, remember?"

Desperation had started to creep in.

"He's got a three-bedroom semi and wants to make a home for me and the kids. And the baby, of course."

"Baby?"

"Yeah." Naba's voice dropped and so did her eyes as she studied her pudgy little hands. "There's a baby coming." This was the fifth time she'd had to say these words to

Doudou and it was never easy, even now, with a wedding in sight.

Penda had not moved during all of this. She watched the other two, her fingers idle on the carpet. She saw Doudou draw himself up straight as he turned to face Naba.

"What about his family?"

"Family?" Naba echoed. "Well... he's got one – mum, dad, a couple of brothers... Hey Dad! Guess what! His granddad was African! From Sierra Leone, I think he said, or was it Nigeria? Anyway, what do you think of that?" Naba delivered this with a beaming smile. "And... and..." she persisted, "I thought we could ask Auntie Mame Koumba to organise things for the wedding. To make it... sorta... ethnic."

Doudou received the news of Cliffie's lineage and the possible involvement of the redoubtable Mame Koumba Seck with a singular lack of enthusiasm. When he first spoke, his tone was dismissive. "Don't talk to me about that troublesome woman!" Then he became more serious, the gravity of his words making them slow and emphatic.

"But when I go meet his father? His uncles? His older brothers? When we go see each other and talk about the marriage?"

Naba's face was very pale as she jumped from the sofa and started pulling on her coat.

"Dad, I think I'll come back some other time. When you're, you've..." Even from where he was sitting, Doudou could see her eyes filling up.

"Why you being so? Naba, I want to do the right thing for you. That's all. I'm your father."

"But Dad," Naba sniffed, "Ever since I came down from Liverpool when I was eighteen, you've been begging me to get married. Every time I'm in the family way, you're telling me to get a decent man who wants to marry me."

Even beneath the coat's camouflage, Doudou could see her body shaking. "Well, I found him! He's got a job. Never been in the nick. He makes me laugh. And he likes me and the kids." Naba was really crying now. "But all you can talk about is... is..."

Doudou went over to console Naba. It took a bit of time but when she left, she managed to give her father a wan smile. But for Penda there was a look of pure accusation.

"*Nidiaye*, what's wrong with our little daughter?" Penda listened as Doudou gave a brief account of what had happened. For a moment, she said nothing.

"But why was she angry with you, her father?"

He raised his eyes to her and gave the single word that explained all the strangeness in creation.

"'Toubab!"

But the unfathomable world of the white man was the furthest thing from Doudou's mind an hour or so later when he and his wife retired for the night. Naba's talk of weddings, and in particular, babies had reminded him of his sacred duty to produce a son. His body told him that tonight was the night to set the whole enterprise into motion. From the moment that Naba had left, Penda saw that unmistakable light in his eyes as he watched her find unnecessary things to do. When at last he reached for her in the darkness of their bedroom, Penda was almost singed by his touch.

Doudou Camara gave himself wholeheartedly to the task, his body shedding the years with every movement, kicking aside any barriers between it and his heart. And so he ploughed his love into the sleek young body that moved tentatively beneath his. He claimed it as his own, that body, the spirit that quickened it and the new life that he would plant in its rich black soil. The sweat poured down like a cleansing rain and when at last the seed of his immortality burst from him, his tightly clenched eyes beheld a vision of his blood line, stretching towards the far horizon, tall and strong, striding over the earth like the sons of Soundiata.

Meanwhile Penda, the happy recipient of her husband's attentions, had her mind on other things. She had developed the uncanny knack of having her body in one place, apparently participating in a given activity while in fact her mind wandered about among the stars. So while all the elements of Doudou Camara's being converged around the ecstatic rite of procreation, Penda meandered through a maze of half-revealed thought and memory. In among all this, one thing was certain. Doudou was out of luck. Penda knew the rhythms of her body well enough to be sure that the longed-for heir had not been made tonight.

Penda got out of bed and went to the window. The room was warm and dark and smelled of love. But it was a love that she did not feel. She reached across to pull a wrapper around her but then stopped. It felt good to be like this, soothed by the dark warmth, without insistent hands violating her nakedness. She looked over at her sleeping husband with a clinical eye. He looked pretty good, considering. She could imagine him under the tangled bedclothes. Apart from a certain lack of suppleness, his body was that of a much younger man. Then there was his face, now in utter repose, somewhat lined but in no way ravaged by the passing years. Only the skin around his neck and his hands gave him away, one being loose and empty-looking, the other rough and calloused. Not that it mattered. He could have been as beautiful as the elegant young men she had seen in Dakar as they took the plane to England. It would have been the same.

Penda looked out of the window and saw the moon drifting in the blackness. When she was a child, she used to creep outside her uncle's house when everyone else was sleeping and watch its luminescence trailing across the sky. It had always seemed like a friend.

She was lucky, she knew; just as Badjene had said, Doudou Camara was a kind man. "And," Penda hugged herself with glee, "he's rich!"

This marriage was indeed a godsend. It had taken her away from the place of her birth, the place that had fed and clothed her, had taught her the ways of its world, had instructed her on how to be a woman in that world, had given her skills and a handbook for living. And yet... from a very early age, Penda had known that this was a place from which she must flee. Somewhere along the way, the village had failed her. In its careless inattention, it had not managed to fill in the spaces left by the parents she'd never known. It had, without ever being aware it was doing so, consigned Penda to the fringes, rescuing her from complete invisibility for only those few days after her return from Banjul, when her mistreatment there had provided an opportunity for the whole village to rail against the perfidy of those who lived in the town. She'd had to wait ten more years to become visible again. When she and her new husband had entered the taxi that was taking them away, Penda had felt the sharp wrench of severance as the waving arms disappeared in a cloud of dust. But she knew that this was the pain she'd prayed for for as long as she could remember.

Doudou made a loud snorting noise and muttered in his sleep.

"Look at him!" Penda said under her breath. "He looks like a newborn drunk on his mother's milk." She could almost see the glow of happiness that surrounded him. A ripple of scorn crossed her face. She and Doudou were so different! Not so long ago, he'd confided to her how he'd felt on the day, months ago, when they had met by chance by the stream. Penda had been astonished at how he'd described the scene, with such lovely words. How, to him, she'd seemed like a queen, walking in the coolness and how, when she'd spoken to him, her words had fallen upon him like a blessing. His eyes had shone so when he'd told her this story that she hadn't had the heart to tell him that all she'd remembered was how much her back had hurt, her knees had hurt, her fingers had hurt and how broadly she'd smiled when, on her arrival in England, she'd seen how the brilliant white machine consumed dirty clothes only to regurgitate clean ones. That's how different they were.

"There are things that he wants that I don't want..." Almost as a reflex, her hand touched her belly. "And there are things that I want that he doesn't..."

Penda pulled her wrapper around her and tied it so that it rode atop her breasts. It was getting cold.

"It is cold and wet today," Penda whispered in heavily accented English.

She stole a furtive glance over her shoulder. Doudou slept on in the lap of the angels. He had not heard the English sounds fall from her lips. Nor did he know that for an hour every day from Monday to Friday – while he was at work – all household duties ceased while Penda tuned in to "Let's speak English!" on TV. She looked at her husband's untroubled face. Yes, her secret was safe.

Glancing around, Penda tiptoed over to the chest of drawers, pulled something out and just as noiselessly returned to her place at the window. She looked at the city streets and found them beautiful. The brick and glass citadel – no matter how ugly or in what state of decay – never failed to speak to her of its possibility. It might look like a labyrinth, but in it there was a road leading somewhere. And as her hand stroked a faded navy and now grey sash, Penda knew exactly how she would get there. By knowing. By speaking with authority. By speaking for herself. These things alone would lead her to the great beyond which had seemed within her grasp on the night that she'd fallen asleep in the cool quiet of Sister Gabriella's school. She twisted the sash in her hands as she grappled with the problem of how to get more knowledge. Right now she felt like a thief, grabbing bits and pieces of it wherever she could. Wasn't there another way, one where she could learn something – anything! – without feeling like she was sneaking off to see a forbidden lover?

She looked over at her sleeping husband and felt herself harden towards him. As decent as he was, the last thing he would want was a wife who wanted to go to school. Could she ever make him understand that that was what she burned for above all other things?

Penda started pacing the floor and mumbling to herself. A sense of powerlessness rose like bile within her. Would the road ahead be barred to her while she spent her life keeping her eye on the pot of patience? She wrung the sash viciously and cast a chilling look at the man couched in innocent sleep.

"Will you deny me this, Doudou Camara? Will you?" she said between clenched teeth as she strode back and forth across the face of the window. Her breath came in uneven bursts as wave after wave of emotion broke over her. "And now all this talk of babies..." As soon as the thought was formed, she stopped dead in her tracks. An uncontrollable trembling overtook her. Out of the sadness of her past rose a vision peopled with children running, children laughing, or wailing after some summary chastisement, children making the long walk to school, returning with precious exercise books – the lucky ones! Babies with sticky eyes and runny noses and streaming bowels, babies dead from light-ning attacks of fever. Looking down on these pitiful speci-mens were the women of the village, their bodies bulging with the successors to the sick and dying babies. Every last female, from the smallest girl child to the oldest crone, everyone had, in the agony of Penda's mind, a belly bloated into a monumental and everlasting pregnancy from which there was no deliverance.

Penda clapped her hands over her eyes as terror gripped her. She wanted to run. She wanted to weep. She felt she would go mad.

At last the fit subsided. She stood like a statute at the

window, her ears no longer hearing the sounds from the street below, her eyes no longer following the plaintive circuit of the moon above. All that moved were her hands, busy beneath the dark blue cotton cloth, pressing hard on her belly, so smooth and firm and flat. So beautiful, yet so treacherous. For beneath that band of muscle lay an awesome power that was in a permanent state of vigilance, waiting for, longing for, the tiny scrap of life that would make it whole and set in motion the wheels of eternity. Penda pressed hard on her belly but knew that her desperate hands were no match for the lurking force that would propel her life into that of another. But she did not want the assurance of life eternal by what issued from her womb. She just wanted a life, her own life, where she would know something other than how to be the perfect wife, a life surrounded by the bright toys of the toubab, but most of all, a life free of the choking ties of the African family. One of Penda's hands flew up to her mouth as though stopping those foul thoughts from oozing out into the night air. An African woman who did not want to hold her own child, at least not yet – it went against all the laws of nature. And yet, that is what she was. For a second time the dark wings of madness beat in her eyes. But the sensation was fleeting.

"I'm not in the village any more. I'm in the land of the toubab," she thought. "Everything's different here."

Maybe, just maybe, she would be delivered from her destiny and, once and for all, defeat the enemy within.

"Penda!"

She whirled around and found Doudou sitting upright on their bed, alarm etched on every feature. He had awoken and seen Penda at the window, the music of her body singing a mournful song.

"What's wrong? What's happened?"

Penda stood her ground, resisting his demand to know. At that moment a cloud moved from the face of the moon and its beams threw pools of light into the dark space between Doudou and his wife, between Penda and her husband. Penda felt the moonlight on her face; felt it like the caress of a lover. But she knew it for what it was, the tainted touch of yet another enemy. That same moon that pulled up the ocean tides month by month by month, the moon that pretended to be her friend yet reached down into her most secret self and made it vulnerable to the desires to men. A great calm descended on her as she assembled all of her artillery. But as she crossed the room, no one would have known she was about to wage war. For Doudou, she had never looked lovelier as, framed by moonlight, she sat down beside him.

"*Nidiaye*," she said, lowering her eyes. "Since I came to live with you in England, you've shown me nothing but kindness." She paused. "Never has my life been more pleasant, more easy." The truth of these words rang out in her voice. "But... but ..."

"What is it? What is making you unhappy?"

"Oh *Nidiaye*! I am not unhappy. You have done me a great honour by making me your wife..."

"But what?"

"Well, you see..." Penda leaned closer and then stopped. "To be a more worthy companion, I would like to learn English."

"What? Is that all?" Doudou looked hugely relieved. "You'll learn it quickly enough – you'll pick it up! Just like I did."

Penda said nothing for a moment but remained where she was, her head and shoulders very close to his. Doudou found himself forgetting what Penda had just said. The hastily tied knot that was keeping the wrapper afloat was causing him distress.

"No, *Nidiaye*." Her voice was a whisper. "I would like to go to school. So that I can read it and write it. English! I want to be able to speak Toubab!"

The softness of her words did not disguise their serious intent and were heard by Doudou even through the deafening clamour of her nearness. He straightened up a little, trying to clear his mind. What did this mean? Was this a challenge to his authority? Would it mean that two years from now, she, speaking perfect English, would be wearing the trousers in the family? He looked at her bowed head, could still hear her tremulous voice. No! What would this mean? It would mean that she could now go to Safeways by herself and he would be hailed as a modern husband.

"Well, I don't know," he said, not wanting to appear to have capitulated too quickly. She did not look up but pulled away from him a fraction of a centimetre. Her shoulders trembled a little. "'Well I suppose it can't do any harm..." Doudou did not complete his sentence for Penda had fallen on her knees before him.

"Allah be praised for sending me such a good man," she cried as an embarrassed Doudou pulled her to her feet. In her mind she knew this to be true as she thought of some of the hardened wife beaters she'd known in the village.

"I will allow you to learn English. The Council puts on courses. For 'immigrants'. That's what they call us. But only," and here Doudou's voice took on the stern tones that he had used much earlier with Naba, "but only if your duties as a wife don't suffer."

Penda stood up and gave Doudou a beatific smile as she felt the moonlight streaming around her.

"Don't worry, *Nidiaye*, I take my duties as a wife very seriously." And with a slow hand, she untied the knot which fixed the wrapper around her. As the cloth slid to the floor, Penda's shining eyes saw the beginning of the road where she would be at nobody's mercy, where she could speak and be heard, where she would find ways, in this land of the toubab, of being something other than somebody's wife or somebody's mother. And when she reached for him, it was he who was singed by her touch. And it was he who prayed that God would give strength to his sixty-year old heart in the face of this explosion of youthful passion. They came together from two different points of the mind's planet but nevertheless, for that moment, they came together and they were together.

After the long night was over and the dawn nosed through the net curtains, both Penda and Doudou awoke to a silent contemplation of what had gone before. To Penda, those hours in the dark had been the herald to the first day of a new life. But for Doudou, although he had married Penda months ago, it was and would always be his wedding night.

"One man's life is like a teardrop in the sea of creation," Doudou said to himself, thinking also how easy it had become, since his marriage, to retrieve these old sayings that had previously been locked away, beyond his reach. One man's life... the thought held in Doudou's mind for a long while but eventually a persistent sound intruded.

The noise of drumming was loud even though Doudou was separated from it by a winding staircase and a couple of closed doors. He looked down through the window at the front garden which was full of people come to welcome a new child to the world. There were a few white faces huddled in corners but for the most part, this garden in Barkingside was under siege by an invading army from Africa. The "soldiers" were, in the main, female and they dazzled the pale beauty of the English springtime with their brilliant boubous which billowed in the light breeze. The husbands of this gorgeous infantry shied away from the limelight – christenings always seemed to them to be women's business – tending rather to congregate around the doorway and in the hail. There they found security in being together, smoking, drinking the profane substances of the toubab, talking men's talk, trying not to see what the drumming was doing to their wives. But in the end, they couldn't keep their eyes off the dancers. The sounds of the two deep-throated toumba drums and the soprano wail of the tama sought out the spirits of the women and unleashed them on the suburban English air, transforming it and them. In Josephine's large garden, the women, representing all Gambian families in a 100 mile radius, danced the dances of their ancestors, the ones that the British colonisers had tried to ban so many years ago on the grounds of their lewd and corrupting nature. But, for the women, everything – housework, husbands, children, being an immigrant on the cold soil of England – all of this was swallowed up in the liberation of the dance.

Doudou watched them and felt the throb of the rhythms coming from the rooms below. Slowly he turned his back on this scene and faced another, quite different, wholly detached from the swirl of noise, movement and colour. It appeared as an ancient tableau, dimly-lit, silent. The room had become a universe in which all life drew its breath from two scarcely-moving figures seated at its centre. A young mother nursed her baby. She bent her head low, feasting her eyes on the child drawing sustenance from her body. The child's eyes were sealed in sleep as his mouth sucked in rhythmic ecstasy. His body was relaxed as his mother's breast and arms provided a warm cradle in which to rest. Baby and mother were two separate entities, but the snip of a cord seemed only to confirm their essential oneness.

Doudou looked away, a powerful sense of exclusion twisting his insides. Yet part of him was glad as he reviewed the landscape of his childhood memory and found it populated with innumerable scenes like this one. He went over and touched the baby's head. His hand shot back as though it had been burned. The baby's mother chuckled.

"You should know better than to touch the soft spot."

Doudou looked down at the pulsating stretch of skin at

the crown of the child's head, exposed and vulnerable as the twin plates of bone made their slow journey towards one another.

Doudou shuddered a little as his fingers still felt the timid assault of the throbbing membrane. With a sigh, he moved back to the window.

This is the way I am now, Doudou thought. The slightest thing disturbs me. Ever since... He forced his eyes to focus on the happenings in the garden and in the street. First of all, Josephine's neighbours had abandoned their posts behind net curtains and were at their open doors, gaping, not sure whether to join in the revelry or call the police. A circle of women had formed and at its centre was the unmistakable figure of Mame Koumba Seck, unofficial cultural attaché of this African militia, undisputed organiser of all events Gambian in Southern England. Mame was not a small woman, neither was she young but as the youth with the talking drum approached her, her body proclaimed the joy of being female, with feet to pound, hips to roll and yards of diaphanous cloth to send shimmering into the sunlight.

"*Djigeni!*" sighed Doudou. "Women! You just don't know what to do with them."

Mame Koumba Seck's boubou appeared to be shot through with silver as she whipped it around her, accentuating the movements of a remarkably supple pelvis as she was urged on by the drummer's fingers and the clapping hands of the women around her.

"*Djigeni!*" he repeated, turning his weary eyes from the festivities. What was a man to do with them? He doubted whether even the old man in the taxi would have been able to remain calm in the face of what he, Doudou, had had to live through. He didn't even remember what it was he had been looking for when his guileless fingers had ventured into Penda's drawer and seen the small packet lying there.

But he did remember how clumsy his fingers had been as he had turned the packet over and seen the line of innocent-looking pills which went round the perimeter of the packet. He'd turned it over again and seen the words, Sun, Mon, Tues going in an orderly row underneath each pill. This silver packet of death had reposed under Penda's "English For Beginners" workbook.

Doudou tried to force back the memory but, like a freak wave, it overwhelmed him. He remembered how his hand had trembled as he ran shouting, waving the packet under Penda's nose as she first denied knowledge of it, then admitted it, then dropped sobbing to her knees, pleading with him to let her use them. How he'd raised his hand to strike her but, seeing her cowed and whimpering on the floor, how his arm had dropped to his side like a stone. And how his rage had returned the next day with the visit of the milk-faced, lank-haired agent of Satan – Sue, Penda's English teacher – who had raised her voice at him in his own home and accused him of being cruel and of wanting to make his wife a baby-machine. And how silent the flat was after Sue and Penda, carrying her book, her pills and little else, had slammed their way out into the wintry street. And how he'd wanted to weep for his wife and his son and his dreams, all now dead with the slamming of that door.

"Dad! Dad!"

Doudou wrenched free of his thoughts and saw that Naba was standing right next to him, her baby lying forgotten in her arms.

"You mustn't get on so. You look like you've seen a ghost. Dad, you've got to put it all behind you."

Both Doudou's face and voice were grim as he said, "I don't know what you're talking about."

"Yes, you do," she said quietly. "Penda."

It took a particular effort for her to push out the last two syllables as they had been unilaterally banned from use in the presence of Doudou three months ago, when the news of Penda's departure first broke. The ban had been waived only once, a few weeks later when an article appeared in the Ilford Recorder. "Gambian Woman Victim of Abuse", ran the headline. The article centred around an interview with a certain Sue Majors who condemned "patriarchal practices" in Ilford's West African community where young women and girls were being denied their fundamental human rights by being forced into heavy domestic labour and child-bearing. She outlined the case of Mrs. Penda Camara who, fearing for her life, had had to flee from her husband's home and go into hiding, all because she wanted to continue her education. Sue Majors had gone on to say that efforts were being made with the Home Office to regularise Penda Camara's situation and she was personally committed to having Penda's name put on the Priority Council Housing list as well as making application for an educational grant. The article had ended with a few words from Penda. "I come to this country for a new life."

Doudou had said nothing as his daughters and some of his countrymen had railed at the villainy of Penda, of her ingratitude, her treachery. From Josephine to the oldest Gambian, the consensus was absolute; she had dishonoured her country; she had dishonoured her sex. She was, in fact, just a white woman wearing black skin. And the old men had muttered darkly about *nit kou nioul* – black men – having to stand up to this worldwide conspiracy. Ideas for her censure – each one more extreme than the last – were tossed about like so many colourful balloons. But in the end it had all fizzled out, leaving Doudou in the darkness. He found things to do, arranging and rearranging the furniture to the way it was before Penda had first set foot in it as a new bride. But he just couldn't remember how things had been then. On his way to bed, he'd seen a copy of the article lying on the floor. Despite himself, he'd picked it up. The words swam about indolently as his eyes locked onto the two faces in the photograph. He spent a long time on Sue Majors, the wife-stealer, the one on whom he placed the entire blame for filling Penda's head up with toubab nonsense, making her forget who she was and what role she had to play in this world. He could see the gleam of the zealot in her eyes. He had seen that same radiance in the faces of the Mouride pilgrims on their way to Touba. He could see the sharp angle of her shoulders set in a line of purpose and determination. Everything about her declared that Sue Majors had found a cause.

Doudou found the other face in the picture much harder to read. Positioned next to the white woman with the thin well-defined mouth and straight hair, Penda seemed almost veiled, the darkness of the printer's ink smudging her features. Doudou searched for the beauty that had lit up these very rooms but found none. But there was something in the way that she looked at Sue Majors that told Doudou that there was no worship, that complete trust was an item which would be withheld, even from whomever wished to participate in her rescue. And there was the difference in the tilt of Penda's chin – a sense of something lost but also something found. When Doudou had at last put down the paper, he knew beyond all doubt that reconciliation would not ever be possible, that his wife was striking out on her own down a new road.

A hand clasped Doudou's wrist and gave it a shake. Doudou looked down at Naba's mute face and saw his own misery reflected in it. He felt a stab of guilt.

"Naba," he said with false cheeriness, "go downstairs. There's people waiting to see you. Your guests, your children. Your husband! Look. Little Doudou is sleeping sound, sound. I go watch him for you."

Naba hesitated then laid the baby in his cot and, squeezing her father's arm again, left. Doudou turned his back on the child and started pacing the room. The sounds from downstairs had altered. The drumming had ceased. There was the clash of large pots being uncovered and the expectant buzz of those whose stomachs were soon to be filled. Rich aromas stole through the crack beneath the door. Doudou gave a passing thought to the food. No, he thought, I won't bother. Nothing has any taste these days.

Suddenly, the baby started to cry. Doudou was startled. He had not expected this. Within seconds, that same baby who had slept so placidly in his mother's arms, was exercising his lungs in a very serious fashion. Doudou picked him up and held him at arm's length as the angry infant's noise, somewhere between mewing and neighing, continued unabated.

The door opened and in strode Mame Koumba Seck

"*Hai!*" she said, visibly puffing up. "Doudou Camara, what do you think you're doing?"

In two or three robust steps, she had crossed the room and snatched the child from his grandfather. Doudou retreated to the window. In a whirl of powder, baby wipes and zinc ointment, Mame Koumba changed the baby's nappy. A look of astonishment crossed the baby's face, his mouth closed and the thickly fringed eyelids fluttered shut.

"Doudou Camara," she said briskly, "the food is ready. Go down and eat and leave this child to someone who knows what they're doing."

"I will not be eating." Doudou's voice was flat.

"*Hai!*" Maine Koumba exclaimed. "People labour for days to prepare satisfying dishes to honour Doudou Camara's son."

"Grandson, not son."

"It's the same thing! The fruit of your loins has given him life. It is the same. But as I was saying, you now wish to cause offence to those who laboured..."

"Mame Koumba! Enough!" The baby lying in Mame Koumba's arms jerked his arms up at the harsh, heavy sound then with a sigh, resumed his sleep. Doudou had not noticed and continued the barrage. "I will not go down there and be the sport of all those people!"

"The people downstairs have come for this child. Your namesake, remember? Like you, he bears the name of the Prophet – Mamadou. I will not call his English names. They do damage to the ears. But your daughter Jeynaba gave him your name. That's why people are here."

"They have come in such numbers because of... of... that woman I brought here to help out her family in the Gambia." Anger flared from every pore of Doudou's body. "They have come to pity or to mock. Even you should have the wit to see that!" Mame Koumba placed the baby in its cot and, hands on ample hips, looked Doudou square in the face.

"The insolence of men is matched only by their stupidity!"

Doudou's eyes widened. His mouth opened in retort as he wrestled with the problem of which ritual insult of women to use. No sound issued forth and they stood in an aggressive silence for a full minute. In the end, it was Mame who relented.

"The girl you married is not like you and me, Doudou. She was born in a different time – although I know some very old women in my village who would have been like Penda if they'd had the chance." She sighed and looked a little wistful. "But the thing is, you have to understand that there is new kind of African woman these days."

"I prefer the old kind," Doudou murmured. All of his anger had drained away and he stood with his shoulders hunched over.

"Do my ears deceive me? Am I hearing Doudou Camara say these words?" and Mame Koumba exploded into peals of laughter, making her gold bracelets sing in accompaniment.

"What have I said? Why are you laughing?"

"Because you never knew the old kind! Always too busy chasing the toubab!" Mame Koumba's sides shook and her eyes watered as the ghastly humour of Doudou's words hit home.

"You are a hard woman," Doudou said at last, when the laughter had subsided and Mame Koumba stood wiping her eyes.

"I'm not hard. Maybe the truth is." Mame Koumba bent over and tied the baby to her back. At the door, she turned. "But another truth is that you have four children and little Doudou here makes your twelfth grandchild. They're not what you would have had if you'd stayed in the Gambia. But they're what you have. And there's Africa in them all." Mame Koumba's face was very still, the baby on her back was very still and there was a quiet about her solid, vigorous body. "Be glad, Doudou Camara. Be glad."

She left him alone. From nowhere, the old riddle came to his mind. When does the lion fear the gazelle? When God forgets to... In a flash Doudou was at her heels as she approached the staircase.

"Mame Koumba Seck!"

"What is it, Doudou Camara?"

"Do you remember how to dance the Patchanga? Or are you too old?"

"*Hai!*" she exclaimed. "Let us just eat our fill first and then we will let the children decide which one of us is old!"

ENDANGERED SPECIES

ENDANGERED SPECIES

The taxi stopped at a break in the dark, dripping hedges that bordered the road. From the narrow gap emerged the featureless figure of a man wearing a crumpled hat. Julia got out of the car and felt the rain on her face.

"You must be the janitor."

"Yes, ma'am."

Julia turned her back on the man in the hat, instructed the taxi driver to get her suitcase, counted out thirty-five dollars and, without a word, dismissed him. She again addressed the man in the hat, never once looking at him.

"I'm Julia Griffin. Mr. Harrigan must've told you about me. And what do they call you?"

There was a slight pause.

"My name is Clarence Ellsworth Bean."

"Yes, but what am I to call you?" she said impatiently, as a raindrop found a space between her collar and her neck.

"You can call me Mr. Bean."

This corner of the February night was lit only by a few street lamps but Julia now saw the man quite clearly. His words had given him definition. She saw his brown, weather-beaten face, not lined but folded into a series of deep furrows, saw the hint of power under the shapeless raincoat. Age seemed to press down on his shoulders but his head remained unbowed beneath the ancient brimless hat. Something about him – was it the leathery brown skin? – reminded her of her father. She dismissed that thought instantly. At another point in her life, she might have been impressed. But this moment of flight from her desk in a building that nudged the sky, from the weariness of her mind, from the madness of her grief, to these islands lost in a heaving ocean, the "still-vex'd Bermoothes", the Isles of Devils, this moment had no space for the grandeur of another soul. She had come here to face her own demons and could not be bothered with the absurd dignity of some janitor.

"Well then, Mr. Bean," she said, "we'd better be on our way. Wouldn't want to hold you up. Life's too short to be used up with mindless activity such as doing the job one is paid to do." How easy it was to take an instantaneous dislike to someone, she reflected. He started up the outboard motor and assisted Julia into the precarious-looking boat. They set off across the water. Everything was black – the choppy waves, the moonless sky, the drizzling rain. If the wind could have had a colour, it would have been black too. Julia sat huddled in the boat but in less than four minutes the tense little journey was over. Mr. Bean secured the boat, picked up her suitcase and, at a brisk pace, headed towards a light flickering behind the swaying trees.

As she struggled to get out of the boat, Julia cursed Mr. Bean for leaving her. She raised one foot and aimed it at the stone steps of the landing. There was nothing to support her but water and air and they were both churning around in the darkness. She longed for the solid rock but all matter had been transformed into the lurching of the drunken boat. She managed to scramble ashore but the feeling of being suspended in an element both insubstantial and hostile, far from the solidity of earth - this feeling remained, even as she trudged up the path to Star Island House, the holiday home of Tom Harrigan and until recently – five months, two weeks and two days, to be precise – of Milly Harrigan. But now Milly was gone. And so was Julia's strong grip on the world.

Mr. Bean had lit up the house and when she walked into the living room Julia found him bent over, lighting a fire in the brick fireplace. The artificial fire-starter was already ablaze as were the carefully positioned balls of newspaper. Little tongues of flame were starting to run along the spines of several pieces of reddish brown wood. The fire's fragrance scented the air.

Julia stood in the middle of the room. Everything about her was aggressive – the lean muscles of her limbs, the short leather skirt, the high-heeled ankle boots, the flawless make-up, the tight black hair cropped so low that her scalp shimmered.

"What's that?" asked Julia.

"Cedar."

"No," she snapped. "I mean, what on earth do I need with a fire?"

"Bermuda's chilly this time of year. And this house is real damp. Mrs. H used to love..."

The fire roared in her ears. The heavy perfume of the wood threatened to suffocate her. Yet she held on.

"As you can see, I'm not your Mrs. H. I have just come from the snow and ice of New York City. On the plane they told us the temperature here was a balmy 67 degrees. In some parts of the world that's bikini weather!" She tossed her head and Mr. Bean could see hard bright stars flashing in the lobes of her ears. "I don't need your quaint but totally unnecessary fire. I do not need it!" These words shot from Julia's mouth as though from a Smith and Wesson. Mr. Bean watched her with steady eyes.

"I just want to be left alone." There was no gunfire any more, just a dull matter-of-factness. It made Mr. Bean move toward the door.

"Well... um... um... ma'am... with Mr. Harrigan and Mrs.

163

H, I come over Star Island twice a week. Wednesday evenings with the order from the supermarket and Saturday afternoon to do the yard and anything in the house. I'll do the same for you."

Julia stared vacantly at the fire, not seeming to take anything in.

Mr. Bean continued. "There's a second boat moored on the far side of the island. On Saturday, I'll come and teach you how to use it..."

"Don't bother. As long as you bring me a few groceries once a week, there's absolutely no reason for me to go to the mainland."

"Don't you want the newspapers? Mrs. H liked..."

"No!"

"So I suppose you don't want me to bring your mail from the post office either." Mr. Bean's voice had taken on a weary tone.

Julia raised her eyes and gave a hard little laugh. "Mr. Bean," she said, "not that it's any of your business, but no-one knows I'm here. Just Tom Harrigan. And now you. I intend to keep it that way." She turned on her heel and walked off, mumbling "Good Night!" over her shoulder.

Mr. Bean stood for a moment, shaking his head, then put up his collar and stepped out into the night. He immediately turned back and stood hesitating in the living room. At last he shouted out, "Ma'am? Ma'am! On Saturdays I always bring my grandson, Seth." The only response was the crackling of the fire and the swishing of branches dancing in the wind.

Shrugging, Mr. Bean hurried home, four minutes across the water, right across the road from the gap in the dripping hedges. When he closed his door behind him, he picked up a letter lying on the kitchen table. He'd received it over a week ago and now he reread it, especially the last few sentences. "She'll probably not be very nice to be near at the beginning. She's got quite a sharp tongue. She's used it against me enough times! But you have to understand. She's very upset. It's as though Milly's death is only just starting to sink in. I'm asking you to bear with her, Clarence. She's not as bad as she seems."

"Didn't get that right, did you, Mr. Harrigan!" Mr. Bean put down the letter. "She's as evil a female as these seventy-four years have seen..." Still grumbling, he switched on the outside light for Seth, went to bed and drifted off to sleep thinking of his beloved Mrs. H and the glory days on Star Island.

Under the covers of a huge four-poster bed with the night fretting around her, Julia too thought of Mrs. H. Except she hated when people called Milly that. She'd always had a problem with Milly's names. Milly sounded too much like Silly. Millicent smacked of some Victorian schoolmarm. But they paled in comparison to Mrs. H! How unbearably matronly, how insufferably middle-class, how invincibly mumsy! Yet Julia had to admit that these words did describe some of what Milly had been. What a contrast to those she would use to describe herself – sharp, bright, tough, chic – single sounds that fell on the ears like jabs from a prizefighter's glove. Julia had never believed in the theory that opposites attract – she had a string of broken relationships that could attest to that. But an unlikely friendship had ambushed Julia and Milly in their youth. And even now, twenty-six years later with Milly dead and gone, she was still held captive by it.

Julia jumped out of bed and started roaming through the house. Everywhere there was the pervasive smell of burning wood and outside, the wind was increasingly boisterous. Although she shared this star-shaped coral islet with no other living soul, although she was alone with the night voices pressing in on her, she was not afraid. She concentrated on the rooms. They were all commodious and spare, but what little furniture there was was of good quality. The tips of her fingers slid smoothly over chairbacks and tabletops. Even in the dark, she knew that they had been polished for her arrival. That awful Mr. Bean. She moved from room to room, her hands alive to the texture of the surfaces. Occasionally, she switched on a light for a brief spell but on the whole seemed happy to conduct her keen inspection of the premises in the dark. At last, she allowed herself the luxury of being still.

Just like their house in Hastings, she thought. The exact same Tom-and-Milly feel about it! She started to laugh a little, feeling that same odd mixture of comfort and unease that characterised many of her responses to Milly. The laughter continued, ringing out around the empty house.

"But where is it?" she said out loud. "Where's the dreaded Family Room? It's got to be around here someplace."

It was. The next door along the hall had a large brass key in the lock. She opened it and stepped into the only cluttered space in the house. Milly had worked on the premise that if there was one room that was officially a mess, there was a small chance that the rest of the house could be kept in order. Mr. Bean had not been there. Dust was everywhere – on the bicycles, dolls houses, board games, card tables, on the huge television and its attendant pile of cassettes bearing the name Nintendo. Innumerable childish masterpieces adorned the walls. Covering the entire surface of the door was an almost life-sized poster of Tom, Milly and the six little Harrigans wearing Disney hats and grinning hugely. As usual, Julia saw the little Harrigans as an undifferentiated mass despite the fact that one stood six feet tall, another sprouted a head full of embryonic blonde dreadlocks, one squinted behind thick glasses, another – the only one not sporting the Disney ears – surveyed the world with the aggressive ennui of the thirteen year old, still another flashed a smile full of steel wires, while the last one

– the youngest – pointed to her oversized T shirt which proclaimed that she was "10 Today". Milly's brood. Julia knew them well, collectively and individually, and would even admit to liking them but at this moment, on this God-forsaken, wind-blasted island, she could only see them as the result of Milly's wilful act of madness. Six children in eight years! No wonder one of those overworked breasts had produced a lump that would not stop growing.

So senseless! Julia turned away and stared straight ahead in this room which gave silent testimony to the noisy harmony of this family. The demanding childish voices boomed in her ears, obliterating the sounds of the night. They are not to blame, she said several times. No one is. Reluctantly, she faced the poster again. She studied the two adult faces, her eyes narrowing with the effort. On closer scrutiny, Tom's smile had something of a grimace about it, as though the magic of Disney's kingdom was wearing thin. There was a rigidity about the whole face – the fixed smile, the staring eyes, the taut lines around the mouth – that revealed a person locked into the knowledge that the smiling woman next to him was not going to get well. Beneath the ridiculous Mickey Mouse ears, pain was stamped all over him. Julia sighed. It had taken her a quarter of a century to forgive Tom. First of all for his colour, his freckled, reddish-white Boston Irish skin. Then for being the kind of man she claimed to despise but in reality had been looking for all her life, the "boring" kind – dependable, loving, kind – the type that would make her feel safe and sane. Lastly she forgave Tom Harrigan for being Milly's dearest and closest friend. This had been the hardest of all, although Julia had constantly denied the jealousy she'd felt. After all, he was Milly's husband! But Milly's death had levelled all that out. Like a bloody great bulldozer.

Her eyes finally came to rest on Milly. She was at the centre of the picture, her natural place. The picture had been taken about a year ago, the Disney trip being followed by a week on Star Island. Milly had felt her illness closing in on her, had wanted to make farewell journeys. Yet there was nothing on that lovely face except delight, as though a ride on the "Space Mountain" roller coaster with a pack of adolescents was the high point of her life.

She always had that capacity for joy, thought Julia, finding a chair and setting it right in front of the poster. Yes always...

She remembered the first time she'd met Milly, twenty-six years before, when they were both freshmen at Wellesley College. It was September 1968. Julia had stood in the middle of her room feeling like a piece of flotsam washed up on a glittering beach, light years away from the ungenteel end of Long Island and even further away from the mean streets of Bedford Stuyvesant which, although she and her family had left them five years before, remained her spiritual home. She'd felt as though she had landed in an alien place, where everything, from its food to its vowels, had a strange, bloodless feel to it. A black dot in a white, white world, that's what she was. But even at eighteen, Julia had not been one to allow herself to be overwhelmed by anything, least of all by feelings of vulnerability. She'd closed her eyes and forced her mind to have thoughts that would make her strong, would let her survive this. The images came: slain heroes lying in pools of their own blood; Watts in flames; beautiful brothers wearing black glasses and black berets and black souls, toting rifles with stunning ease, flaunting the virility of their bodies and the fearlessness of their minds. Julia had felt her dark brown skin burning bright and her hair bloom around her head like a fierce black halo. In the middle of her dormitory room, she'd remembered who she was. Then there'd been a knock at the door. Julia had opened it and there had stood Milly. It had been hate at first sight.

"Excuse me. But may I use your powder room?" Many years later, Milly had told Julia that all she could remember of this encounter was Julia's open mouth and her incredulous, staring eyes.

"My what?" Julia's eyes had travelled slowly down this apparition, taking in the yellowish-brown skin, the sleek hair curling up on the shoulders, the pale blue sweater set – this was the nearest Julia had ever been to cashmere – the string of fat pearls, the wool skirt just brushing the knees, the blue knee-socks and the crocodile shoes.

"Your powder room! Mine's 'hors de service'. There's a man in there fixing it now, I'm just down the hall." These lines had been delivered in a breathless rush as the girl followed the direction of Julia's pointed finger. When she'd reached the bathroom door, she'd turned and said, "I'm Milly. Millicent, really, but that's too old-fashioned, don't you think?"

Julia had been left staring at the closed bathroom door, re-evaluating her decision to come to Wellesley. Was this how Wellesley's espoused aim of promoting minority women translated into action? Would all the other black women be like this sun-burned Alice-in-Wonderland? She had not yet unpacked – maybe she should leave right now.

Milly had re-emerged, beaming a mega-watt smile at Julia.

"Why, I don't even know your name."

"No, you don't, do you?" There had been a lengthy pause. Julia had finally relented. "It's Julia."

"Well, Julia, I've got to run. Mom and Dad are helping me unpack." She'd stopped just outside the doorway. "You know, I've got this funny feeling we're going to be great friends."

"A feeling I don't happen to share," Julia had said without a moment's hesitation. She'd watched as Milly's bright, open face had crumpled inward, more in amazement than hurt. Sharp words were clearly not part of her daily diet. But Julia had not finished. "But you can use my john – I mean my powder room – any time." Julia had walked off, her narrow hips moving in an exaggerated street swagger.

As she sat there twenty-six years later looking at Milly's picture, the memory of this scene unfolded in Julia's mind with an almost unbearable poignancy. Not everyone, thought Julia, could tell the difference between being bitchy for the hell of it and being bitchy because you're scared. But Milly had known, even way back then because she'd followed Julia back into her room and she'd said in an unhurried voice, "Yes, I know we're going to be friends. Why, you could even say I'm convinced of it."

Julia had looked at her in utter surprise and behind those misty brown eyes, she'd thought she'd seen something gleaming, something tough and enduring, so incongruous in the milk-fed blandness of the rest of her face. Even then, it had been there.

From this inauspicious beginning, a strange friendship had been born, although it looked more like war. Julia was the aggressor, determined to liberate, by force if necessary, Milly's tender bourgeois heart. During that first year, Julia had placed a mirror in front of her friend and made her face the my-daddy-is-a-dentist syndrome, the I-am-a-black-American-princess syndrome, the with-my-light-skin-and-long-hair-I'm-prettier-than-all-you-dark-skinned-nappy-headed-bitches syndrome. Most of that year, Milly had spent either shedding apologetic tears or reading thick tomes by the likes of Fanon or Du Bois. By the end of the summer semester, Julia had felt that she had achieved some measure of success. Milly had cut her hair and was watching with awe as a dense reddish-brown mass sprang from her head. Her own virgin hair had not seen the light of day since Milly's first year at elementary school.

But Julia's victories were only partial. When Milly had

sold her pearls and given the proceeds to a local day-care centre, Julia had berated this as the knee-jerk instinct of liberal philanthropy rather than the act of a true revolutionary. Milly had not cried but had looked at Julia for longer than a moment and said, "Because that's what you are, right?" Julia was stung by this implied rebuke and had walked away from Milly for a full week. When a short time later, Milly had packed up several boxes of cashmeres and silks and taken them to the Salvation Army, Julia had said nothing but felt that this was indeed a significant step. At least now Milly would look as though she belonged to the "Young, Gifted and Black" generation. But Julia's pleasure was short-lived when she discovered, to her horror, that, in place of the Doris Day look, Milly had opted for a form of dress that consisted of yards of variegated cloth which fell a few inches shy of her ankles. She now looked like she needed the services of the Salvation Army. Julia, wearing the obligatory African robes or skintight jeans, had been appalled. But Milly had smiled sweetly and continued to swathe her body in this singular mode of attire from which she did not deviate for the rest of her life. But Julia's quest for Milly's soul was so ardent that she did something which, at that time, was virtually unthinkable. She ceased judging her friend on appearances. It was the first great lesson of her friendship with Milly and one which, over the next twenty-six years, she had to keep learning.

The second lesson was trust. Julia had no reason to trust Milly. Their pre-college lives were as different as two lives could be. Milly's parents belonged to the upper echelons of the black middle class, the fair-skinned Washington D.C. middle class at that. College education, the top black colleges, of course, could be found in the family for the past fifty years. Milly's father had his practice and his home in a salubrious nook of Virginia, but once a month he did his civic duty and drove to Washington to give a free dental clinic to poor black people. That was the group Julia belonged to, America's urban, disenfranchised, disfigured, disturbed and disturbing black underbelly. It was only by dint of the efforts of Julia's steel-clad mother that the family had been heaved out of the morass into the comparative safety of Long Island. Not everyone in the family had survived the journey to higher ground. Teddy, Julia's beloved brother and confidante – the only real point of light in her early life – had been sucked back down into the underworld. At the age of twenty-two, just as Julia was completing her second year at Wellesley, Teddy had died of a heroin overdose. Julia had turned to Milly, her strangely dressed, politically incorrect friend. It was the first of many times when Milly would be the rock and Julia the rain-drenched bird seeking shelter from the storm.

All so long ago. From the time of Teddy's death till now, the two lives – Milly's and Julia's – had remained discrete yet intertwined with Julia flying solo, first as an academic and then switching to a brilliant career in publishing, pushing for black, radical and feminist literature. Milly had gone the way of the nurturer, baking her own bread, growing her own vegetables, giving succour to all-comers. She gave Julia home-cooked food and somewhere to restore her body and her soul. Julia gave her reading lists and temporary access to the world of abstract ideas and hard cash. All those years of talking and tears, of that mutual exchange, had been the bedrock of Julia's life, only Julia had not realised it until now.

Julia got up from in front of the Disneyworld poster. She felt cold and the muscles at the back of her legs ached. That Mr. Whatever had been right. It was much colder than she'd expected. She pulled on a robe she'd found in a closet, took a few steps forward and then retraced them. She stopped suddenly. She felt something strange happening to her. Her hands fluttered around her like the wings of a wounded

172

bird. The wind outside wailed and the waves slapped against the rocks of the island. She closed the door of the Family Room then locked it, no longer able to bear the burden of all that memory. With a sudden certainty of purpose, she made for the front door and threw it open, letting in the night. She leaned back and flung the key into the dark, in the direction of the thickest grove of casuarina. Just as she threw it, the moon broke from behind a bank of clouds and for a fragment of a second, Julia saw the key blazing across the sky. Then the darkness consumed it.

Back inside, Julia was drawn towards the fire, her outstretched hands seeming to want to snatch its heat. Her whole life needed rekindling to drive out the cold that had been settling in her breast ever since she'd heard Milly say, "It's malignant." Now, after two and a half years of struggle, hope and despair, of the final goodbye, of the funeral arranged and lived through, of the motherless children consoled, of the grieving husband propped up and relaunched into life – only now did Julia see the extent to which the cold had insinuated itself into her bones. She pressed herself against the fire's grate, coming within a whisper of singeing the down on her arms, yet the crackling flames had no power against the cold which had sent such deep and searching roots into Julia's body. She started to shiver. Rows of bumps flashed across her skin. The muscles that only a few minutes before had ached in a vague and listless way were now the site of stabbing pains, as though a freezing blade were continually slicing into her flesh. Julia sank to the floor in terror, her arms crossed around her. Was it pain like this that Milly had felt at the end, she wondered, as her arms and her back fell beneath the assault. Although she attempted to gather herself into a ball, her body would no longer move at her command. The trembling doubled in intensity. She tried to cry out but there was only silence. Somewhere deep inside her, deeper than the roots of the strange bitter tree, rose a feeble voice of resistance which was as ancient in her as her life's breath. She would not be prevented from moving, from speaking, not by anyone or anything.

Gritting her teeth, she concentrated on straightening her left leg, then her right. Movement by cruel movement, she staggered towards her bedroom. As she approached the Family Room, the pains returned, weakening her knees and sending her crashing against the locked door. The icicles around her throat shattered. "Why do they always leave me?" she screamed in a voice that ripped through all other sounds of the night. It rang out over the sound of the fire, the wailing of the wind, the mocking applause of the waves. It howled across the water onto the mainland, finally merging with the grumbling voice of the open ocean.

Julia continued her journey and with a supreme effort, made it to the four-poster bed where she collapsed, saturating the sheets with her sweat.

As promised, Mr. Bean returned to the island on Saturday with his grandson Seth. Seen from behind, the two men showed all the signs of a shared blood. Both scraped six feet, both had shoulders set at almost perfect right angles to narrow necks, both walked like gunslingers. But seen head on, they were very different. Although not fat, Mr. Bean's body was solid and just a little menacing as though if you were in collision with it, you would know. This air of controlled aggression was at complete odds with Mr. Bean's face, which, though not quite beatific, was well on its way to being so. There was a calm lodged beneath the furrows of his brow and his eyes, hooded and dark, reflected a hard-won wisdom. Seth, on the other hand, was like a shiny new penny. His complexion was golden with only a trace of darkness above his upper lip. His bones were long and thin and the only danger you ran here was being inadvertently impaled on one of those sharp elbows. He was a gangly youth of twenty, new, bright, golden, like the dawning day. And yet there was something about him that ruffled his grandfather's brow, that made Mr. Bean look at Seth without his usual serenity. Maybe it was the shadow which often settled over Seth's eyes. Maybe it was his reluctance to smile.

"We got to go carefully with this one," Mr. Bean said. "She's a disaster waiting to happen." He slowed his pace almost to a halt. "Hard to believe that that woman was Mrs. H's best friend. But Mr. Harrigan swears down she was."

Seth said nothing, dragging his sneakered toes through the gravel.

"Don't let her get you going," Mr. Bean continued. "There's nothing she likes better than a fight. But I've known people like her before. Thirty-odd years in the hotels, you can handle anything. People have a gripe about something and they want to take it out on you. But I won't let her make me lose my temper... I learned how to control it a long time ago working Maintenance at Hamilton Princess. And I'm not about to start losing it now, no matter how much I'd love to give that woman a good cussing... I owe that much to Mrs. H."

"Whatever you say, Pa."

Mr. Bean started walking again, giving Seth an exasperated look.

"But you couldn't care less one way or the other, could you, son?"

Seth stopped, but avoided his grandfather's eyes.

"I don't understand why you get so hyped about these people. What they do is not our business. You do a job for them, they pay you. That's it." He shrugged. "To me, they're just rich white folks."

"But they're not!" Mr. Bean protested. "Why do you

always say that? You know very well what colour Mrs. H was. O.K. Mr. Harrigan's white but he's a decent kinda..."

"The dude with the money's white and that's all that counts," retorted Seth.

Mr. Bean stopped and looked out over the tops of the trees. "Let's just drop it," he said flatly. "You'll think what you like anyway."

He took out his keys and opened the door, calling as he went. There was no answer. He and Seth stood in the middle of the living room looking around. There was no sign of life. Piles of white ash were the sole reminders of the fire of two days before. Otherwise everything was exactly as it had been then. Even the suitcase stood untouched in the doorway. Still calling out Julia's name, Mr. Bean went into the kitchen. The food he had left in the fridge had not been disturbed, neither was there a cup or plate on the table or in the sink. The furrows in Mr. Bean's brow deepened.

"Seth," he said, "Have a look around outside. Maybe she's gone for a walk." Mr. Bean watched him go and found his thoughts shifting from the missing Julia to his grandson. What was it about the boy that bothered him most? Was it that aimlessness that showed itself so clearly in his shambling walk, the same aimlessness that had caused him to drop out of college the year before? Or was it the shadow which often darkened his eyes, making him look so angry?

Mr. Bean wondered why he should be entrusted with Seth in what should have been a peaceful and well-earned retirement. But life had other plans for him. A few years ago, a stroke had taken Miriam, his bride of forty-eight years, robbing him of the prospect of sharing with her that Caribbean cruise, maybe a few great-grands, and certainly many more evenings spent sitting out on the porch. Instead, last year, his poor troubled daughter Rachel handed Seth over to him as she fled to the ragged anonymity of the American metropolis. Her cry was desperate. "Save him, Dad! I know

I can't." So he was trying to save Seth, in the only way he knew how, with a combination of work, good food, regular habits and – this was the hard one – a measure of trust. But Mr. Bean was not sure about what kind of job he was doing. He thought that Seth loved him. But was that enough?

Mr. Bean heard a noise and, snapping out of the downward drift of his thoughts, he hurried towards the main bedroom. The sound was an odd one, somewhere between a shout and a moan. He knocked. The sound continued. He knocked again. It became louder. He tried the doorknob, found it unlocked and poked his head around the door. The heavy, closed draperies made the room stuffy and almost completely dark but in a few moments, Mr. Bean's eyes grew accustomed to the gloom. The covers of the bed heaved and twisted. There seemed to be a wrestling match going on beneath them, to the accompaniment of the shouting, moaning lament.

Indecision was not an emotion with which Mr. Bean was familiar but it came to him now, raising one of his feet in flight away from this scene and propelling his other towards it. Outside, some low grey thunderclouds grumbled as they passed. He went over to the clamorous bed and stopped at a shape that looked like a head.

"Miss Griffin! Miss Griffin!" His voice was powerful and created a space between the noise inside and the noise outside. The writhing creature beneath the covers seemed to hear him.

"Miss Griffin! It's me. Mr. Bean! Are you all right?"

A dark brown hand emerged and gripped the pale bedspread. With tentative little jerks, the cover was pulled down and Julia's head was revealed. In the obscurity, it looked as though a fine veil covered Julia's face but it was just an impression caused by the fact that Julia had not opened her eyes. There was something about that secret, silent, veiled face. Not knowing what else to do, Mr. Bean busied himself.

177

"What we need is some fresh air," he said and hurried over to the window. Mr. Bean fumbled with the drawstrings of the curtains, with the window sashes, with the heavy wooden shutters. Behind him, he heard movement and wondered whether she had resumed her fight with whatever was under the sheets. He turned around.

Julia was standing, naked, looking at him.

Mr. Bean stumbled backwards while his eyes wildly searched for the nearest exit. He thought of calling out for Seth but knew that would make matters worse.

Julia took a few steps towards him. The light from the newly opened window made it impossible for him not to see her in the most minute detail. Despite his fear, despite the voice in his head repeating, "Get thee behind me, Satan!", the clear daylight from God's sky made him see her. There was no escape. It was a youthful body. Nowhere had the skin been pulled and stretched and left with long tracks looking like tyre marks on a rutted road. Nowhere on this landscape was there the spongy, pitted evidence of fatty tissue, unchallenged and triumphant. Everywhere this body was lean – very lean – smooth and beautiful. Mr. Bean hung his head, feeling the shameful stirring in his genitals. His mind flew to Miriam and her familiar flesh that the years had softened and folded and spread. He remembered the temptations he had faced during their long life together when he had been beckoned away from that flesh. He remembered – as though he needed to be reminded – that he had never strayed. He had been a faithful husband. It was one of the achievements of his life of which he was most proud.

Julia started moaning again, this time very quietly. She stood as still as a statue, with only her bottom lip quivering a little. Mr. Bean looked into her face and felt the flicker of desire he had known only moments before, splutter and die stone dead. Here was a face ravaged by innumerable wars which, in the cruel daylight, defeated the classic design of the bones beneath it. It was a gaunt, weary face, with two deeply-cut lines running from her nostrils past the corners of her mouth. Her eyes, now wide open, resided in two dark caverns; they seemed quite dead. The fluttering light from the window made her alternately look like a bruised old woman or an abandoned child. Mr. Bean gazed at the un-moving, unseeing face with a combination of fascination, revulsion and fear. But the longer he looked, the more these were overridden by a new emotion, one that he never would have dreamed he could feel for that foul-mouthed hussy he had met a few days before. Pity. The same pity he would have felt for an injured animal lying in the road, he told himself.

He looked around the room and saw a robe lying on the floor. Very slowly, very gently, he moved towards it. Julia's empty eyes followed him. She continued to produce the terrifying moaning sound. Mr. Bean picked up the robe and draped it over Julia's shoulders. She jumped as though from an electric shock and began to shiver. With clumsy fingers, Mr. Bean put the robe onto Julia and tied the belt. She did not help him, neither did she resist. It was like dressing a doll except that Julia was actually drawing breath, was still emitting the plaintive moan and, as Mr. Bean discovered to his dismay, was giving off a heavy and offensive odour.

Mr. Bean sat her on the edge of the bed and went to find Seth who was out in the yard fiddling with a walkman. Mr. Bean approached him almost at a run.

"Take the keys! Go back home and get my address book. Bring it back and make haste!"

Seth looked bewildered but immediately set off towards the dock, shouting, "What's going on?" over his shoulder.

"The woman's sick. Real sick."

Mr. Bean found Julia where he had left her, except that she was lying on her side, as though she had just keeled over. He bent close to make sure she was breathing. She was, though the only movement to be seen was a slight tremor that rippled up and down her body. Satisfied that she was not dead, Mr. Bean pulled her more fully onto the bed and arranged the covers over her. He rushed to the kitchen, sweating and swearing and flinging open cupboard doors in search of something to feed to Julia.

"Where the ass is that boy?" he said opening a tin of soup. "Sorry, Miriam," he muttered as a reflex, "but this thing can't happen. Not here, not in Mrs. H's house!" The can opener was not doing a neat job and Mr. Bean's finger caught on a jagged edge. He dropped the tin and put his finger to his mouth in time to see thick red soup splatter onto the floor.

"Shit!" he said. "Sorry Miriam." Mr. Bean stopped for a moment in the midst of his turmoil and noted that conversation with his wife had survived her death. Then, looking in the direction of the bedroom, he shouted, "What the hell's wrong with her anyway? She's got to be on something!" Mr. Bean sat down, feeling suddenly old. He sucked the blood from his finger and somehow that calmed him. He cleaned up the mess, put the rest of the soup on the stove and just as it had come to the boil, heard Seth's step at the doorway.

"What took you so long?"

Seth knew that was not really a question to be answered so he remained silent, as his grandfather took the book from him and dialled a long-distance number.

"Mr. Harrigan? Yes this is Clarence Bean. Yes, fine... But we're in trouble here. Your friend, Miss Griffin... Well I don't know what's wrong with her. But she's sick... I don't know what to do."

While Mr. Bean was explaining to Tom Harrigan what was happening with Julia, Seth peeped in at her, still profoundly asleep. So she is black, thought Seth in mild surprise. I wonder how much screwing she had to do to get to a place like this...

"Seth!" The boy turned around quickly, wondering yet

again if his grandfather's penetrating eyes could read his thoughts.

"Help me out here," Mr. Bean said. "Prop her up and don't let her fall over. I'll be back in a minute with the soup."

Seth had to struggle with Julia's passive weight but by the time Mr. Bean returned, Seth had her sitting with her back against the headboard. Mr. Bean's hand shook as he guided the spoon to her mouth. Her eyes were open but her mouth remained firmly shut.

"Just see if you can open her mouth, Seth," said Mr. Bean, very aware of his own lack of skill as a nurse. For his part, Seth felt no awkwardness and in one or two movements, had secured a crack into which the warm red soup could pass. For an awful moment, Julia held it in her mouth and refused to swallow. Seth tapped her on the cheek and she swallowed. Mr. Bean smiled and gave her another spoonful.

"What did the bossman say?" asked Seth.

"He said he would phone around a couple of doctor friends of his, then call me back. But in the meantime, we should try to see if she'd eat something." Mr. Bean was starting to get into a rhythm with the spoon. It reminded him of when his children were babies, on the rare occasions that Miriam had allowed him to feed them. He'd enjoyed it but hadn't been able to show it to Miriam who had very clear ideas about what was "woman's work". "He didn't think it was anything to do with drugs," he added. "According to Mr. Harrigan, she's been against that all her life."

"I've heard that before..."

"What?"

"Nothing." Seth was sitting next to Julia, holding her head straight. "One thing though, Pa, your friend here, she reeks!"

Mr. Bean laughed. "I told Mr. Harrigan that. You can't usually get a rise out of him, being that he's a lawyer and all but I could tell that really shocked him."

The phone rang.

"That must be him. See if you can give her some more."

Seth shifted his malodorous patient in his arms so that he could feed her alone. There seemed to be a bit more life in her although her head was still heavy. By the time Mr. Bean returned, the soup plate was empty and Julia was asleep again, with only the occasional groan and shiver breaking into the pattern of her breathing.

"You did a good job, son," said Mr. Bean. "Let's talk in the kitchen."

Over cups of sweet tea, Mr. Bean briefed Seth on his second phone conversation. Tom Harrigan had spoken to two doctors, Julia's and a psychiatrist friend. They were in agreement. Milly's death had finally caught up with Julia. Something about being on Star Island had made her drop her guard and let in a troupe of demons. Julia's own doctor also said that Julia had complained for several months of not being able to eat or sleep properly. And, as the psychiatrist said, food, rest and time are Nature's own antidotes to grief.

"That's all fine. Sounds like something you'd hear on Oprah," Seth said. "But what I saw in there was pretty scary. What are we supposed to do now?"

"Just watch her. Very closely. The fact that she took the soup is a good sign. But she's not out of the woods yet. If she's not walking about and talking and eating in the next couple of days, we'll have to get her down St. Brendan's." Mr. Bean stood up. "In the meantime, I'm going to have to stay here and see she eats."

"But Pa..."

"Look! You've got to work on Monday. The Bank of Bermuda won't take kindly to any cock-and-bull story about you having to take care of a crazy American tourist."

Seth shook his head, a look of incredulity loosening his features. "Pa, I wasn't offering to stay with her. Not in this life. But neither should you."

"I'm staying." Mr. Bean spoke quietly and Seth knew the matter was settled. Mr. Bean wiped his hand across his forehead. "But, Lord, how I wish your grandmother was here!" He got up and looked out the window. "Now! You best be getting back. It'll be dark soon and the weather's making up."

They walked outside together. The sky was low and dark and the trees on the island hissed as the wind blew through them.

"Tomorrow morning you can bring me a change of clothes and some of that stew from the freezer. And... and son, take it easy this weekend. Watch yourself, especially with some of those friends of yours..."

"What about my friends?" The boy's eyes flashed. "What did my friends ever do to you? Do I say anything about your friends?"

In the quiet of his mind, Mr. Bean thought about what he would have done twenty years ago if one of his sons had spoken to him like that. Fetched him one box around the ears. But times are different, I'm different and this boy is different.

"Seth," he said resting his hand on the boy's shoulder. "Just watch yourself." Mr. Bean saw the anger evaporate and was glad. Even when the noise of the outboard motor had died away, Mr. Bean remained outside. The air was chilly and damp and the light in the west was fading fast. The day seemed exhausted. A few wet-looking sparrows alighted on the telephone wires, fluffing up their straggly feathers before flying off again over the water. Seeing them gave Mr. Bean an idea. Yes, that's what I'll do, he said to himself, first thing tomorrow.

The night passed without incident, with Julia sleeping a deep and silent sleep. Mr. Bean had located a folding bed which he placed next to the four poster. At about seven, she opened her eyes. He fed her tea made with condensed milk which, after a moment's hesitation, she gulped down. Mr.

Bean ran a shallow bath and led Julia to the bathroom. That's when hostilities broke out. Mr. Bean was astonished at how strong she was. She fought a woman's fight – dirty – with a lot of scratching and biting and kicking while he just stood there, powerless to do anything except take the blows and prevent her from escaping. Every now and then, when she landed a blow that hurt him or at least injured his pride, he felt like retaliating with one ringing slap. But he desisted and when at last she wore herself out, he whisked off the robe and put her in the tepid water. With the washcloth poised in one hand and soap in the other, he was suddenly overcome with the indecency of the situation. Giving a bath to a total stranger, and a woman at that, one who, when in her right mind, was as evil as the day was long! What next? Mr. Bean set to work, sloughing away the grime and sweat and the sour secretions of Julia's madness. She sat quietly with her head drooping down. When the job was done and Mr. Bean was helping Julia out of the bath, she said, "Don't leave me. Stay." Her eyes looked right through him as if searching out some other person visible only to her. The words were clearly enunciated and when he heard them, Mr. Bean felt a little rush of pleasure. No matter who she was addressing, wasn't it a step forward that she was talking at all? Dressing her was easier than he'd expected – she actually assisted – and as he was doing it, he wondered who she was talking to. A husband? A lover? Had to be. The words she'd spoken had been full of longing. So, thought Mr. Bean, as he finished buttoning up the blue satin pyjamas he'd found in her suitcase, so, this tough lady has a heart, just like the rest of us.

He sat her in a chair by the open window. A pale yellow sun lit up the sky and the sea was flat. A quiet winter's day. The fiends on Devil's Island seemed appeased. Mr. Bean left her and went to the shed outside. This had always been his favourite part of the house. It was the kind of shed he had always wanted himself, large, orderly and full of all the gadgetry he had been able to persuade Tom Harrigan to buy. "You use them, Clarence," Milly used to say, "Tom's a sweetheart but Mr. Fixit, he ain't!" That was another thing about the shed. It was where he and Milly had had their endless conversations about any and every thing, while Milly passed him the tools. It's where the little Harrigans had come, drawn to their mother like a magnet, bouncing in and out, poking around, jumping about. Then Tom Harrigan would come, calling Milly – how that man loved to call his wife's name! – and he would be looking a bit disconsolate, as though he were missing out on something. But Milly would tease him and give him a hug and all would be well again. And this was the place where Mr. Bean had wept the tears of a child after burying his own wife, the place where Milly had known how to listen and what to say, the place where Milly had wept with him in Miriam's name. Mr. Bean glanced around him and felt a surge of ownership.

He set to work, assembling planks of wood, hammer, nails, saw. He had clamped a piece of wood on to the work table and was about to begin sawing when he became aware of eyes watching him. Even though Julia's face was veiled and distant, the blue satin pyjamas added a splash of glamour to the shed. Mr. Bean felt his body clench with resentment. In her long, unfashionable clothes, Mrs. H always seemed to fit in with the practical, workmanlike atmosphere of the place. Now here comes Park Avenue! Chastising himself for having such uncharitable thoughts, he dusted off the stool – Mrs. H's stool! – and beckoned Julia to sit down. With all the ebullience of an automaton, she did. Mr. Bean sighed. He almost preferred her fighting.

"I'm making a bluebird box," he said at last. "I'd been promising to make one for Mrs. H for the longest time but never got around to it. And then... well you know what happened then..." He shot a quick glance over at Julia. She just sat, blank-faced.

"As far as I know, no bluebird has ever nested on Star Island." He finished a piece of wood and started measuring another one. "They make stops here, though. That's how Mrs. H came to know about them. Saw one on the phone wire. She couldn't believe how pretty it was." He clamped the wood and sawed it cleanly. He stretched a web of words over the silence.

"She asked me about the bluebirds and I told her. That they belong here. What's the word? Anaemic? Ingenious? Somethin'... Anyway, nowadays, they're dying out. What do they call it? An endangered species." He looked outside as though expecting one to hop right in. "The starlings and the sparrows are the ones they have to watch. When the eggs hatch, those bad boys just swoop down and mash up the bluebird nest." He sawed another piece of wood. "It's only people that can save them. People – the biggest killers of all! Ain't that something?" He glanced over at Julia. She had not moved a muscle. Mr. Bean seemed now almost to be talking to himself as he ran his hand delicately across the wood. "These boxes are the only real hope we have of keeping them safe, especially when they're young... Even then, it's not certain. Those other birds are real vicious..."

"Nobody kept me safe. Not Teddy. Not Milly, not even Milly... All ran out on me. Every last one."

Mr. Bean dropped his saw and rushed over to Julia.

"Miss Griffin! You're all right! You're talking! You really are!" He kept squeezing her hand, his smiling face close to hers. She looked startled at this sudden and intimate commotion. Mr. Bean's face was covered in confusion as he watched the thick veil fall across Julia's eyes. Silence descended and Mr. Bean crept back to his work station and resumed his work in a fever, sawing, hammering, banging – trying to banish the bristling silence into which Julia had fallen.

Over the span of hours, the bluebird box started to take shape. He made sure that the edges of the box locked together in a flawless fit, that the entry hole was perfectly circular and smooth, that the wood was sanded to an extra fine finish and then primed and painted in an unobtrusive grey. Twice Julia moved around, once going into the house, the other time walking down to the dock and walking straight back. Both times Mr. Bean stood still, not wanting to follow, praying that she would return.

Some time in the middle of the afternoon, Seth came and the two men ate together. The meal had started with a party of three, with Julia, Seth and Mr. Bean facing a dish prepared by one of the ladies from the Church. (Mr. Bean was a great favourite among the unattached Sisters who overwhelmed his widower's table with their creations.) After the first mouthful, however, Julia spat hers out and went into her room, slamming the door behind her. The two men stared after her. Mr. Bean did not look Seth in the eye but muttered into his food, "This thing's not over yet."

Later, Seth helped Mr. Bean anchor the pole that would support the bird box in a concrete bed. After much adjusting, the pole stood straight. In twenty-four hours, when the concrete was set, Mr. Bean would fit the box onto the pole and the job would be complete.

Seth gave a huge yawn.

"Had a hard night?" Mr. Bean asked, noticing for the first time how tired Seth looked. "I told you, those guys are going to wear you out."

"Why do you always think that it's my aceboys' fault if I'm tired. Don't I have a girlfriend?"

"Yep," Mr. Bean replied, getting up. "But I see that you're just yawning. If it was your girlfriend, you'd be yawning and smiling!" They both chuckled and Mr. Bean decided not to pursue the matter any further. Soon afterwards, Seth left to get himself ready for the working week ahead. Mr. Bean watched the little boat cut through the unruffled water and was thankful for Seth's teller's job at the bank. As soul-destroying as it might be – and Mr. Bean could only believe what his grandson told him – it kept the boy off the streets and put some honest money in his pockets. And it kept him away from those shifty-looking individuals who seemed always to be on Seth's horizon.

Later that night, Tom Harrigan phoned. Mr. Bean gave a progress report, that Julia was walking around, that she no longer had that unholy smell, that she was eating a little and that she had said a few sentences and then had clammed up. When Tom Harrigan suggested that he should come and get Julia, Mr. Bean said no, without really knowing why. But he knew at some instinctive level, that going back to the full-blown madness of the City was not what Julia needed. Tom Harrigan was not easily convinced but in the end allowed himself to be persuaded to adopt a "Wait and See" policy. For the next few days, anyway. When Mr. Bean came off the phone, he found that Julia had come in on those padded feet of hers. Her eyes were bright and something resembling a smile tickled the corners of her lips. Although she said nothing, she gave Mr. Bean a hardly perceptible nod which Mr. Bean took to mean thank you.

There were times in the week that followed when Mr. Bean almost regretted his intervention on Julia's behalf. She was very difficult to handle. She never fought him again – on Monday morning she had gone into the bathroom and slammed the door in his somewhat disappointed face – and she now ate without any coercion. But all other aspects of her behaviour were bizarre. You could never know what kind of day she was going to have. Would it be a crying day, a screaming day, a death-like sleeping day or a wound-up-like-a-clockwork-toy day? It was all exhausting to Mr. Bean, especially the common denominator of all days, the lack of speech. His only defence against this was to keep to his tried and tested routine of early rising, plain food and work. Julia seemed oblivious to whatever he did, attending only to the devils that pursued her.

But still Mr. Bean kept Tom Harrigan at bay.

Seth would come every evening. He brought food, clothes, his grandfather's old radio and news of mainland Bermuda. Every day, he would try to persuade Mr. Bean to come home, to let the rich lawyer take this woman away back to the City.

"That's what made her crazy in the first place," Mr. Bean had said, seeing the incomprehension in the boy's eyes.

"But Pa, you don't know this woman! Why do you even care?"

Mr. Bean had paused to think for a minute. "I care because... because I have to care." That was all he had been able to think to say and Seth had not asked again.

Every night Tom Harrigan would call and Mr. Bean would give him the latest bulletin on Julia. Mr. Bean never tried to "tidy up" the events of the day, even when he noticed that Julia started sitting in on the phone calls. His graphic descriptions of her goings-on elicited no response from Julia, as she sat there with a bored expression on her face. But she sat there nonetheless.

The following Sunday – a week after the putting up of the bird box, a full week of silence – Tom Harrigan called at his usual time. He had an agenda. He had decided to come to Bermuda, not necessarily to bring her back but to have her "seen". He would be coming with his psychiatrist friend. Mr. Bean hesitated for a moment. Then in his slow and measured way, he put forward his case, pleading for more time for Julia, arguing, although it was not true, that he thought he saw a bit of progress, arguing that what she needed most was to be left undisturbed. But Tom Harrigan would not be moved.

"So when will you and the doctor be coming?" Mr. Bean asked at last. "I'll get Dennis – you know, my son with the taxi – to come and pick you up..."

"Give that here! Come on, give that thing to me right now!" Mr. Bean almost lost his balance as he felt himself being thrust aside and the phone snatched from his hand.

"Tom? Julia here." Even in his shocked state, Mr. Bean could hear Julia's voice shaking.

"You heard right. You're damn right it's me. Who the hell else do you think it is!"

Emotion clouded Julia's words as she tried to control her trembling. "Leave me alone, you hear!" Julia was breathing hard. "And you can take your trip and and your goddamn shrink and stick em where the sun don't shine!"

It sounded like anger but Mr. Bean could see that Julia's spirit was being convulsed by its sudden journey out of the shadows into the light. Raw communication after deep silence. It had Julia on the rack.

"Tom," she said again, riding roughshod over Tom Harrigan's exclamations, moderating her breath, playing for time. Mr. Bean watched as Julia lowered her head and searched deep down in herself for composure. She used to be so sharp, so focused... But since landing on this rock, all of her mind's hard contours had disintegrated. She closed her eyes and summoned all of those diffuse and battered energies to her aid.

"Tom," she said once more, and this time her voice was firm. "Let me say this in words of one syllable so that you'll understand. Don't come! Do not even think of coming!" Tom Harrigan's voice on the other end fell silent and a few moments passed as he readjusted himself to Julia's altered tone. During that time, Mr. Bean witnessed a startling physical transformation overtake Julia. Although standing there in a dishevelled tracksuit, her bearing and pose, the new authority in her voice, gave Mr. Bean a startling glimpse into the world from which Julia had fled, a world where, in her power suits and high-heeled shoes, she was in total charge.

Tom Harrigan finally found his voice and, in the sudden stillness of the room, Mr. Bean could hear the quiet and patient tone he adopted to reply. It was the tone of the professional at work. He spoke for what seemed a very long time during which Julia's body never lost its feral look. At last, he seemed to have run out of things to say.

Julia took a deep breath.

"You're not the only one who loved Milly, you know. She may have been your wife, but she was my... my dearest friend." Mr. Bean thought he heard a sound at the other end – the room was so quiet! – the sound of a voice catching in a sob. "She wouldn't have wanted you to swoop down on me, all guns blazing," Julia continued. "Intruding on... on my time here." Despite the occasional pause, Julia's monologue proceeded in a confident flow which inhibited any possibility of a reply from Tom Harrigan.

"She would have told you, 'If she wants to act up, Tom, just let her. She's been holding on to too much for too long. It's time she let some of it go.' Don't you think she would have said that, Tom?" Julia stopped again and the worlds on both ends of the telephone line were suddenly flooded with Milly's presence as Julia's voice made a near perfect imitation of Milly's slow, faintly Southern lilt. "'Let her be, Tom. Let her be. The fresh air and sunshine'll make her better.' Don't you think she would have said that, Tom?" There was that sound again, that quiet little sob. Mr. Bean lowered his head, feeling as though he had stumbled into some fearful intimacy.

Tom Harrigan did not come to the island to have Julia "seen". Instead he spent the next few days gazing out from a plate-glass tower in the sky, while the neurotic metropolis whirled below. It was not that Julia had re-ignited his longing for Milly. No, he wore his loss like a badge of honour, permanently fixed to his breast. His exchange with Julia had been deeply unsettling for some other reason. But what was it? As he replayed the phone call over in his mind, the same thing kept coming back again and again. Milly's words coming out of Julia's mouth! The uncanny similarity of the sound, the unerring correctness of the spirit behind the words. Julia was dead right. Milly would have said just that. How was it that Julia had known and he had not? Tom felt his head tightening into a migraine.

Julia too was profoundly affected by this conversation. But whereas the encounter had made Tom look inward, it had the reverse effect on Julia, stirring her to make a few tentative steps out of the dark place into which she had become almost comfortably bunkered. She started to move around the house more; she started to talk to Mr. Bean. Just a little. But enough to make Mr. Bean feel that some semblance of normality was returning and that he could return home with a reasonably clear conscience. A few days later, Julia walked down to the dock with him. Mr. Bean had to make a conscious effort to restrain his natural vigour to accommodate Julia's pace and when they finally arrived at the dock, he saw that her eyes had glazed over. She said goodbye without emotion and he watched her walk back up the path, every step a battle against an overpowering inertia.

The image of Julia dragging her grief up the gravel path haunted Mr. Bean as he sped across the water, even when he opened the door of his house and found his five sons and their families and assorted friends waiting for him in an impromptu welcome-home party. He'd been away almost two weeks and had been missed. Some of the smaller grandchildren crowded around him, hugging his knees. In the corner stood Seth, the architect of these festivities, a smile playing at his lips. Mr. Bean noticed an array of pies on his table and a few of the Church ladies giving him quizzical looks. He'd never come to care for them when they'd been sick! And still he thought of Julia. At the height of the party, he slipped outside into the darkness. The bitter chill of the February night took direct aim at his arthritic joints and hit their mark. Rubbing the knuckles of his right hand, he located the light on Star Island dock. There were some casuarinas right next to it and as these bent before the wind, the light seemed to flicker. Mr. Bean went back into his house but its warmth brought him no solace.

Julia too looked out over the water. She had braved the sharp tooth of the wind and returned to the dock. She located the light from the jetty across the Sound. It beamed strong and unwavering. She imagined Mr. Bean enfolded in the bosom of his family. Images of Milly and Tom and the little Harrigans sprang up before her, even as she squeezed her eyes shut against them. Then there'd been Teddy, whose face came to her in daylight colours. She could hear his laugh. He'd been so funny. He'd been able to make her laugh away the stern eyes of her mother and the hopeless ones of her father. But laughing didn't always keep him from crying and in the end there had been the bitter mockery of the hypodermic needle. That light over there, she thought to herself, raising a trembling finger towards the mainland, it could go off in a second and never be seen again. She turned her back to the water and the light and walked wearily back to the house.

After that night, an uneasy truce settled over them. Mr. Bean started off by making a daily trip to Star Island. She was functioning: eating, keeping herself and the house clean, engaging in occasional conversation. He felt like a fussy mother hen. He cut back the trips to five times a week, then four, finally three. She was not a casualty of life any more but neither was she a participant. Whatever he did, she just watched. He painted the shed and planted a vegetable garden. She took no interest, still lost in another sphere. They spent their time thus, he watchful, she drifting... Every Saturday Seth came along, adding a jarring note to the strange melody, the young man casting disapproving eyes on this peculiar relationship. And so the days rolled into weeks and the weeks nibbled away at the chilly winds and soaking rains and white-washed water on the Sound. Without them even noticing, the winter was gone.

One day, in mid-April, Mr. Bean made his now habitual Monday morning trip to Star Island. The morning was brimming with colour but Mr. Bean did not see it. He was distracted. Seth had come in very late the night before and only just about made it to work in the morning. It was becoming increasingly difficult to keep him on the straight and narrow. "Bad company," he muttered as he tied up the boat. Thoughts of what to do about the boy engulfed him as he made his way to the house. When he saw Julia suddenly standing before him on the path, he was startled. He stared at her. Apart from appearing from nowhere, there was something different about her. He scanned her face. It was lit up from within by some strong and mysterious flame.

She put a finger up to her lips and said "Shhh!" With the other hand, she grabbed his arm and pulled him off the path into the undergrowth. They were heading for the house but via the most circuitous route. Mr. Bean tried to control his panic. What was happening here? Had the February Julia returned? As she pulled him through the tangle of cherry, sage and stinging nettle, he remembered, with a shudder, the screamer, the fighter, the stripper. He had no wish to be lost in the bushes with any of these. Yet there was something irresistible about her grip and the determination with which she pulled him forward brooked no opposition. When they were within sight of the side of the house, she stopped. She turned to him and said, "Shhh!" once more. Her skin glowed and her eyes were lit up like small fires.

"Look!" she whispered and pulled back some bushes.

At first Mr. Bean didn't see anything out of the ordinary. Everything in the yard was as he had left it a few days before.

Then he saw it. In a pool of sunlight on the smooth lawn stood a bluebird. It was quite near to where Mr. Bean and Julia were crouched but it was not aware of their presence. It was not feeding but seemed to be just standing there enjoying the sun on its glorious plumage. The two watchers, feeling like voyeurs at a midnight window, held their breath and exchanged smiles. The bluebird was joined by its mate. They bowed to one another and then, on their green stage, began an elaborate dance. One had more brilliant colours but as they bobbed and twirled, amber breast touching amber breast, indigo wing brushing indigo wing, it was clear that each was beautiful to the other. When at last the dance was over, they fluffed up their feathers and, of a single accord, raised themselves off the ground and into the branches of a tree. A moment or two passed and, with the same unity of purpose, they flew off, merging quickly into the blueness of the sky.

Julia and Mr. Bean crawled from their hiding place. Julia ran out onto the space recently vacated by the bluebirds, bobbing and twirling in a cumbersome human version of their dance. With her arms raised she spun around, feeling the sun reaching down and driving out midwinter from her bones. She felt the sun's healing hands upon her, stroking away her fear and sadness, bursting, with one massive pull, the chains that bound her. Freeing her... Mr. Bean laughed as Julia danced in the sunshine, knowing, without knowing how, that this was more than a dance.

Julia and Mr. Bean spent the rest of the day talking. Mostly about Milly. They both felt sorry that she had not witnessed the dance of the bluebirds. They knew she would have loved it. Julia told Mr. Bean about her years at college with Milly, how she'd bullied her, how Milly had mothered her. She told him how disaster had struck in their last semester at Wellesley; how Milly had met this white law student; how she'd broken the hearts of several aspiring black doctors, architects and company executives and the hearts of her parents; how she'd alienated every single black person she knew. How she'd married Tom anyway. And how she, Julia, had not spoken to Milly for eight long years.

"So how did you two get back together again?" Mr. Bean asked, hardly believing that he was sitting in the sunshine having a pleasant conversation with this woman who, up to now, had been either mad or bad.

"It was a pure fluke," said Julia, her voice brightening with the memory. "I don't believe in Fate but this was one strange coincidence. We ran into each other in the middle of Manhattan. Literally. Can you believe that?" Her mouth curled into a smile that made her look very young. "I was just starting out in publishing – I eventually got tired of being at school – and so it was hustle, hustle, hustle. I was running along the sidewalk, with a million other New Yorkers, when I collided with a vehicle." Julia glanced over at Mr. Bean and saw with satisfaction that her powers of storytelling were returning. "It looked like a down-sized car without a motor but what it was was..." She paused for effect. "The biggest bloody stroller you'd ever seen! There were two grisly chocolate-covered babies in it, a person who had just learned to walk clinging to it, bags slung all over it. Pushing this monstrosity was what can best be described as the world's hugest belly on legs. Who was it? Former Miss Coloured Teen America. Former graduate of the Julia Griffin Academy of Black Studies. Current holder of the Gerber Outstanding Achievement Award!"

Mr. Bean thought he had been following up until this point, but now looked perplexed.

"Who? What?"

"It was Milly, silly!" Julia threw her head back and laughed until tears rolled down her cheeks, "It was only her voice as she cooed at Child X or Child Y that gave her away. She told me later that my eyes kept moving between the

196

belly and the babies, the babies and the belly. The horror! The horror! I must have been quite a sight."

Julia wiped her eyes with the back of her hand. "So we made up right there on Fifth Avenue. Then she took me back to the hotel to meet The Husband..."

She went on to give Mr. Bean an account of that momentous meeting. They'd found Tom, red-haired and freckled, pouring over a sheaf of papers in the middle of a huge toy-strewn hotel room. Only Tom could have thought of going to a business meeting accompanied by three babies and a pregnant wife. But the meeting was to last for a week – too long to be away from them. Well, enough said about that! Julia, Milly and the children had tumbled into the room, laughing. Tom had liberated the babies from their pushchair and then had gone over and gathered his wife into his arms.

He and Julia had eyed one another.

"So you're Supersperm," said Julia crisply.

"And you're Julia," Tom countered.

"How do you know who I am?"

Tom had kissed the top of Milly's head.

"Oh! It's just the occasional thing that's been said to me every single day for the last eight years!" With one arm around Milly, Tom had leaned towards Julia with an out-stretched hand. "I'm happy to meet you at last."

Julia had stared at his hand. It was milk-white with a sprinkling of reddish-brown spots. She could see the palm, very pale but slashed by a series of clear brown lines. This no-nonsense hand seemed to be extended in friendship. Julia had hesitated for a moment and then closed her own dark brown fingers around his.

"Yes... Yes..." was all she'd been able to say while she'd watched as Tom's other hand had pressed into Milly's shoulder.

Julia closed her eyes and laughed. "We did become good

friends, you know. After I'd given him ten to twenty years of pure hell, of course."

Mr. Bean shook his head, smiling. Being with Julia was like being in the path of a whirlwind sweeping over the face of the ocean, whipping up the waves and sending them spinning into the lightness of air. It was exhilarating, scary and not meant for those intent on a quiet life. He shook his head again, thinking of the wildness of her, the fury of her passions, the greedy way she consumed life. So different from all those I have loved in my seventy-something years, he thought. And yet when he looked at her again from beneath those hooded lids, what he felt was not far from love.

For several more hours, Julia's high spirits continued unabated while Mr. Bean lay back, almost speechless, as she put on her electrifying show. When at last he announced that he was leaving, Julia walked with him to the dock. The walk made her quieter. On the way down, they checked the bluebird box but there was no sign of nesting yet. Mr. Bean was in the boat when Julia said, "Milly was more than a person. She was like a place I could run to, where I could be as brilliant or as dumb as I liked. Nowhere else in my life was there a place like that." For the second time that day, Mr. Bean saw Julia's eyes fill with tears. His heart felt large and sore within him.

"Where do they go, Mr. Bean?" she asked.

"Who?"

"The dead."

Mr. Bean felt a constriction in his chest as he saw himself fall in the path of Julia's grief, returned to her with the unexpectedness of a squall in the middle of a summer day.

"It helps if you believe in heaven," he said, knowing what her response would be.

"And if you don't? What then?"

Julia's eyes were full of earnest entreaty. Mr. Bean wished he could give her some word of comfort that would make the pain go away. "Let not your heart be troubled... In my Father's house are many mansions..." he began. "All I know for sure is... For those of us that's left, life goes on... The sun always rises."

Julia looked at him long and hard.

Mr. Bean's prediction that life would go on proved to be accurate. Everywhere on Star Island rain-muted freesias had given way to the white blooms of lilies. The touch of the air was tentative, not yet showing the full-blown sensuality of high summer. Julia saw all of this but remained unmoved.

With the coming of the warm weather, Mr. Bean had hoped for a major breakthrough with Julia. But it didn't quite happen. She was neither happy nor unhappy. She seemed to have reached a plateau and was content to meander along it. The reawakening earth around her left her cold. But she was starting to look better. Her eyes no longer sank back into her face; her hair had grown and raised itself into little tufts all over her head; and she had put on a bit of weight. But Mr. Bean was disappointed when Julia showed no further signs of that spectacular joie de vivre that had come bubbling up on the day of the bluebirds.

It did not return when Tom Harrigan came to stay, even though she became quite animated, arguing with him constantly, exchanging barbs with the familiarity of old friends: "No wonder men are scared of you, Julia. Just look at the way you stand. Like you're ready to crush a man's skull. Or worse."

"Any man who is wimpish enough to be intimidated by me will get just what he deserves!"

"Spoken like the seasoned campaigner that you are."

"Tom, what you need is one good fuck. Sort out your uptight New England prudish ass once and for all. And hey! – I'd even oblige. Just so you'd know how it's really done."

199

"Frankly, my dear, I'd prefer a night with the Harvard Law Review." It was like a routine that they had worked out over years. They did not speak of Milly, although she was there between them, almost as palpable as flesh.

And still the joy did not return. Not even, when, on the day of Tom's departure, Mr. Bean discovered a few twigs in the bluebird box. Not even then did Julia exude the delight in living that she had shown that day. She just smiled without a word.

Tom Harrigan went back to the City. As he and Mr. Bean crossed over to the mainland, Tom thanked Mr. Bean for looking after Julia.

"Anybody would've done it!" he exclaimed in surprise. Tom's laughter could be heard over the coughing of the outboard motor. "Wouldn't they?"

"Clarence, I live in a place where people don't want to see what's ugly or sick. They'll step over a dying junkie or hurry past a filthy bag lady. But you..." he shook his head. "You stopped and gave a hand. And that makes you part of a dying breed. Certainly in the States. And probably even here in 'paradise'." He paused. "She is grateful, you know. She may not show it but she is."

"All I know is, she's lucky to have you, Mr. H."

"Not really," said Tom in a suddenly quiet voice. "I have to hang on to Julia, pain in-the-butt as she is. Just as she has to hang on to me. She was an important part of Milly's life. Of our life." Tom had found it difficult to share his wife. He had often wished that he had fallen in love with someone whom he alone could love. But it was his fate to love someone whom the whole world loved. Milly had never belonged only to him. It was through her friendship with Julia that he had learned this.

He turned his head away and looked out over the water, reluctant to let Mr. Bean see the emotion moving in his face. It had been a hard lesson that had stretched across his entire marriage. He liked Julia. He liked her verve, her humour, her sense of drama. He had a wry appreciation of these qualities so different from his own. He knew she had another side, one rarely seen, a side that was both tender and vulnerable. He knew that there was a secret garden, stoutly defended against legions of predatory lovers, glimpsed by only one person. His wife Milly. And that knowledge had cast its shadow down a long corridor of years.

At first he had tried to explain the closeness of the friendship on the grounds of race. Would he ever be able to fully bridge that gap? Was it because of this that he had so embraced Milly's desire to have baby after baby after baby? "From your white and my black, look at this beautiful thing we've made," she'd said to him as she'd handed him their first child. No, it wasn't race that kept Julia and Milly together. Then he'd argued – only to himself, of course – that it was this Women's Movement thing, this spirit of the age, with women moving forward, breaking new ground, recreating themselves. For a long time, Tom had held to this theory and had even once or twice chuckled with male friends whose wives also had stridently feminist women friends. Although part of him felt ashamed about doing this, there had been comfort in that chuckling, to feel that his unease was shared. Then Milly had got sick and Tom had realised that neither race nor gender politics could explain away the magnitude of Julia's devotion to his family. She had been the tireless footsoldier when he himself had fallen apart, when the children had lashed out, when Milly's spirits had sagged. Julia had been the rock.

Milly did love me, Tom said. He may have even said it out loud but by this time he was completely unaware of his surroundings, of the salt spray on his face, of the rhythmic sound of the outboard as it cut across the Sound. From their earliest days together, he had never doubted Milly's love. It informed everything she did – in her thoughtfulness, her teasing, in the way she told him when he was arrogant or tedious. It showed in their lovemaking which was good right up to the end. Maybe some of the fire had gone, but that was to be expected in a house full of children. Yes, that part of their lives was solid. But still, Tom laboured with the thought of Julia and what it was that lay at the heart of her relationship with Milly. He wondered what Julia saw in her mind when she thought of Milly. It was a torment to him. If he could have been granted one wish, it would be that this thing be laid to rest forever.

The noise of the boat's engine changed and Tom saw that they had reached the other side.

Mr. Bean did not appear to have noticed Tom's distraction. He was concerned with tying up the boat. Tom got out. "Clarence, I couldn't let go of Julia, even if I wanted to."

Mr. Bean looked surprised. There had been a full three minute break in the conversation. He had thought it was over.

"Julia's part of the family. Part of us all." As he spoke, Tom realised that he was as near to a resolution as he would ever be, that life would probably allow him to get no closer to the truth than this. "Maybe it's just as well," he continued in a low voice.

"What you say, Mr. H?"

"Oh, nothing, Clarence. Just talking to myself."

After Tom Harrigan had left, Mr. Bean felt happier. Although far from radiant, Julia seemed all right and was certainly no longer "funny in the head". His area of concern shifted to Seth who was becoming more and more uncommunicative and had started to stage disappearing acts at the weekends. His friends, whom Mr. Bean pictured as snarling, circling wolves, were becoming visible presences at the house. They were civil to the old man but had the tendency to stop talking whenever he entered the room. Mr. Bean so felt he was losing a grip of the situation that he even considered foregoing his yearly trip as part of his local bowling team. This was shocking news for Mr. Bean's family who knew that for the last fifteen years this trip to the Bowling Tournament in Philadelphia was one of the high points of their father's calendar. They urged him to look at the facts. Seth continued to hold down a job, he never asked for money and although he went missing some of the time, he usually kept his appointments with his family. The boy was, after all, almost twenty-one. He was doing better than most.

In the end, Mr. Bean put aside his fears and went. Before going, he assured Julia that Seth would come three times during his ten-day absence and that there was no need for her to worry. She said she was sure the boy would be fine and, to Mr. Bean's embarrassment and surprise, embraced him warmly as he stepped into the little boat and set off across the water.

As she stood waving on the dock, Julia felt surprised at herself – that she was sad at seeing him go, that she was sad for someone other than Milly, Teddy or herself, that she was feeling anything at all that was different from the deadening paralysis of her grief. Her step was light as she walked back to the house. For the first time, she noticed the scent of sage in the air.

In this state of returning vigour, Julia started to read, to explore the tiny island and, occasionally, to switch on the radio. She was listening to a newscast one afternoon, trying to work out the mysteries of local politics, when she heard a noise outside. It was Seth, coming up the path with another young man. Each was carrying a bag of groceries. They were laughing loudly and play-fighting, swinging the bags around and throwing mock punches. Twice, objects from the bags spilled out and the youths had to scramble about on the ground to pick them up.

"Hey you guys, take it easy!" Julia shouted from the

doorway, half laughing, half annoyed at their skylarking. Seth stopped in his tracks and the other youth followed suit.

"You hear something, Spragga?" They both cupped a hand around an ear.

"Nah!" Spragga said. "Just some longtail dropping some crap. They so full of shit, it goes bang when it hits the ground!" The two youths doubled over at Spragga's wit and pushed by Julia who stood at the door, open-mouthed at this version of Seth and his sidekick.

Sniggering, the boys went into the kitchen and started throwing the bags around again. When they pushed past her with their hard male bodies, Julia had felt a moment of pure fear, but now that they had resumed their childish games, anger boiled within her. She wished she'd taken up that martial arts course she'd been promising herself for so long.

"You know what a longtail is?" the heavy voice of Seth's friend said.

"She's a bird, man. Comes and stops by here from those cold countries." Seth's words were punctuated with giggles.

"Yeah," the heavy voice said, much more controlled and emphatic. "But what about the other kind? The kind with legs and arms and eyes and ears..."

"And dollar bills!" From where she was sitting in the living room, straight-backed and seething, Julia could hear Seth's voice slurring. "But you know, Spragga, the kind with wings and the kind with legs are just the same. They all come down here to get..."

"Some heat!" both voices chorused and once again dissolved into helpless laughter.

"And we can sure help them out there, can't we, Spraggs!"

The anxiety Julia had felt at the doorway returned. Ninety-nine per cent of her wanted to go in there and curse them and their mothers until they wept with shame. She had made grown men cry before! But that had been on her own turf where she knew the rules. Hell, she'd made the rules! But this was different. There were two of them, they were bigger than her and their particular brand of meanness made her suspect that what was coursing through their veins was not just blood. So she decided not to confront them. But she'd be damned if they thought she'd scurry off and lock herself in her room. No way! She'd sit it out until they'd heaved their rear ends off this island.

The raucous sounds in the kitchen continued for a few more minutes. Then Julia heard Seth and Spragga coming out. She sat very still as they approached. They were about to go through the door when Seth stopped and turned to where Julia was sitting.

"One thing though, Spragga, man, one thing I want you to know." In the light from the open door Julia could clearly see his pupils were dilated, in open contradiction to the sober expression on the rest of his face. "I want you to know that I hate them."

"Who?"

"All of them. Them who fly here, take what they need and fly out again. Don't matter what colour they are. Sometimes I think the black ones are worse cause I know that just yesterday, they were just like us." Seth's mouth curled into an ugly line. "Look at this place! A private island. Can you dig that? I tell you, I hate these bastards. Them with enough money to be free."

Seth spoke as though Star Island had vanished and he was addressing a vast rally of his peers. Julia sat without moving, without breathing.

"Hey, don't start getting deep on me," said Spragga. "All's I know is that I'm a businessman. And if you want to be free on this rock, you'll become one too." Spragga smiled, revealing large even teeth, white, except for one in the front, which glinted gold. "Someday soon I'm going to have me an empire. Right there on Angle Street. You just watch!"

Julia still sat motionless, long after the outboard engine

could no longer be heard. When she did at last get up, she set about locking up the house against the night and other dangers. She banged and slammed windows and doors in her rage. Why did this have to happen? Just as her life was becoming manageable. Seth's last words about wanting to be free had cut through her, even as his body had cast a shadow of menace over hers. She would have never guessed that Mr. Bean's surly, aimless grandson could have had thoughts of freedom. It reminded her of her early days at Wellesley when she had been wedded to a whole culture of freedom-seekers. Black was power; black was beautiful. Now, in her mid-forties, freedom on the printed page was her bread and butter, the commodity that paid the mortgage on her smart duplex overlooking Central Park. She thought of her chic apartment and she heard Seth's raw words. Her head started to throb.

What was she to do? Should she report the incident to the police? She had, after all, felt threatened by those two wild-eyed youths. No. No police. She still had an instinctive reaction against them dating back to her childhood. But suppose Seth and company made a return visit. What then? She paced the floor, rubbing her forehead, swearing. Suddenly she went silent as she remembered Seth's eyes whose irises had been swallowed up by their black inner core. Telling Mr. Bean that his grandson had been abusive was one thing. Telling him that he was involved with drugs was another.

"Oh God!" Julia slumped into a chair. Brother Teddy had cured her of flirtations with any pill or powder promising paradise; the void that he'd left had also shown her the dangers of caring. The long string of failed relationships with men bore witness to the protective walls she'd put up. Then she'd dared to care about Milly and look where it had left her. On the brink of lunacy. Oh no, she said, blocking out Mr. Bean's furrowed face. Caring's just too hard for some people.

A week later, Mr. Bean came for his regular Wednesday visit. Julia had not seen Seth again. When Mr. Bean asked how everything had gone, she told him that everything had been just fine. When she asked him about his tournament, he said it was O.K. She pressed him for details. "We won," he said in a flat tone and went outside into the shed. When he'd finished his work, Julia accompanied him to the dock. A pair of bluebirds flew busily in and out of the box. No one noticed.

Just before Mr. Bean started up the engine, he said, with studied casualness, "Oh, by the way, he's moved out. Seth, that is. Gone to live with a friend."

Julia felt it was time to be going back to the City. The thought had come to her as soon as she'd seen Mr. Bean's dull eyes and the droop of his shoulders as he'd steered the boat across the water. It was not that she had any appetite for the life she'd left back there. Could the thing that kept her at her desk twelve hours a day have any possible merit, or was it just a job, well paid and tailor-made for a workaholic like herself? And had the causes that she'd championed all her adult life become smudged with the dirty thumbprint of commerce? Then there was her life outside of work. What life? No friends. Next to Milly, all the others seemed like grinning puppets. No family. Six years ago, she'd bought her parents a house in Florida and had not seen them since. No lovers. Since she'd buried Milly, she'd felt the need for some purification and had not been able to bear the thought of a man's hand on her. No, there would not be much to go back to. Not a cat or a goldfish mourned in her absence. Yet she could not stay and look at Mr. Bean's face. She had known enough suffering. She did not need to see any more.

But despite her decision, Julia found it hard to rouse herself to go. Dawn followed dusk in relentless procession and May swept in with flowers and sunlight. Mr. Bean continued to come, as regular as the sun, not visibly unhappy but invisibly, deeply so. He looked after Star Island House and the garden, not quite mechanically but with less vigour, brightening only when telling Julia, with his unconscious schoolmaster's manner, about this wild flower or that lizard or some bird. He climbed a ladder and plucked an egg from the bluebird box and let her hold the pale, blue-veined jewel in her palm. By the time he'd replaced it, with the utmost gentleness, the brightness in his face had gone.

Then one day, Mr. Bean didn't come. Julia spent an anxious evening and a sleepless night. At first light, she phoned Tom Harrigan who chided her for waking him and also for not having the common sense to get Mr. Bean's number long ago. Eventually he gave her a series of numbers where he might be reached. Julia called Mr. Bean's number several times but there was no response. Just as she was summoning up the courage to phone one of Mr. Bean's children, she heard the familiar noise of an approaching outboard motor. Julia ran down the path in time to see him getting out of the boat and securing it. Relief flooded through her as she saw the dark coloured clothes, the angular shoulders, the narrow neck, the back bent to its task. She stopped running. He turned and walked towards her. The strong sunlight toyed with her vision and she blinked. When she opened her eyes, the truth was clear. It was not Mr. Bean.

"Ma'am," the man said, "I'm Johnny Bean. I come to tell you Pops is in the hospital. Heart attack."

A man of few words, thought Julia, trying to distract herself from the disturbing resemblance between this man and her Mr. Bean, trying also not to hear the gravity of his message.

"I also come to ask you if you seen Seth. We can't find him. Since he quit his job, no one knows where he lives."

He's gone into business, Julia almost heard herself say, but instead she bit her lower lip and maintained her silence.

"Now Pops is calling for him. So if you know anything, we'd appreciate..."

Julia had stalled on the words "calling for". That's what dying people do. They "call for" priests for benedictions, lawyers for legacies, old loves for reminiscences, past enemies for forgiveness, wayward children for promises. He was calling for Seth.

Julia spun on her heel and went running towards the house. "I have no idea where Seth is!" she shouted. "I'm sorry. I can't help you." She ran back to the house without stopping and slammed the door behind her. She listened and after several minutes heard the outboard motor take off across the Sound.

The rest of the day was spent in feverish activity. She washed clothes, scrubbed the kitchen, wrote letters and made phone calls. Her journey back to the metropolis was at hand. When everything on her mental list had been ticked off, she fell into bed, sinking instantly into a deep, dreamless sleep from which she awakened early the next morning, exhausted. The previous day's energy was gone and she dragged herself around the house in slow motion.

The phone rang. It was Tom Harrigan enquiring about Mr. Bean. Her replies were terse and monosyllabic and the conversation was soon over. She went outside. For those with eyes to see, the morning was fresh and beautiful – but not for Julia. She wandered in and out of the shed, past the vegetable garden, down to the water's edge, around to the far side of the island. By the time she came back to the house, she had made up her mind to see Mr. Bean. Every feeling told her to cut her losses and run – every feeling but one. Was it gratitude, obligation, or, in Milly's phrase, "plain manners"? "Whatever," she said to herself as she hunted for the keys to the other boat moored on the north side of Star Island. "Whatever! I just need to see him is all."

Julia was at last ready to go. She stood outside fumbling to close the door. Her head was feeling very heavy and her hands were shaking so much that she dropped the keys. As she bent to pick them up, she became aware of sharp little noises raining onto her. She shook her head as though to dislodge them from her hair. They only got louder. Julia prayed that her mind was not starting to buckle again. When she raised her head, she laughed out loud when she saw several birds flying low overhead. For some reason, Julia stopped to look at them more closely. They were all sparrows, small, brown and muscular. There was something joyous about their movements, almost like jubilation, as they flitted up and down and around, all of them seeming to describe rough spheres around one central point. Julia scanned the air until she found the fixed point of their ecstasy. A grey wooden box with twigs tumbling out of the hole in its side.

She started running and shouting at the same moment. The sparrows were jolted out of their bliss, her harsh cries sending them flying to the cover of the trees. She kept screaming at them as she grabbed a stepladder from the shed and snapped it open underneath the bluebird box.

She was too late. The massacre was already accomplished. Crushed blue-veined shells, bloody, matted feathers, chicks with their heads shoved in. As Julia slowly descended the ladder, a flash of dark blue shot past her. She watched the two birds hover in the air for an endless moment, their beady eyes on the box, their wings seeming heavy. Then they turned themselves around and reached for the open sky.

Julia went inside and made a phone call, then walked to the north side of the island and found the boat. With a combination of trial, error and profanity, she started it and made her way across the water. She was clear-headed and sure of her new objective. To find Seth and take him to his grandfather.

At the jetty on the other side, she found Dennis and

Johnny Bean waiting. She'd been lucky and had found both of them at Dennis's house, next door to his father's, when she'd called. As they drove towards town in Dennis's taxi, she told them about Seth's visit with his friend Spragga and about a place called Angle Street. As she looked from the taxi, it dawned on her that she was seeing the mainland for the first time. When her plane had touched down four months ago, night had already fallen.

Now, here was Bermuda, visible to her for the first time. Despite the urgency of the need to find Seth, Dennis's taxi maintained its "tour-guide" pace, like a show horse long since broken out of the habit of running with the wind. In the front seat, the two brothers talked, quietly, spasmodically, trying to sketch out some plan to find the errant boy. The words brushed over Julia as her eyes focused on the ribbon of road that edged the thin and rocky curves of the island. She already knew the blues of the water, the shifting, colour-spawning sea. She knew the cloud-flecked blue of the sky, all brightness and shine. But look at these houses, with their pristine white roofs, their pink, yellow and blue stone walls, their flower-filled gardens, the rich green of their lawns and geometrically correct hedges. Look at the buses – pink!; the cars, all in mint condition, the little mopeds buzzing along like freshly-painted dragonflies. What did this place remind her of? There were echoes of other places Julia had seen but this island sang its own distinctive song. So clean, so neat, so beautifully, so innocently packaged. Julia's natural cynicism sprang into action, wishing to dissect the beauty, to reveal its murky, beating heart. When she got out of the car, her attention was so drawn by the fine pastel buildings, wondering at the same time at the source of the wealth that had built them, that Dennis Bean had to call back to her, "Miss... umm... Miss... We should be getting along over Angle Street now." Dennis and Johnny Bean were staring at her.

"Angle what? Oh! Sorry! Sorry!" She felt the blood rush to her face, ashamed at having so totally forgotten why she was there. "Of course! Let's get going."

For the next few minutes, they walked up Church Street, past the City Hall, so white it almost hurt the eye, past the sombre pomp of the Cathedral of the Most Holy Trinity, past the functional triumph of the Central Post Office, past the clock tower of the Sessions House, dozing in the hot afternoon sun. Julia noted that the people they passed, white, beige, brown and black, looked as well heeled and well dressed as the houses and the gardens and the citadels of public power.

They turned left and a large grey church came into view. A group of immaculate matrons were hurrying up its steps and organ music swelled from the open door. Julia and Mr. Bean's sons were just in time to witness the approach of a small fleet of identical cars, gleaming and bedecked with white ribbon. Julia craned her neck around and was rewarded with a glimpse of the bride. It was enough to justify a smug quote from one of her favourite movies. "She looks like a big meringue."

This tableau had so engaged Julia that it took a few minutes before she became aware of the new street she was on. Something had changed. From the moment they had passed that church, the world had become darker.

"We call this the Block," Johnny Bean said.

"Our own little Harlem," added Dennis with a smirk.

Julia gave a polite smile. When did Harlem look this good? But she saw what they meant. The molecules that made up the air on this street were grittier, harsher. Paint peeled; the odd window was boarded up and swirls of graffiti adorned the walls. The white faces which only a short time ago had exuded such comfort and ease were now completely absent. Those who lounged on the street, waiting for the night to fall, seemed neither young nor old, neither happy nor sad.

Dennis Bean approached a man with a baseball cap turned backwards on his head and a bottle-shaped brown bag in his hand.

"Hey, mate, what's happenin'?" Dennis, the less taciturn of the brothers, stopped and looked at Johnny who gave him an almost imperceptible nod. Julia could see they were both out of their depth, swimming in shark-infested waters. Dennis pressed on. "I'm trying to find this boy Earl Brangman. Young fella. His people are from down the country. Bailey's Bay, I believe. His uncle used to be a bus driver." The man in the baseball cap took a swig from his bottle, then seemed to study Dennis's right ear. "They call him Spragga. Know him?"

The man in the cap dislodged a plug of phlegm from his throat and shot it from his lips. It landed, glistening, a few centimetres from Johnny's shoe. He unsheathed two rows of disorderly teeth. At last he turned muddy eyes towards Dennis.

"Nah! Don't know no Spragga. So you best just step. Go on, step!" He started to snigger. Dennis, Johnny and Julia began to back away. The man stood up straight and raised his voice. "But leave the piece here! What you two old faggots goin with a piece like that anyway? Leave her with me!" Johnny and Dennis moved to surround Julia with the solidity of their bodies as the man's cackling rang out down the street. Although they drifted around the Block and Angle Street for almost a full hour – there was nothing to be learnt. Back in Dennis's taxi, Julia was the first to revive.

"Can you take me to see your father?" she asked and somehow the gloom was dispersed.

A few days before, Mr. Bean had been transferred from Intensive Care to a general ward. When they walked into his room, he was sitting propped up on a small hill of pillows, looking out of the window, a half-smile softening his mouth. Julia was relieved to see that there was a minimum of machinery around his bed, although his right arm was attached to a drip. His face brightened when he saw them although there seemed a moment's reluctance to pull his eyes away from the horizon. Julia pressed her lips against his forehead and then stepped back in dismay. His eyes were filled with such warmth but there was a new fragility about him that frightened her. She dropped her gaze. The awkward silence held and was only broken minutes later, by the arrival of the doctor, a tall, muscular young man with a pony tail.

"Hey, Clarence, how you doin?" he said, taking Mr. Bean's chart and flashing a youthful smile at everyone.

"Oh God," Julia groaned to herself, "If that's a doctor, just call me Grandma Moses." Mr. Bean shifted on his hill of pillows, looking with a combination of amusement and disbelief at this vision of a child with a stethoscope.

"Not too bad for an old man," Mr. Bean answered, chuckling.

"Not bad! You're a bloody marvel! Look at this chart!" He thrust the chart under Mr. Bean's nose and snatched it away again. "And to what do you attribute this impressive rally?" The young doctor's eyes lit on Julia. "Aha! I think I've cracked it!" He glanced over at Mr. Bean. "Why, Clarence, you crafty old dog, you." He put down the chart and advanced upon Julia with an outstretched hand and the unabashed smile of a suitor. Julia did not flinch and stood her ground, pushing out her chin. Mr. Bean and Sons looked on as the battle was joined.

"And who, pray tell, is this vision of loveliness?" He cast a look over the shoulder to his patient. "Is this gorgeous creature your daughter? Clarence, have you been holding out on me, bringing me only your salt-of-the-earth sons and hiding away this jewel?" He grasped her hand and kissed it. Despite herself, the corners of Julia's mouth twitched.

"That's one tired line, Dr. Kildare," she responded. "What you need is a line transplant."

"Oh! A wit as well as a beauty!"

Julia took her cue from Mr. Bean who seemed highly entertained by the doctor's ardour. She would play along for a little while longer, if it would keep that smile on his face. That particular smile, wide and toothy, not the one he'd had on his face when she'd come into his room. Too wistful by far, as though he wanted to be in some different place. So Julia played along with the doctor.

"So Clarence, do I have your permission to court your daughter?" he asked, giving a mock bow to Julia. Mr. Bean laughed out, moved in such a way that the drip pulled at his arm, gave a frown then laughed again.

"Lovely lady," the doctor tried again, "What would a man have to do to get your number?"

"Well," Julia said, striking a Mae West pose. "A man wouldn't have to do much at all." Pause. "A boy, on the other hand, would have his work cut out for him."

"Suppose I managed to grow up real fast..."

"I don't doubt that you're capable of... of growth." As she said this, her eyes slid down the length of his trunk. "But – as in any other occupation in life – real men are born, not made, by growth or anything else."

The Bean brothers' eyes were round, as though they were watching a blue movie. But their father was entranced.

As the skirmish continued, with Julia plucking the feathers of the unfortunate cockerel one by one, she watched Mr. Bean out of the corner of her eye. At the first sign of him flagging, she would bail out of this immediately.

She was ready to bail out anyway. A sense of unease was setting in as she systematically dismantled her young victim's ego. Although he still appeared light and jokey, she knew she was getting to him. What was worse was that she was on automatic pilot, with the rebuffs coming sharper and faster, without the least effort on her part. She had done this so many times before. And she was weary of it. Even for laughs. But wasn't it just like life that although she was trifling with this youth for all the best reasons – to keep Mr. Bean from thinking of his illness – she was trifling with him all the same? What was it that Tom had once said about her? "Imprisoned by her own persona." Sounds just like Tom! Pompous! How did Milly put up with him? Still, not far from the truth...

"You mean to say that unrequited love for you is to be my destiny?"

Julia was relieved to see that this little piece of theatre was drawing to a close. Dr. Kildare had had enough.

"I'm afraid so, sonny..."

The doctor shrugged his shoulders and turned towards Mr. Bean, his smile waxy but intact.

"But I'd watch that, if I were you," Julia said. "All that turning and twisting when you're around me. Gonna get yourself one almighty stiff... neck" And again her eyes fell to just below waist level.

The doctor excused himself and left the room.

He was soon followed by Mr. Bean's sons who left, a little flustered, saying they would return later. Julia pulled up a chair and took Mr. Bean's hand. He was shaking his head and grinning.

"I think your sons were shocked."

"Poor them!"

They both laughed.

"I hoped you wouldn't go without saying goodbye," he said at last.

"Who said I'm going anywhere?"

"There's no reason for you to stay. You're better."

"How do you know that?"

"Just look at you!" Mr. Bean's eyes were warm upon her. Julia looked away.

"Looks are deceiving, Mr. Bean. For all you know, I could still be out to lunch." She made a wavy gesture near to her head.

"I guess I could be wrong. But I don't think so." He smoothed his sheet with his free hand. "Whatever ailed you was in here." He tapped his heart. "And I think it's better. Me now, I've got real heart trouble. The old ticker's just not what it used to be." He smiled and this time, the wistful half-smile had returned.

Julia said nothing and as the moments passed, she began to feel more and more choked. She didn't like Mr. Bean talking about his heart and she didn't like him talking about hers. She didn't think she could agree that hers was better. Maybe not as sick but certainly not better. Still empty, still cold – look at how she'd demolished the poor doctor! What had he ever done to her to deserve death by public humiliation? It was so easy for her to skewer men on her hook and watch them flap. She'd done it since she was in her early teens. And, as surely as she was sitting in this hospital room, she was a phoney and she knew it. Her much-vaunted sexuality was as fraudulent as a two dollar bill. It came from nowhere and it went nowhere. Every sexual encounter had been just that, a physical exchange, my body for yours. She had never truly given herself and now as she saw Mr. Bean tapping his heart, she confessed to herself that she had spent her life in longing, wishing only to be able to bestow that gift on the right person.

Then there was Mr. Bean's heart. Why did it have to go and screw up now? And why the hell was he so serene about it all? Didn't he know there were people here who needed him?

Julia dropped Mr. Bean's hand as though it were on fire. "I've got to go!" In one brisk movement, she was on her feet and heading for the door.

"Miss Griffin! What's the matter? Did I say something?" Mr. Bean looked bewildered.

"No! Of course not. I've just remembered something. I've got to go!" Her voice was brittle. "I'll be back... sometime..." She ran from the room.

Mr. Bean sank back into his pillows, bemused, and wondering what he had said to have changed her mood so. On the other side of the door, Julia furiously swiped at the tears burning her cheeks.

The next few hours were very hectic. She went back to Star Island, threw herself across the four-poster bed, cursed the Fates that had led her here, thought about Mr. Bean's kind eyes, the needle in the soft flesh of his arm, thought about the ravaged bluebird's nest, about Milly and Teddy, passed her life in review – again! – decided she was tired of doing that, got up, got dressed and went back to town.

Darkness had now fallen and Julia was back on the Block. She was sitting in a bar, alone, surrounded by overpowering music and the people of the night. Her dress was a hair's breadth away from being overtly provocative. Her skirt was cut short, her top was cut low, her metallic earrings glinted in the light. Her hair, which she had not combed for four months, raised itself off her scalp in a multi-pronged challenge. With a shade too much make-up and a touch too much perfume, the costume was perfect. She did not look like a whore but more like a good-time girl who would drop in on the Scene when occasion or necessity required it. Julia was satisfied with her appearance. As the night lay sprawled before her, she felt confident that she would be able to play the part well.

A man came up and asked if she wanted to dance. She studied him. He had on a collarless pale grey silk shirt and beautifully tailored trousers. A thin gold chain winked around his neck.

"No thanks. I'm waiting for someone," she said and turned her head away in a gesture that was unmistakable. There was nothing further to discuss. The man she was looking for, someone who could help her achieve her objective, was certainly not some elegant accountant trying to escape his wife for a couple of hours.

Several other men approached her and were dismissed in like manner. No-one fitted the bill. He was either too smooth, like the silk-clad accountant or too rough and reminiscent of the charmer in the baseball cap. She needed someone with his finger on the pulse of the street and yet who could also walk through the pastel-coloured metropolis unnoticed. Not easy. But Julia was patient and while she nursed her black rum and ginger beer, she watched the life being lived within the swinging doors of this bar.

The name of the game was commerce. Everything was for sale. Pills, powders, rocks, resins; flesh – male and female; flesh – young and not so young, with buyers and sellers in equal supply. Julia watched all of this and felt the full weight of her forty-three years. She'd been here before – in the great city from which she had fled, in the many places to which she had travelled. In dream and in nightmare. She had been to this place before.

The waitress placed a fresh drink in front of her. Julia glanced up in query, the waitress raised her chin in the direction of a man sitting at the bar who then nodded with great formality. Julia smiled; she knew she had found her companion for the night.

The man came and sat across from her but continued to look at his drink. He seemed like a man in hiding, camouflaged, and despite the flashing lights from the dance floor behind him, he appeared to be plunged in impenetrable shadow. Black circles ringed his eyes as though a tongue of flame had blown across his face, scorching it. He sat at Julia's table without saying a word. They remained like this, not talking, not touching. Smoke drifted overhead, people drank and laughed; on the dance floor couples ground deeply into one another as the music slowed. Time passed and still the man did not speak. Julia, who until now had felt she was an old hand at mind games, started to feel outclassed. She knew that her poise would soon abandon her. It did. She ran a nervous hand along her leg while the other tugged at an earring.

"What can I do for you, lady?" The man's voice was low and much more cultivated than Julia had expected. For a moment she considered playing him along for a while with something like "Who said you could do something for me?" But a look at the man's cavernous eyes told her that all posturing would be pointless.

"I'm looking for Spragga Brangman. Where can I find him?"

"Why do you want him?"

She wanted to tell him it was none of his business but once again a warning voice pulled her up short.

"I don't. I want the kid who hangs with him. Kid called Seth." She found that she was regaining her confidence even though she knew she was in the presence of danger. "And I want him without Spragga." She looked him straight in the eye. "And no, I'm not Babylon."

The man opened his mouth in a caricature of a smile.

"Why should I?"

She couldn't get over his voice. It reminded her of one of her professors at college. She slipped the strap of her handbag from around her neck and, in an unobtrusive gesture, revealed the corners of five crisp green notes with 100 on them. Seconds later, the bag was once more reposing in its accustomed place across her chest.

"That should not be a problem," he said in his scholarly way, his eyes darting in and out of the crowd.

"But," she leaned over and whispered, her sense of unease rising again. "You take me to Seth. You get the money. That's it, you get nothing more."

The man turned his sneering smile on her. Julia felt her body being stripped and appraised. "There's nothing more that I want," he said simply. Julia was not pacified. If this was the last man on earth, she would not trust him.

Over the next three hours, they hit three other bars, all in the same area. In each one, Julia hoped for a breakthrough. In each one she was disappointed. The pattern was always the same. They would find a seat on the fringe of the action, they would order drinks (Julia was now drinking just ginger beer), the man would disappear into the throng and be seen in sparse conversation with the odd person, he would return to their table and they would leave. In the course of the evening, they might have exchanged thirty words. Eventually, they returned to their original bar. Julia was beginning to tire of the whole thing and wondered at her sanity for having embarked upon it. She went to the toilet and came back determined to call it a day.

"I've found him," the man said, getting up. "I'll take you to him right now. He's just around the corner."

Julia's heart started to pound.

"How do you know he's there?"

"He's been home all night," the man said in his smooth voice. "I've just been waiting all this time to make sure he's by himself." Then he added, "Lady, we just been killing time."

"You mean..." Julia started to splutter, her anger fuelled by the smug look on the man's face. But before she had time to say more, the man nodded towards the door. There, gold tooth flashing, a ripe young girl on either arm, stood Spragga, looking approvingly at his own image in the glass. He and his entourage pushed to the middle of the dance floor and demonstrated how unfettered their collective pelvises were.

"Now!" ordered the man and he and Julia slipped out onto the street.

Although it was well past midnight, the air was hot and Julia felt her clothing beginning to cling even more closely than in the sweaty bar. The Block was alive with people in high gear and cars prowling. Near to them stood a parked car, with a woman standing next to its rear fender and a woman

221

leaning into the driver's window. Nothing could be seen of the leaning woman except for a very short sequined blue dress moulded around a firm body. The woman at the back of the car was stringy and worn and seemed intensely interested in the conversation that was going on at the front. As the woman in blue turned to speak to the other, she swept Julia with a vacant stare. She could have been no more than thirteen.

Julia and the man turned left and immediately things became quieter, this part of Angle Street having none of the Block's hard glamour. A dark red wall proclaimed the sovereignty of the One Way crew over this stretch of territory. Mainly these houses were in darkness, their occupants trying to get some sleep on yet another noisy Saturday night. The man stopped in front of a house which had a wooden verandah jutting out over the ground floor entrance. He went to the door and beckoned Julia to follow. She hesitated and then joined him in the stifling gloom.

There was a large window to their right. A point of light inside illuminated the closed curtains.

"Well, this is it. He's in there."

"How do I know that?" Julia's voice carried a toughness she did not feel.

"Lady, are you going to waste my time?"

"The deal was for you to deliver me to Seth, not some doorway."

For a split second, the man came out of hiding as anger flooded his eyes. He took a step towards her. Even in the deep shadow beneath the verandah, each could see the other's eyes. Julia remembered how when she was a little girl, her brother Teddy would tell her to stare down anyone who wanted to hurt her. As she locked her eyes on his, she also tightly crossed her arms across her bosom and handbag. They remained frozen into these postures of hostility as the man considered his next move.

A fluke of providence saved them both. A figure suddenly pulled open the curtains and with equal haste pulled them shut again. It had not been long enough for him to notice them outside but long enough for them to recognise the tall gangly youth with the broad shoulders and the narrow neck, the signature of his clan.

Julia reached in her bag and handed over the money. The man's fingers closed around the notes but his arm remained loosely extended as though waiting for the command to snap back to its normal place. He seemed engrossed in thought and for one mad moment, Julia wondered if he was going to give the money back.

"That boy's a loser, you know. He'll never make it in this business."

"That's what I'm counting on." The extended arm clutching the money hung like a lifeless phallus. Julia could not take her eyes off it.

"What are you? Some sort of missionary? Salvation Army?"

"Do I look like one?"

"Hey," the man said, still heedless of his dangling arm, which had become an object of horror for Julia. "Everybody down here's in disguise."

Julia gave a short laugh. "Whatever else I am, I'm no fucking saint." She stopped laughing. "I just want to take him back to his family."

"Lady, for every kid that goes back, there's ten, twenty more to take his place." He shook his head. "I never took you for someone to waste her time." Giving her one long, last look, he summoned back his arm, pocketed the money, took a few silent steps and was absorbed into the darkness.

Julia knocked at the door, not wanting an instant more to contemplate the great wave of fear that was rearing up in her mind. Action alone could keep it from crashing down and swamping her. She knocked again and heard footsteps approaching. She held her breath and one small objective part of her brain informed her that she did not have the slightest idea what she would do once the door opened.

"How come you're back already? Spragga, man, didn't I tell you I needed some sleep? How come you can't just leave me..." The whining came to an abrupt end as Julia swept past Seth into the living room. He followed her, stumbling, bleary-eyed, holding one hand on top of his head.

"You!"

Julia sat down and placed her hands in her lap.

"What the hell are you doing in my goddamn house? Get out, bitch! Get the hell out!"

Julia continued to sit, pushing back the cuticles on her left hand.

"What did I tell you? I told you to go. I'll call the cops!" Julia glanced up at him then returned her attention to her hands. "Get out!" Seth shouted, a bead of sweat breaking free from his hairline and carving a path down the side of his face. "Who sent you? Who the hell sent you?" He kept circling the chair where Julia was sitting, screaming at her to leave, sometimes pushing his sour breath and frowsy body very close to her. Apart from the motion of her fingers, Julia did not move as the harangue went on. The tears at the fringe of Seth's voice made him completely without menace.

In due course, he stopped, drying up in the middle of a sentence. He flopped down on the floor and put his head in his hands. He was so still and his breathing so regular that Julia wondered whether he had dropped off to sleep. She threaded her way through the clutter and bent towards him.

"Don't touch me!" He spat out the words, not looking up.

"All right, Seth," Julia said, returning to her chair. "You see, I'm back over here. I won't touch you. I just want to talk."

He drew his knees up and rested his head on them. There

seemed no energy in his body; it was exhausted, spent. When he did eventually speak, every word required of him real exertion.

"So who sent you? My Pa, I bet. Him and you always were tight. Too tight. It was disgusting!" Julia's forehead creased and she shook her head. Seth saw nothing of this, with his head still lolling on his knees. "And what kind of man would send a woman down here to get me? What kind of man is he anyway?"

While he had been talking, Julia had been assessing him. Was he high? Was he drunk? Was he just tired? Was he all three? The empty bottles and dead spliffs decorating the room indicated that the first two were more than likely. But this last speech of his was lucid enough to make Julia believe that tonight at least he had not taken too much and what little he had taken had brought him no relief. More than anything, Seth was weary.

"What kind of man is he, I ask you?" he repeated.

"A very sick man, Seth. Your grandfather's had a heart attack."

Seth's head jerked up and he turned red glaring eyes on her.

"You're lying!" He jumped up, knocking over a plate of half-eaten food which landed on the floor with a thud. He became wild and uncoordinated again, stumbling around, shouting.

"It's a lie! He sent you here to tell me lies! It's a trick to get me to come back." He never took his eyes off Julia. "But it won't work. You hear me! I won't go and nobody can make me!" His voice had become shrill and childlike. Even Seth heard it and the shock of it quieted him.

When Julia rose to go to him, she had him in her sights. As she crossed the dishevelled room, every step brought the terror in Seth's eyes closer. Step by step, she approached the field of fear which was now cast about him. She knew that a month ago, she would have retreated from a task such as this as from a yawning precipice. Why even this afternoon, she had fled from the room when she'd seen love in Mr. Bean's eyes. But now the moment was upon her. She could run no more.

"Seth, it's no lie or trick. You know I wouldn't lie about your grandfather." It was a simple truth and Seth heard it. She lay her hand on his thin shoulder and the movement beneath the grimy shirt was like the fluttering of some winged creature.

"We have to go and see him." Julia spoke slowly, aiming each word at Seth's ear. "He wants to see you. You, Seth." She felt her own breathing alter and start to come in irregular bursts. "I know it's late but we have to go now. We have to get you cleaned up and go right now!"

Seth slumped against her. She steadied him as her eyes searched for a door which might lead to a place where one might find running water. Could this bijou residence possibly have a powder room, she wondered as she inhaled Seth's unwashed body.

When the first door knob that she tried opened onto a squalid little cupboard containing a toilet and a shower stall, Julia began to believe in answered prayer. But it proved to be a false dawn as Seth began to baulk at moving from Spragga's dank foxhole to a place where his humiliation would be on parade. He began to beat his breast and say he couldn't face his grandfather's disappointment. To all of this, Julia said that the only person Mr. Bean was calling for was him. That made him pause for a brief moment but then the lament resumed, the wallowing in shame and self-pity. Julia was reminded why social work and the other "caring" professions had never been an option. People got on her nerves too quickly. She was tired and had had enough of this boy's snivelling.

"I thought you said you wanted to be free," she said at last.

Maybe it was the sharpness of her tone that caught his attention. Or maybe it was the word "free". He shut up and looked hard at her.

"Yeah. I remember the speech you made about it at Star Island House. Sounded pretty impressive." She sensed a change in him. "Let me tell you. That freedom thing. It's hard to come by at the best of times. I'm still trying to find it." There was a sound of scoffing that angered Julia. "Hey! It's not just not having money that can make you a prisoner. There's a whole lot of other things that can do it too." She sensed again she had his full attention. As much of a pain as this boy was, Julia had to concede that he seemed to recognise the truth when he heard it

"I can't tell you where to go to get free. You're going to have to find that out yourself. But one thing's for sure. You're less free here than anywhere else."

He dropped his eyes, refusing to look at the rank despair of this stricken room. When he raised his eyes, he made strange squinting movements as though he were consciously trying to clear away the fog from his mind.

"I'll get ready." He was unsteady again. "But you might have to give me a hand."

So Julia helped Seth to get clean for his grandfather. She coaxed the shower nozzle to work at full blast, she passed him soap and towels, she ransacked the bedroom until she unearthed some clean clothes, she ironed them, she found a comb and combed his wet hair. The only thing she did not do was to go into the bathroom and scrub him down. At last, Seth stood before her, clean, shiny. Julia brushed a microscopic speck off his shirt and lifted his chin with her finger for a fragment of a second. Then, grabbing Seth's hand, she pulled him into the street. Again, luck was with her as a lone taxi cruised by and stopped just ahead of them.

The events of the day were starting to catch up with Julia as she and Seth leaned back in the taxi on their way to the hospital. She glanced over at Seth. His clothes lay smooth and flush on his spare frame. The gold lights of his skin shone as did the damp sheen of his hair. He looked freshly-minted, reborn and, in his present condition, could have walked the immaculate streets of the pastel city with the best of them. But she knew that inside Seth was wrestling with a great disturbance, trying to put aside his weakness and fear, plumbing the depths for the strength to face whatever awaited him at the end of the taxi ride. Seth was not aware of Julia's eyes studying him, nor did he hear her sigh and look away.

Julia put her fingers to her temple. It had been a very long day. She felt tension and weariness knotting the muscles of her neck. She rolled down the window and was greeted by a canopy of pale stars and the cool night air. She let the night soothe her with the tender darkness of its hand.

The taxi set them down in front of the hospital and they hurried inside. They were met by two security guards and the receptionist on duty. A brief but animated exchange ensued with Julia switching into her power-broker stance and manner. Seth held back but soon found himself being pulled into the elevator. Nothing was said as the lighted panel flashed 2, 3, 4. The door opened.

"I thought you said he was in Memorial Ward," muttered Seth as they moved along the darkened corridor.

"No," Julia answered flatly. "He's back in Intensive Care."

Seth stopped and appeared to take root in the concrete floor. Julia tugged at his arm. But Seth had become fused to the floor and Julia had to stop.

"You think I can stand this? You think I want to go in there?" The words swelled in Julia's throat with a suffocating intensity. "But we've got to go. You hear? Both of us!" Instead of trying to propel him by force, she put her arm around his waist and guided him the rest of the way as though he were a blind man.

The nurses in Intensive Care spoke in low, solicitous

tones and, with a minimum of fuss, took them to where Mr. Bean lay.

Beeping monitors and winking screens stood like sentries at his head. Both arms were pierced with thin tubes and a large plastic one was taped to his mouth. His chest rose and fell with the same rhythm as that of the machine next to him which had the motion of a bellows.

As if by an unspoken accord, Julia and Seth sat down on either side of him, each taking one of his hands in theirs. Julia found the fine roughness of the hand pleasing as she explored its landscape of ancient scars. Mr. Bean's hand was as cool as a slab of marble, as the air breathing through the trees outside.

She looked over at Seth. His head was bowed in prayer. What deal is he trying to strike with God, she wondered, loathing herself for asking such a question. She stared at the motion of Mr. Bean's chest and tried not to think about all the technological trickery that was keeping it rising and falling in this unnaturally precise way.

"Is he still here?" she wanted to ask Seth. "Is he still in this room or are we too late? Has he gone already?" But she dared not trespass on Seth's ardent petitioning on his grandfather's behalf. She continued to stroke the hand, that craftsman's hand that she had seen so often in its strength, its compassion and delicacy, digging the earth, fashioning wood, grasping heavy loads, rubbing away its own arthritic pain, cradling a tiny bird's egg in its palm. Now it was still. Julia could form no words of supplication to the great spirit beyond this steel and glass room, that spirit breathing out there in the dark. She had no words. She could find no words. So with Mr. Bean's hand in hers, she leaned back in her chair and slept.

She was back on Star Island, with Mr. Bean. They were crouched low among cherry and sage and fennel. Behind them was the house – Milly's house – nestled quietly among the casuarinas. They had pulled back some of the undergrowth and were watching the courtship ritual of a pair of resplendent birds. Dark blue and amber feathers touched and spun in the sunlight. The watchers looked on in silence at the twirling, bobbing passion of the dancers. The dance was reaching its climax. The birds became rigid and seemed to wait for some signal. Then of one accord, they broke free from the heaviness of earth and rose into the sky. Julia and Mr. Bean ran out onto the green grass, laughing and spinning in the sunshine. And from the cover of the trees, a host of bluebirds appeared, joyous and free, and in such great numbers that they almost blotted out the sun.

"Miss Griffin! Miss Griffin!" Julia felt someone shaking her shoulder roughly.

"Miss Griffin! Something's happening!" Seth's voice was urgent. Julia snapped back into consciousness.

Mr. Bean's face, which had been as still as his hand, seemed to have changed. The movement in it was so minute that it was almost invisible. But nevertheless it was there. The nurse was already in the room, studying numbers and charts and equipment. Julia and Seth studied Mr. Bean's face where there seemed to be a random eruption of twitching. Slowly, very slowly, the movement became concentrated in one place, his eyes. His eyebrows went up and down several times and then the dark screen of his eyelids rose like an old and massive drawbridge.

His eyes looked as though they had been washed clean. A strong light shone behind them. His head remained perfectly still but his eyes moved first to Seth then to Julia. The light burned fiercely as first Seth then Julia felt his limp hand gain power and squeeze theirs in benediction.

The drawbridge clanged shut and the hands tumbled back into their peaceful sleep. More nurses bustled in and out, sidestepping Julia and Seth who stood like dazed paratroopers after the landing.

"Has he gone?" Julia managed to ask at last.

"No," the nurse said. "But he's had a turn for the worse. The doctor's on his way. And I've called the rest of the family."

Julia waited with Seth until the others came. He clung to her as they felt a coldness start to travel from Mr. Bean's fingers and make its inexorable journey into the rest of his body. They watched the numbers on the machines. They watched them fall and fall and fall. When Dennis and Johnny and the rest of the clan arrived, they embraced her and Seth and put the boy up at his grandfather's head as they encircled the bed.

Julia slipped out of the room. As she left Intensive Care, she saw the young doctor with the ponytail and gave him a small sad smile. She decided to take the four flights of stairs down. A strange calm enfolded her. When she reached the ground floor, it struck her that today was supposed to be the day of her return home, to the great city where the buildings nudge the sky. She would go back, maybe not today, but another day. Soon. She looked up and saw a rose-coloured dawn breaking over the trees. A new day. A new beginning.

A car stopped in front of her.

"Need a cab, lady?" the driver asked.

"Yes. Star Island Dock. Southampton."

"Oh," the driver said. "I just brought some folks from up there." He glanced at her in his rear-view mirror.

"Yes," she said in a whisper. Her breath was uneven. "I... I... know them." Their eyes held for a moment then he looked away.

"Look at that sky," he said. "It's going to be a beautiful day."

They both looked out at the blush of light curving across the heavens.

"Yes," said Julia, putting on her sunglasses. She leaned back in her seat and embraced the warm release of tears.